Mexico Trilogy

MEXICO TRILOGY

D.N. STUEFLOTEN

Normal

Published by FC2 with support given by English Department Unit for
Contemporary Literature at Illinois State University, the Illinois Arts
Council, and the National Endowment for the Arts

Address all inquiries to: FC2, Unit for Contemporary Literature, Campus
Box 4241, Illinois State University, Normal, IL 61790-4241

Mexico Trilogy
D.N. Stuefloten

ISBN: Paper, 1-57366-019-1

Book design: David A. Dean
Cover design: Todd Bushman

Produced and printed in the United States of America

Maya originally published by FC2, 1992. *The Ethiopian Exhibition* originally
published by Black Ice Books, 1994.

NATIONAL
ENDOWMENT
FOR THE
ARTS

This program is
partially supported by
a grant from the
Illinois Arts Council.

PREFACE

I had been living for seven years in California. Inexplicably I was unable to write. One day—it was April 1, 1987—I loaded my typewriter and some clothes onto my motorcycle and drove into Mexico. Crossing the northern deserts, my old Honda had five flat tires, a sure sign, I thought, that I was a fool to be making this journey; or else—such is the ambiguity of signs—that I had been a fool to put it off for so long. I arrived finally in Manzanillo, a seaport below Puerto Vallarta. I moved into an abandoned house in a coconut grove next to the ocean. I wrote daily, unexpectedly, in a café on the plaza. In three months the first draft of *The Ethiopian Exhibition* was complete.

Mexico has been good to me in its own peculiar way. It is a country cruel and beautiful, passive, violent, imitative and original. In a life spent obsessively wandering around the world, I had never before encountered a place I disliked so intensely, or found so fertile. When *Ethiopia* was finished I roved for a couple years east and west, north and south. Everywhere I went I found pieces of a new novel, which I called *Maya*. There were bits of it waiting for me in the Yucatan, in San Ándres Tuxtla and Santiago Tuxtla, in Tlacotalpan and Uruapan, in Lagos de Moreno and Morelia. One night in Xalapa, laid low by a recurrence of malaria, I saw *Maya* unreel before my eyes like a flickering kinescope. I was in the Hotel Limón, a monstrosity of tile where sounds echoed from wall to wall: whispers became roars, the dripping fountain a hailstorm. My malarial dreams were a cacophony too: they reverberated within my own skull. After *Maya* I retreated to Pátzcuaro, a 400-year-old town in the mountains of Michoacán. Everything ran downward, blood from the slaughterhouse, sewage from the cluttering shacks, into the lake below. It seemed the natural place for *The Queen of Las Vegas*, my third Mexican novel. It rose out of the miasma like the regal whore she was.

I do not pretend that these short novels are about Mexico. In my own mind they are about America, that sprawling country to the north. But of course I cannot be sure of that either. The novels are united by recurring themes, recurring metaphors, recurring characters, but beyond that I am certain only of my memories, real or imagined, and the despair I so often felt—and the passion—as I roamed the Mexican hinterlands. And, of course, Yasmeen: she rose from her own miasma to briefly illuminate some of these more harrowing passages. It is to her—wherever she lies—that this volume is dedicated.

—D.N. Stuefloten
Aguascalientes, Mexico, 1996

CONTENTS

THE ETHIOPIAN EXHIBITION

PART I THE EXHIBITION

I

THE IRIDESCENT
BIRDS OF ETHIOPIA

On the Ethiopian plains, night falls at six o'clock. It is impossible to say with certainty why this is so. Later we shall discuss this more completely. Examples shall be given. In each case the horizon reddens. Stars appear. The last baboon climbs into his cave. The first hyena emerges from his lair. The diurnal birds—all of them are gray—fall silent. The nocturnal birds begin to sing. These nocturnal birds are brilliantly plumaged, even ornate. Their voices differ from those of the daytime birds. The daytime songs are as harsh as the countryside. They can be heard everywhere, even in the cities. The nighttime songs are seldom heard near human habitation. They are oddly melodious. Such songs can rouse unease. There are stories about some of these songs, and their effects on humans, that may be called incredible. Some of these stories will be discussed. This book may be seen as a discussion of these stories. No one alive today, however, can vouch for them. Perhaps no one alive today has seen a nocturnal bird. They are known, nevertheless, to have iridescent feathers. These feathers, however it is known, are said to be several feet in length. The eyes of these birds are said to be black and expressionless. These birds are capable of gliding soundlessly for miles. These birds are predators. They are most iridescent when hungry. There are tales of glowing birds carrying off children. We believe these stories are true. Infants vanish during the night. In daylight there is wailing. People gnash their teeth.

The bifurcation of Ethiopia between day and night is virtually absolute. In truth Ethiopia is two countries. It is rare for anyone—any man, and beast—to know them both.

2
THE FOUR
CYLINDER INDIAN

A plume of dust rises from the wheels of a motorcycle. The rider of
the motorcycle is John Twelve. He is a ferengie—a foreigner. Carried
on his motorcycle are specimen jars, notebooks, cameras, a small
typewriter, and items of personal wear. On his head he wears a leather
helmet and goggles. Already he is covered in dust. The motorcycle is
a four cylinder in-line Indian. It is quite ancient. Its motor can be heard
for some distance: thump-thump-thump-thump, thump-thump-
thump-thump. He purchased it on the docks. Does it run? he asked the
owner, a plump man wearing a fez. The plump man puffed and blew
as though insulted. Yet he started the machine only with difficulty.
There was no paint left on the machine. It was eaten with rust. No tread
was on the tires. Spare parts would probably never be available, not
even in Ethiopia. Yet the ferengie paid money for this machine, plus
the leather helmet, the goggles, and some cracked saddlebags. It is into
these saddlebags that he stuffs his equipment. More items are strapped
across the gas tank. All this occurs in daylight. As he rides across the
Ethiopian plains a plume of dust rises from his wheels. This plume of
dust is visible in the distant villages.

Nearby a black Abyssinian on a white pony watches. He wears a
shamma, a loosely draped garment. He looks towards the horizon. The
sun is already low. The pony wheels. His hooves are delicate. Even at
a trot they raise scarcely any dust and create scarcely any noise.

3
DESPAIR

He is overwhelmed suddenly by despair. There is no ready explanation for such a thing. It happens during the brief moment of twilight. He pulls off the road and puts his face in his hands.

At such moments it is his nature to question everything. He is a man alone. He has no family. Although he has his studies, it seems that everything else has deserted him. There is no purpose to anything, least of all his life. Bitterness sucks away his vital spirit. He feels emptied. Later we will spend more time examining his despair. We shall try to make his despair palpable. Perhaps if his despair is given dimension, and texture, and color—perhaps if we can discover the sound of his despair—perhaps then we may understand it. Or perhaps we will discover it is a canker that will never be understood, not in Ethiopia, not elsewhere; and never be healed, not by day, not by night.

4
THE RAGING
TRUCKS OF ETHIOPIA

It is dark. He lies in his sleeping bag. A tarp is spread from the branches of a thorn tree over him and his motorcycle.

When the trucks begin to pass it is not clear if John Twelve is asleep or awake. His face grimaces, but his eyes remain closed. The trucks whine and snarl and snap up the hills and around the curves. Few have mufflers. The noise is intense. The trucks seem endless. They start shortly after dark, and stop shortly before morning. In Ethiopia trucks travel only at night. Their headlights throw shadows which veer across the landscape. They are festooned with other lights—red and green lights, blue and gold ones. The trucks themselves are painted bright colors, sometimes many colors. During the day they are hidden. Only their wreckage can be found in daylight hours. Trucks go off the road and plow through trees and into cliffs, and sometimes villages. On some dangerous stretches of road there are wrecked trucks stacked one next to another. Families live in some of these wrecks: in the huge trailers, twisted or not, and in the cabs, still reeking of oil. Lines of wash are strung from truck to trailer and trailer to thorn tree. Children play in the shadows. Children are born in the huge aluminum caverns.

But at night the trucks race through the countryside. The roads, deserted all day, fill with diesel rigs and gasoline rigs, with semi-trailers and doubles, loaded and overloaded with goods that we can only imagine. They roar and they howl. There is silence only briefly, after a crash. Broken glass falls onto sheet metal hoods. Air hisses one last time from the giant brakes. Perhaps blood drips. Then the howling of the engines begins again. The trucks rage all night, all night, until the Ethiopian dawn.

5
THE SHAPE OF DESPAIR

Despair follows him like a plume of dust.

This plume of dust rises from the wheels of his motorcycle and hangs in the air for miles behind him. The plume of dust is visible from villages some distance away. The Ethiopians who live in these villages stop their tasks to watch. They squat in the shadows of their mud huts. They see how the eddies of wind in the air above John's motorcycle give the plume of dust a shape.

John, on his motorcycle, is unaware of this. He is deafened by the thumping of his four cylinder, in-line engine. He is aware of the constant vibration which batters his body. He is aware of the struggle to keep his machine upright and in a straight line. He is aware of the dryness of the air on the Ethiopian plain, and the heat of the sun, and the buffeting of the wind. He is aware of his despair, but he does not realize it is taking a shape in the plume of dust which follows him. He does not realize his despair is taking the shape of a giant locust. The natives in the villages see the locust. They watch the mandibles take form, and the powerful legs, and the primitive wings. They are aware of the locust in their own lives. The locust has swarmed across their land stripping it of their crops. They know how difficult it is to kill a single locust, with its armored body. They understand the devouring hunger of the locust. The natives in the villages watch the locust take shape. They watch the yellow sunlight, as it mingles with the dust, turn the locust green.

John, on his motorcycle, is unaware of the locust following him in the plume of dust. He cannot see it poised above him. We see it. We cannot alter this. We can only watch, like the villagers, as despair takes the form of a giant insect in the plume of dust which follows John across the Ethiopian plain.

6
THE PHOSPHORESCENT
ANIMALS OF ETHIOPIA

It is dark. Like an animal he burrows into the bushes. He pulls his sleeping bag over his face. The motorcycle next to him pings and hisses as it cools. The other daytime animals have gone to their burrows also. They are replaced by nighttime animals. These animals have black, glittering eyes. They are feral creatures. They stalk each other beneath the wild fig trees, the tall acacias, olive trees with gnarled and bent limbs, bottle trees with their pulpy bark, and flowering magnolias. From above—from the vantage of a soaring Ethiopian bird—the earth seems covered with unceasing movement. This is especially true during the mating season. The females become phosphorescent. Their sexual organs glow. They circle through the bushes, followed by the males. The female rodents, ferrets, wild cats, including the spotted leopard, even the female hyenas glow. Their organs of sexuality glow. They produce a kind of incense, particular to each breed. The male creatures follow the females, sniffing at the glowing vulvas. Coupling occurs after midnight. The phosphorescence increases. There is a rhythmic pulsing to this glow. The odors become as strong as crushed flowers. The male animals snarl and snap at each other. The females, odoriferous and phosphorescent, growl also. Their movements become jerky— short steps to the right, quick turns to the left. Sometimes they leave trails of phosphorescence, along which bound the males of their breed.

When coupling occurs the odors become even stronger. Trees blossom at this time. If there is rain, the rain smells like perfume. Above all of this glide the iridescent birds.

John sleeps. Perhaps his sleep is uneasy. Images flash, with a phosphorescence of their own, in his brain. When the Ethiopian dawn arrives, with a cracking sound, like thunder, he sits up, gasping.

7
An Ethiopian Street

John descends from the Ethiopian plateau and enters a town along the coast. It has a harbor. There are green trees in the central square. He takes a room in a hotel which overlooks this square.

The streets of this Ethiopian town are filled with children of both sexes, priests wearing white turbans signifying their high office, chiefs and grandees and other important officials wearing peaked caps and carrying scimitars on their hips, slaves, generally black and nearly nude, gun bearers and retainers and zebanias, who are private soldiers, and merchants in long djellabas. The only females, aside from the few children, are old. They are mostly beggars, and sit in doorways, counting beads. All of these people, except the slaves and the old women, are constantly moving to and fro and making noises. The old women, as we have said, sit in doorways. The slaves stand silently, often stork-like, on one leg.

John walks down the crowded street. He hears Arabic, Spanish, French and occasionally English words, all spoken loudly and rapidly. Bitches with rows of swinging teats, puppies with stiff hind legs, and mastiffs drooling down their jaws pass underfoot. The air is hot and dusty. Because there is only a narrow strip of flat land between the ocean and the hills, soon the street ends. It becomes a stairway. The stairway rises steeply, and crookedly, up the hill. Houses are stacked here, one on top of another. No engineer, no architect had a hand in them. The houses are made of mud bricks, concrete, wood, and stone, and no corner is square. Clothes are hung on lines from house to house. Doorways are low; windows have shutters across them. The stairs turn right, then left, and become narrower as John climbs upward. For a long time only children watch him. The children have bare bellies. They stand with fingers in mouths. They stand in every doorway, and at every turning of the stairs.

8
THE BLAZING SUN
OF ETHIOPIA

The stairs turn left. John turns left, still ascending. Above, turning to her left, a woman descends.

It is late afternoon. The sun blazes. The whitewashed buildings shine in this blazing sunlight. It is not clear why this woman is descending an Ethiopian stairway during daylight. She is swathed head to toe. She is mostly swathed in white. Her veil is black. The tip of one shoe, as it descends to the next step, is black. It is pointed, like the triangular head of a viper. Perhaps the shoe is patent leather. We can see it descend, like the pointed head of a snake, to the step below. Everything except this pointed shoe, the veil, and her eyes is white. Her eyes, veil, and shoe are black. The eyes are iridescent. This iridescence is similar to the iridescence flies have when they cluster on a piece of raw meat. As the black patent shoe descends, it emerges more fully from the hem of the robe. The ankle is sheathed in black nylon, perhaps black silk. Like the eyes, like the shoe, like the veil, there is an iridescence to the ankle. Perhaps this iridescence is a trick of the blazing sunlight.

The sun blazes down. The man and the woman stand at the turning of the stairs. They stand like this for some time. No one can say why she has appeared like this. Her iridescent eyes are visible. Except for these eyes, the black veil, the black shoe, and the black-sheathed ankle, she is obscured entirely by her white garments. Then she is gone. The sun continues to blaze. Perhaps she has turned and mounted the steps. Perhaps she slipped away, elsewhere. John stands in the blazing sun, above his own shadow. Then he moves too. He leaps up the stairs. He finds only low doorways, a slinking dog, and two children, naked and dirty, sucking at their fingers.

9
THE ETHIOPIAN WIND

A breeze rises from the sea. It moves inland. It tugs at John's clothes.

He looks down at the harbor and the tin roofs of the town. He can see camels moving in the streets, and mules, horses, a few ancient motorcars. Three ships are tied at the dock. Train tracks run from the docks alongside a lagoon and then westward, into the hinterland. The train itself arrives weekly, bearing grain, scrap metal, sugar cane, and slaves. All are sent overseas, the grain being traded for bread, the scrap metal to return as rifles and cheap watches, the sugar cane processed into Coca Cola. Only the slaves, we understand, remain overseas, in the kitchens of restaurants in Paris, Brussels, and New York.

John climbs higher. His shirt is dark with sweat and clings to his skin. The breeze is moist and hot. It causes the wooden shutters on the windows of the small, crooked houses to clatter. Doors creak back and forth in their doorways. The sheets of tin which form roofs clang as the wind from the sea lifts them and drops them. These are the only noises except for John's breath. John's breath is like the wind, moist and hot. For a moment, while John climbs, the wind and his breath are the same. This can happen in Ethiopia. The Ethiopian wind rises from the sea, just as humans rose from the sea. No man can remember the primitive sea, but his cells remember. His bones remember. When this wind joins with a man's breath there is a moment when these cells, these bones, rejoice. The man feels this as a moment of joy. The moment passes quickly. When the elation is gone, a sadness remains. This sadness is just as deep as the joy. It penetrates into the bones. The body aches in memory of the primitive sea. This is why a man forever yearns to penetrate into the womb of a woman. A woman's womb is saline, like the sea. The male organism, when it penetrates into the womb, recognizes this. Elation and sadness inevitably follow this recognition. These secrets are known in Ethiopia. They have been known ever since the wind first rose from the sea, and blew across an Ethiopian town.

In Ethiopia A Woman's Mouth Is A Sexual Organ

There is a face at a window. It looks down over the bay. It looks down over the steps that John is climbing.

In Ethiopia a woman's mouth is considered a sexual organ. Only young girls are allowed to be seen unveiled, in the same way young girls and boys are allowed to be seen nude playing in the streets. At a certain moment a girl's erotic nature becomes apparent. This event is obvious to anyone within view. Men dream of witnessing this event. If a man witnesses this event, he has a right to carry the girl off. The event may occur at any time, day or night. Forever after this moment she must wear clothes and a veil and cover her hair, which is erotic also. Except for rare circumstance she will not be seen again in daylight, even thus garbed, until she is very old and her sexual power has waned. This is because the erotic power of the Ethiopian woman is so great. Her presence in the streets would prevent the Ethiopian male from performing his proper duties, which are thieving, lying, cheating, and murder.

The woman in the window watches as John mounts the steps. When he looks up he sees her. He sees her just as the Ethiopian wind, warm and moist from the sea, lifts the corner of her veil. Her lips are dark red and fully engorged with blood. The lips draw back as the mouth opens. The teeth are exposed. The fleshy tongue lies across the lower row of these teeth. Deeper within the mouth is the phosphorescent glow of this sexual organ. This glow expands outward with the woman's breath. As this happens, her hand reaches for the wooden shutter of the window. The tips of her fingers are sheathed in long nails. Two of these nails are carved from bamboo; one is silver; the other brass, and encrusted with jewels. They taper to sharp points. The hand, thus sheathed, grasps the edge of the wooden shutter. All this takes place in seconds. Her lips draw back, engorged and heavy with blood. The mouth becomes fully extended. Deep in the throat emanates the phosphorescent glow. This glow begins to pulse. The sheathed fingers grasp the edge of the wooden shutter and draw it closed.

Immediately the wind from the sea dies.

II

THE WEIGHT OF DESPAIR

In Ethiopia the air has a weight. Normally no one is aware of this. When the air is very still, however, this weight may be tangible. It may be felt as the weight of despair.

This weight is composed of the dying exhalations of men, women, and children. Whenever a man is murdered his last breath adds to the weight of the air. Whenever a child dies at birth, the passing of his soul adds weight to the air. The pain of his mother, although it may not be visible in the air, adds weight. During times of war, when villages are destroyed, and whole cities, and sometimes whole races, the increase in the weight of the air can cause a man to stagger. Not all men are aware of this. Cruel men are not aware of the weight they are adding to the air by each cruel gesture. In many countries this weight is taken for granted, and the people think nothing of mass bombings, or mass exploitations, or mass cruelties. Often if such people come to Ethiopia they feel, if not the weight of the air, a vague oppression. The weight of the air, which they have helped increase, gives them unease. They ascribe this unease to the sight of begging children or the dirt on the streets or the careless way food is prepared for them. But in truth it is the weight of the air, which they do not wish to feel.

When John reaches the top of the stairs he is bent nearly double by the weight of the air. He staggers to the wall of a ruined building. He sinks weakly into its shade. The weight of human suffering is so great in the Ethiopian air that he is scarcely able to breathe it.

12

THE PARIAH DOGS
OF ETHIOPIA

In Ethiopia a man in a weakened state will be attacked by creatures eager to respond to that condition. In Ethiopia this is a natural law. The creatures that now come forward to attack John in his weakened state are pariah dogs.

Pariah dogs live on the fringes of all Ethiopian towns. They live in ruined buildings, in groves of trees that have fallen into disuse, and in the refuse pits that encircle even the smallest village. These pariah dogs, in response to John's weakness, come forward in a half circle around him. Their heads are low to the ground. Their ears lie flat. Lips are drawn back to reveal canine fangs. More emerge from doorways, from holes in the crumbling walls, and leap down from windows. If we watch the scene from above, we may admire its classic simplicity. The setting is perfect. The sea at this hour is jewel-like. It is clear and pure as an amethyst. The ruins where John and the pariah dogs enact their drama are on a promontory overlooking this sea.

In Ethiopia the pariah dogs, although not liked, are expected to perform their role with honor. The tragedy they sometimes bring is the price one pays for being a member of the larger drama of all living things. The frenzy of the pariah dogs, when they rip into their victim, tearing off arms, chunks of flesh, scrambling amongst themselves for choice bits of entrails, liver, or spleen, is not seen as an aberration but as an example of the ferocity which exists in nature, and which thus needs expression. It can no more be avoided than the Ethiopian air, or the fall of night, or the lonely cries of a grieving widow. John, a ferengie, is unaware of the larger nature, or even the classic lines, of his role. He does not understand what every Ethiopian knows, that when confronted by pariah dogs one must exhibit either resignation or dominance. The signs of resignation would signal the pariah dogs to attack. The signs of dominance would signal them to flee. John's posture is that of a frightened man, which provokes the pariah dogs to attack, and yet he fights, swinging his arms, kicking out, which frustrates their attack. Because of this confusion the pariah dogs mill about. They snap and snarl, dart in, then retreat. John, backed against the mud brick wall, lashes out. The confrontation cannot come to a satisfactory conclusion. The pariah dogs howl and cry in frustration and anger. In the town below people hear these cries, and pause.

Night falls. The pariah dogs, creatures of the day, slink off into their burrows, their nature wounded. John, a ferengie, a misfit in the Ethiopian landscape, is abandoned to the Ethiopian night.

13
THE SONGS OF
THE ETHIOPIAN NIGHT

It is dark. John Twelve stands alone in the darkness.

He walks through the darkness to the edge of the cliff. He finds his way slowly. He stops when he feels the earth crumbling at his feet. Below him is the town. In the center of the town is the square. The square is full of trees. The trees, in the darkness, are beginning to flower. In Ethiopia the trees flower only at night. As the flowers emerge they begin to glow. Below these flowering trees small animals scurry. The vulvas of the females of these animals glow. All have iridescent eyes. Soon this glow, the glow of the female vulvas and the flowers opening on the trees, is visible from the top of the promontory where John stands. It is at this moment that the nocturnal birds of Ethiopia begin to sing.

They sing as they pass over John's head. They descend from high in the night sky. Their glowing wings are outstretched. Their tips especially glow. Some of these wings are enormous. As these Ethiopian birds glide past John's head he can hear the wind rushing through the glowing feathers. He can feel the wind they create as they pass over his head. The music of these birds is so soft it seems palpable. One could sink one's hands into these songs. One could rest one's head on these songs, just as one could rest one's head on the soft breast of the bird itself. As each bird, descending from high in the night sky, glides over the head of John, its soft song glides over him also. It becomes louder, though no less soft, as the bird approaches. It becomes more distant, though no less beautiful, as the bird glides to the square below. The beauty of each of these songs passing over John's head is unbearable. That is, these songs cannot be borne in the way normal songs are borne. That is the great danger of these songs. They enter into a man's blood. They invade his bones. They will forever ache behind his eyes, at the hinge of his jaw, at the base of his spine. It is a kind of pain. There is no relief from it. As the birds glide over John's head, singing, singing, to the square below, he can feel the softness of each song as clearly as he feels the soft wind of their passing.

14
THE WOMEN OF
THE ETHIOPIAN NIGHT

It is dark, perhaps very dark. From all sides women emerge from this darkness. They are visible in the glow which they themselves cast. Their eyes are iridescent. Each mouth pulses with its glow. A glow emerges from the center of each body. The women come out of the darkness and walk towards John at the edge of the cliff. They do not look at him. They walk towards him and towards the edge of the cliff.

The women are no longer swathed head to toe. They wear fine silks. They wear thin veils and tight dresses. They are garbed in finery from all over the world. Much of their bodies are revealed. Some are almost nude. They step forward in translucent garments. They step forward in high heeled shoes that are iridescent in the darkness. They step forward on legs that shine, sheathed in silk. As these women step towards John, towards the cliff, they make a murmuring noise. It is not clear if this murmuring noise emerges from between the lips on their faces or from the lips, visible or not, that glow between their legs. The murmur is as soft as the songs of the Ethiopian birds. The sound envelops John. The women, murmuring and glowing, walk towards John, walk past him, to the edge of the cliff. They do not pause. They spread their arms and leap into the darkness.

15
THE EDGE OF THE CLIFF

It is dark. John watches the women emerge from the darkness. At the edge of the cliff they spread their arms. John watches their glowing forms descend to the square far below. They join the glowing flowers and the glowing animals and the glowing birds which have come to roost there. They circle, some to the left, some to the right. They go round and round. John watches.

The last woman emerges from the darkness. She pauses at the edge of the cliff. She is the only one to do this. Her iridescent eyes turn. They turn to look at John. Her lips, engorged with blood, draw back from her teeth. The mouth becomes fully extended. The glow that emerges from deep in her mouth begins to pulse. She says nothing, but there is about her a murmuring sound. It is not certain what this sound means, or if it means anything. The iridescent eyes themselves contain no expression. They stare at John. She wears black shoes with high heels. Her legs are sheathed. She pauses at the edge of the cliff—she is the only woman to do so—and stares with her iridescent eyes at John. She stares at him while her mouth is fully extended. Then she spreads her arms. She leans forward into the darkness. She glides to the square far below.

16
INTO THE DARKNESS

It is dark. The glowing Ethiopian woman spreads her arms. John watches her descend. Soon her glow is indistinguishable from the others circling right and left in the square. He watches from the edge of the cliff. There is nothing luminescent about him. We can see no glow coming from his mouth or his body. He stands in darkness. The luminescence is far below. He watches it. Then he steps to the edge of the cliff. The earth crumbles at his feet. He spreads his arms. This can only happen once. He stands in darkness far above the luminescence. There is nothing luminescent about him. He spreads his arms and takes a step forward. The earth beneath him crumbles. The earth beneath him gives way as he leans forward into the darkness.

17
FAITH

It is dark, perhaps very dark. A flower from a tree hangs in the damp air. The flower glows. Luminescence fills the Ethiopian night.

Daylight arrives. The square is empty. Then it fills with murderers and thieves, with petty cheats and foolish liars. They mill about. The sun blazes. It is a daytime world in which everything is visible. There are no secrets. There are no mysteries. We pass down streets made filthy with garbage. Men drop their feces in alleys. Dogs slink from shadow to shadow. The sun blazes on all of them. Cracks spread through concrete walls. Rust eats at the tin roofs of the houses. In the blazing sun even the shadows are harsh. This harshness cannot be avoided. We pass through it. The sun dips towards the horizon. It blazes onto the ocean. We watch the shadows lengthen. Perhaps we can hear a distant murmur. As the sun falls, there is a suggestion of luminescence in the air. It cannot quite be seen, but we have faith it is there. Night will come. In Ethiopia night will always come. We must believe that. Night will come. We will await it.

PART II
THE COMMENTARY

1. On the Ethiopian plains, night falls at six o'clock. And ends at six in the morning. The few minutes of twilight are perfectly balanced. The *equivalence* between day and night is exact. We understand this is not true in other countries, and that the comparative relationship between day and night changes. Why this should be so is not clear. Alfonse de Llovia (*My Life and Observations,* 1653) suggested the lack of balance in other countries was inherent and endemic. That is, the lack of balance exhibited itself in all aspects of the lives of these people. Elehui Cardin claimed to have found seventeen "points of imbalance" in a single composition of music by Johann Bach ("The Etudes of Dissonance," *Proceedings of the Royal Society,* 1912), and we ourselves have argued ("A Theory of Imbalance," *Proceedings,* 1983) that a whole series of dissonances may be postulated from the single fact of this diurnal-nocturnal imbalance. That John Twelve himself had some inkling of this is apparent from the notes he left. He writes them in a rude cafe at the side of a dirt road. The cafe is run by an old woman. She tells him freely that she has had eighteen children, of whom nine died before they were five years old. She squats at his table. Outside the sun is very hot. Three Ethiopian men, already drunk, stand behind him. They watch him make his notes. His handwriting is crabbed, tiny. One of the drunks stabs at the paper with his finger.

"What you do?"

His words are so slurred John cannot understand him.

"What you do? *There!*"

"I am writing," John says with the impatience of one explaining the obvious.

"Why you do that?"

41

"Why?"

The question seems to annoy him. He bends over the paper and writes the word: WHY? Above this word, so large and dark, are the notes about dissonance. The words sprawl across the page, almost unreadable. We have deciphered them with difficulty. *I dreamed last night*, he had written, *I was walking with a group of women. They would not talk to me.* John Twelve, unlike most of his countrymen, was not unsophisticated about metaphor. The meaning of his statement, which the rest of the dream (taking up nearly a third of the page) merely explicates, is clear. The large WHY? below is almost an excessive ornament.

"You journalist?" the drunk demands of John ("Periodista arre?"). He is leaning now across John's right shoulder. His dark finger has left its imprint on the white paper.

"Journalist?" John replies with irritation. "No—scholar."

"Journalist!" says the drunk.

He picks up the paper. It collapses in his hand. The white edges of it stick out from his fist.

"Journalist!" he repeats. He spits onto the dirt floor. The ancient woman—the fat little gnome—giggles. The white paper flying through the air seems to amuse her. All of them laugh uproariously. John pays for his coffee and leaves.

2. *...the owner, a plump man wearing a fez.* The man in the fez, Dar bin Saleh, was actually a thief, and not the owner of the motorcycle. That was why he had difficulty starting the machine. The real owner— insofar as it had a real owner—was a dark, wiry Abyssinian, who watched the transaction from the shadows. His name was Ahmed. He was a murderer. It was his profession. He did not interfere with John's purchase. He watched the money change hands. He then followed Dar bin Saleh and garroted him in an alley behind the Hotel Savoy, taking the money, bin Saleh's wristwatch, and his fine leather belt. Afterwards he went to the police. He reported the motorcycle stolen, and gave the sergeant five Maria Theresa dollars to purchase their action. In this manner he hoped to profit twice, in effect, from the occasion.

The day is hot and sultry. John Twelve parks the Indian motorcycle in front of the Hotel Savoy minutes after Dar bin Saleh, followed by Ahmed, passes it. A policeman strolls by later in the day, but he has not yet been advised of the theft: the five Maria Theresa dollars are not enough to make the sergeant act in haste. In Ethiopia police subsist on bribes, with the amount of the bribe determining the amount of action. They are paid no salary—a great savings to the municipal body—but are expected to earn their keep by the same system as all other Ethiopian males, that is, by lying, cheating, thieving, and murder. In Ethiopia the police mesh perfectly with their society. John Twelve, in his room, knew none of this. From his balcony he could look down at the huge motorcycle. He had expected to purchase a mule or other beast—perhaps a camel—for his journey across Ethiopia, and considers the motorcycle a stroke of luck. That evening he sits at his desk, in the yellow glow of a kerosene lamp, and fills the first page of his

43

notebook with his careful, tiny words. We have read them. His innocence is startling. As F'centa said, in a different context, "Reality has evaded them; they have yet to imagine the horrible truth of their existence."

3. He is a man alone. So too was Ahmed. Murderers are by nature loners, but in Ahmed's case the aloneness was complete. His father, also a murderer, had been killed by his uncle, the great Afaq Torquemond. Of Ahmed's six brothers, three had died of natural causes—typhoid, malaria, and dysentery, respectively—and three had been murdered. Ahmed had murdered one himself, not long after killing his father's uncle. There is often this incestuous quality in families of murderers. Ahmed's three sisters all died young. One was run over at age four by a Mercedes Benz, which was considered something of a distinction. One died at fifteen, while producing Ahmed's stillborn child. The other was murdered by Torquemond, the same uncle who murdered their father. Afaq Torquemond was quite famous. He carried murder to an exemplary extreme. He is reputed to have killed nearly fifty people. This does not put him in the same league as political leaders, who sometimes kill, anonymously, using orders written on slips of paper, many millions of people; or company presidents whose factories produce the pollutants and weapons that maim and kill other millions. Nevertheless, in the sphere of which we speak, Ahmed's father's uncle was considered exemplary. It is difficult to murder many people when you must do it individually, face-to-face, as it were, using primitive implements such as knives, garrotes, bludgeons.

Ahmed was thus quite alone. He had coffee some mornings with friends—other murderers—but their relationship was always marked with wariness. Their common pursuit drew them together, but one does not, at risk of one's life, let down one's guard in their company. In any case, even amongst murderers, he was something of an outsider. He was a thoughtful man, and a literary one. This thoughtfulness is unusual among Ethiopian men in general, and particularly so among murderers. Murder is not an action that one can examine with equanimity. It was Ahmed's burden to be a murderer who reflected on his actions. This quirk in his character caused him considerable pain, but it was a pain he bore with dignity.

Early one morning Ahmed watches John mount his—Ahmed's—motorcycle. The engine thumps loudly. The cracked saddlebags bulge. Another bag is tied across the gas tank. John pulls the leather helmet over his head and buckles it in place. The goggles make his eyes huge. He glances over his shoulder—he does not notice Ahmed—and starts down the road. Ahmed, with the peculiar liquidity which marks his movements, strolls to the bus station.

4. He lies in his sleeping bag. A Camp 7 sleeping bag, rather soiled, purchased in Long Beach, California two years earlier. Ahmed, on the other hand, steps out of the Hotel Puerto Vallarta.

He has dressed for the occasion in a loose silk shirt and gray slacks. He wears gray leather shoes, and no socks. He appears casually elegant. Because of this he stands apart from the crowd of Americans and Canadians who fill the boulevard. The Americans, Canadians and occasional Australians are dressed in resort wear. Resort wear consists mostly of flowered shirts in shades of purple, orange, and yellow, and short baggy pants. The faces, arms, and legs of these Americans and Canadians are bright red. Some have peeling skin. The fatter women have dimpled thighs. The thinner ones, because of the way resort clothing is cut, appear spindly. Ahmed passes through them like a sleek leopard amongst cows.

5. *John...is unaware of this.* A murderer, on the other hand, must be aware of a great many things, simultaneously. That murderers have heightened awareness has been suggested by Arbent Kan, Delorio Santez, and H.P. Hentessy. A successful murderer neither drinks alcohol nor smokes tobacco or opium. The alertness of murderers is legendary. Afaq Torquemond once saved the life of a minister of state when he detected, out of the corner of his eye, the moving shape of a rifle muzzle 300 meters away, deduced instantly who the intended victim must be, and with casual ease interjected a bystander into what he judged to be the line of fire. Torquemond, as every Ethiopian knows, then dispatched the minister himself—when a man is meant to die, he is meant to die—but did the job the way a murderer is supposed to do it: close at hand, in this case with an icepick thrust between the ribs and into the minister's heart. The gunman was set upon by a crowd and torn limb from limb. In Ethiopia, the proprieties are to be observed.

As Ahmed walks from the Hotel Puerto Vallarta and through the throngs of tourists, he observes them all. He notes marriages in disarray, affairs beginning and ending, teenagers glazed with drugs; he sees slack jaws and even slacker eyes; the marks left in the flesh by too many whiskeys, too many fatty foods, too many sweets, steroids, and sexual failures. Out of long habit he singles out the faces of victims and those about to become victims. He is not intending to murder anyone—he has killed recently, after all—but a murderer's skills are never quiet. He must use these skills constantly, not only to hone them, but to protect himself. A murderer is always fair prey to another murderer. Murderers, in fact, and victims are separated by a fine line. Ahmed has pointed this out himself in his elegant monograph. *Your face is mine,* he wrote. *I see you as I see myself, in a mirror. That is how I recognize you.* A murderer in Ethiopia, of course, cannot murder just anyone. He can only murder a victim. In this respect he is like the pariah dogs. He too is an outsider. He functions at the edge of society, and does not belong to it. He is a predator, not a herd animal. His evolutionary job is to cull the herd, and to assist those rare people wise enough to seek out their own death.

But if he is not searching for a victim to murder, he is nonetheless searching. Later we will explain why. Finally he slows his pace. He comes almost to a stop. He drifts across the street, slipping between the crowds of trucks and taxis and jeeps filled with over-fed, over-blond youths. He is stalking. When he stalks he is virtually invisible. The red and white tourists do not notice him. He is a shadow flowing over the sidewalk. When he is satisfied he slips behind his prey.

"Mademoiselle?"

He has touched her shoulder. She turns. Her eyelids lift, slightly. "Yes?"

The single word dooms her.

6. It is dark. Night has fallen in "Puerto Vallarta" as well. This town, gathering American dollars from millions of tourists, is the principal source of hard currency for Ethiopia. The name of the town changes regularly, according to agreement with a certain Latin American country. Next week the town will become Cancun, and the week after that Las Hadas. When night falls in this town, daytime activities do not entirely cease. There is not that precise division which bifurcates the rest of Ethiopia. Thus while John sleeps, surrounded by the glowing animals of the Ethiopian night, in Puerto Vallarta the streets are still filled with foreign tourists. Lights, not animals, glow in the hotels and restaurants and discos. Lamps hover over the street, attracting swarms of flying insects. However, the Ethiopian night does leak into the town. All the electrical power from the humming lines cannot entirely keep it out. This is apparent to even a casual observer. The town seems harsh and dry during daylight. When day is gone the town acquires a kind of charm, perhaps even beauty. The tourists themselves, graceless as they are, notice this. They talk about the nights in Puerto Vallarta. Or Acapulco. Or Ixtapa. They are not aware that they are talking about the magic of the Ethiopian night.

Things that are inconceivable during daylight hours become possible at night. Only an Ethiopian like Ahmed is aware of this. He touches the shoulder of his prey.

"Mademoiselle?"

"Yes?"

Her eyelids lift slightly, then descend. But the rising and lowering of these eyelids has taken place at the exact moment when daylight becomes night. At that moment her soul is illuminated, and the vision thus created cannot be rescinded. Her single word, the single "Yes?" is spoken at the same moment, and likewise cannot be rescinded. Nor can the actions which follow. Moments later she is in his room. Her pants are on the floor. She is bent forward, leaning over a chair. Ahmed spears her from behind. Although her vulva does not glow—she is not an Ethiopian woman—it possesses a satisfying warmth. She is very young, scarcely more than a child, and quite slim, but there is already that dimpling at her thighs that seems to plague American women. Her legs nonetheless are certainly beautiful, especially in the pale light from the window. Ahmed's room is high above Puerto Vallarta; from the window—she now leans against its sill, still bent over, still receiving Ahmed's sexual organ—she can see the long line of vehicles moving in the streets below and the disorganized throng of people moving on the sidewalks. All are illuminated by yellow light. The yellow light rises through the air and dimly illuminates the girl's young breasts. Her shirt, adorned with a pale purple flower, lies on the bed next to Ahmed's trousers. When she lies on the bed, next to this shirt and these trousers, her legs are over Ahmed's shoulders. He holds one of her ankles in his hand. His body is arched. As she looks up at him her eyelids drop even lower. Her mouth, which is slackly open, bears faint traces of lipstick. The lips are bruised. They are thus engorged with blood. The lips of her vulva are likewise engorged with blood. Her liquids may be seen on Ahmed's mouth and, transferred from there, around her mouth as well. When her legs are lowered her heels hook around his ankles. There is a symmetry to their positions. At that moment she takes a deep breath.

The moon has risen. Its yellow glow joins the yellow glow that spills onto the sidewalk from the windows of the shops and restaurants of Puerto Vallarta. Ahmed offers his arm. The girl takes it. She is wearing now a dress, although it is not clear where this dress came from. It is the exact color of twilight. The hour is late; it may be very late. Few people are about. Ahmed leads the girl into what appears to be a restaurant, or perhaps a nightclub. Three people await them at a table. They are Haile Selassie, Sheba Makeda, and Prester John. Of the three of them only Sheba, who has been dead more than 3,000 years, can speak. She looks like a bejeweled hyena.

The girl says her name is Sandi—with an 'i.'

"That is impossible, my dear," says Sheba. "I would like to be kind to you but a name like that is inconceivable. I wont have it on a marquee. I shall give you a name. Provisionally, of course. What do you think of 'Dominique?'"

The girl gives Ahmed a sidewise glance.

"Dominique?" she says.

"Provisionally, of course. What do you say, Ahmed? Is she a domina*tor*—or a domina*tee?*"

Her mouth nearly unhinges with a bray of laughter. Her teeth are yellow stubs. Haile Selassie, next to her, winces. The Queen of Sheba, dead 3,000 years, has terrible breath. Even Dominique, across the table, must draw back from it. She says nothing, however, about this coarse display. Her gaze lingers on Sheba's fingers, each adorned with a rare and precious stone. There is gold strung around her neck. Diamonds hang from each ear. The leopard skin coat, askew on one shoulder, has a broach on which Dominique counts fifteen emeralds, each larger than ten carats. Sheba's open-toed pumps are festooned with rubies. A yellowed toenail—it curves beyond the tip of the shoe— has a sapphire glued to it. Many of these jewels are coarsely faceted. They are uneven in shape. Nevertheless they glow even in this dim room. There is a nimbus of light around this creature. When she leans forward her fat breasts, insecurely housed in her evening gown, flop onto the tabletop. There are rubies in the folds of her flesh. Dominique's eyes, always hooded, become even more secretive. She crosses one nylon-sheathed leg over the other.

"What's the movie about?" she asks.

Her voice is breathless.

She stands on the stage. A single spotlight illuminates her. Perhaps they are in a nightclub after all. She turns slowly. Although there is no music—there is no sound in the room except the whir of Prester John's

Panavision camera—perhaps she is imagining music.

"The film," Ahmed says at last—he is still at the table—"is about the delusionary nature of reality."

The girl turns, and turns.

"The delusionary nature of what we call reality. Or perhaps, my dear, the real nature of delusion."

Sheba barks.

"Do not listen to him, dear Dominique. I will tell you what the film is about. It is about a man who foolishly—or am I being redundant?—a man who foolishly crosses Ethiopia. On a motorcycle, during World War II. A journey that can only be described, if we must describe it, as the triumph of delusion over reality. What else is a summer in Ethiopia? Nowhere else is there such heat. Nowhere else does the sun blaze with such fierceness. While bombers explode over Europe, while Nazis march from triumph to defeat, while Jews cook in ovens and children burn in Dresden, while whole cities are turned into rubble, men into cripples, women into whores—this man, this fool, straddles a four-cylinder motorcycle and crosses Ethiopia—searching for truth, for beauty, for reality! Who could imagine such a thing? Only Ahmed, the great *directeur*, the *haute autor* who dazzles us with images conceived out of the filth of the world! A man who crawls—yes, my dear—a man who crawls through the gutters of our souls to erect monuments to the splendor of imagination! He smells of cordite, Dominique, he stinks of TNT and the hot oil from the engines of tanks, he reeks of the decay of flesh, of burnt limbs, of blood turning black in the sun! And he promises us—listen to me, dear Dominique!—he promises us beauty and the purity of his vision! A madman!" The girl turns, and turns. Although the camera continues to whir, Prester John is no longer visible. Haile Selassie has become a density in the air. Sheba brays once more, spraying the air with jewels of spit. Then she too is gone. Only Ahmed remains.

"He put his hand on my leg."

"Who?"

"That man—"

"Selassie?"

"Yes."

"Ah."

"What does he do? On the movie?"

"He is the producer."

"And you—"

"The director."

"That woman—"

"The Queen. You must have noticed her jewelry. She is fabulously wealthy. She is the principal backer of the film. So she has, of course, special prerogatives. But dont let her put her hand on your leg. And I will speak to Selassie, although it will do little good. I will tell him your legs are mine to fondle."

"Oh....Shall I keep on turning?"

"Slip the dress off your shoulder."

"Like this?"

"Now let it slide to your feet."

". . ."

"Precisely. Precisely, dear Dominique."

7. John descends from the Ethiopian plateau and enters a town along the coast.
This plateau is the dominating feature of Ethiopia. Most of Ethiopia
rises over 8,000 feet above sea level. In its physical features, Ethiopia
rather resembles a hat. It is nearly surrounded by a narrow brim of
lowland desert. The Rift Valley, like a crease in the crown of this hat,
falls off to the south. Some of the central plateau is comprised of level
or rolling plains—the Gojjan, for instance, and the Shoa plains—but
much of it is broken by great canyons. These canyons are the largest,
and the steepest, on earth, as many writers have attested. The Simian
Highlands in the north are so broken with fissures that only one animal,
the Walia Ibex, the most nimble creature alive, can live there. Nothing
else can negotiate the sheer cliffs. The Abbai River—or Blue Nile, as
we understand Westerners call it—has a canyon six thousand feet deep
that is quite impassable. Aside from the Abbai, there are rivers like the
Wabbi Shebali, which rises near Lake Abaya, and the great Hawash,
which vanishes into the sands of Dankaliland. These Dankalis are
lowland savages who kill all who enter their territory. Elsewhere
Ethiopia is populated by Gallas and Abyssinians and Nubians. Slaves,
mostly Nubians, are taken from the west, near the Arrusi escarpment.
In the north central area are Portuguese castles built in the 16th
century by Dom Christoforo da Gama when he came to the aid of the
Christian King Lebna Dengal. Known in Europe as Prester John, he
was being hunted like an animal by the army of the Musselman
Mohammad Gran. When John descends from the plateau he skirts
Dankaliland, and passes near the area where Prester John once hid.
The port town he reaches is on the shore of the Red Sea. The name of the
town, in English, means little apples, although no apples are grown there.

The town is built in front of, up the sides of, and between two hills. The town faces a bay which provides good anchorage. Behind the town is a lagoon which extends several miles to the south. Once canoes skimmed this lagoon. Fishermen cast nets at night. Poets came to gaze at this scene, which was famous throughout Ethiopia. *The nets are sea spray/Fish made from moonlight/Gnarled hands do their work. (Da magan sen maganan/ Dashen sakan dashoi/Korganlagan da mogan dakoi.)* When Puerto Vallarta was built it had to be supplied with electricity. A generating plant was constructed on the edge of the lagoon to create this electricity, which until then was unknown in Ethiopia. In a single year the town of "little apples" tripled in size. A sewer line was built to the sea to accommodate this increase. When it collapsed—the cement was adulterated—the sewage poured into the lagoon, along with the waste products from the generating plant. Soon the sand around the lagoon turned gray. The fish died, and then all the plants except the hardy mangrove. In the center of the lagoon, where the waste from the town met the waste from the plant, the water boiled. A haze of selenium, lead oxide, and mercury vapor filled the air. The prevailing wind blew this haze into the city. Soon children were born deformed. They had incomplete faces. Six fingers became as common as five. Parents would have ten, fifteen, sometimes twenty of these children. Not all would live. Those who did could be seen walking single file down the streets, the ones who had eyes leading the ones who did not. Their parents garbed them in black. On Sundays they limped, they crawled, they were led, they were carried to the church, where the priest thanked God for the town's high level of employment, the highest in Ethiopia.

It is into this town that John Twelve descends. He stops at the outskirts to purchase gasoline. Children rush out to surround him. They carry rags which they wipe over his fenders. Their quick little hands dart into his luggage, looking for loose objects. John tries to wave them away, at first politely, then with desperation. The children grin at him, flashing teeth that are white, brown, and black. All this is on film, captured by Prester John's giant Panavision camera. The children have a single cry:

"Money!"

"Money!"

"Money!"

Gasoline bubbles and spits into the tank. The attendant takes advantage of John's distraction to charge him double, and short-change him as well. From his packs John loses one of his cameras, a pair of shoes, and two bars of soap. The 2 1/2 gallons of gasoline he acquires thus costs him more than $600. Later Ahmed shows the "rushes" of this scene to Dominique, Sheba, and Haile Selassie. Prester John comes back and forth from the lab where he develops the film. They are in the same nightclub, or perhaps restaurant, as before, although it is no longer clear that this nightclub or restaurant is in Puerto Vallarta or in the town John has just entered. Dominique wears her twilight dress. Her legs are sheathed in black nylon. Her feet are shod in black patent shoes with spiked heels. On one finger she wears a sapphire. When the lights are dimmed Ahmed puts his hand on her leg. After a moment Haile Selassie does the same. Dominique's hooded eyes watch the screen.

✛

"Who plays the man on the motorcycle?"

"Does he look familiar?"

"Vaguely."

"You would know him by his stage name. In America he is a rock star. He calls himself 'Fang.'"

✛

Fang grins at the camera. He mugs. He pulls back his lips to reveal his incisors, the incisors from which he takes his name. He is famous for his onstage antics. During his concerts he bites off the heads of small animals—bats, rats, and small cats. He sprays the blood from these animals onto the front rows of his audience. When a young girl—most of his fans are young girls—is sprayed with blood she will faint. Her body will jerk orgasmically. She will not wash for weeks, until the mark—the blood—left by Fang has at last worn away. This is a tradition—that is, this has been going on for about a year, which is as long as most traditions last in America. The ecstasy he rouses has little

57

to do with his music, which is mostly repetitive chords, or his lyrics, which are mostly obscene and blasphemous phrases spoken backwards, or his talents as a performer, which are ordinary. Marat Secord, the great Ethiopian analyst of foreign cultures, would doubtless call him a 'releaser,' a word he coined for another American singer of little talent. (See "Rudy Vallee: A Conspiracy of Hysteria," *Proceedings*, 1939.) Such 'releasers' become the focus of the repressed sexuality of American girls. They are chosen almost at whim, and are discarded as haphazardly. Some of these performers, like Fang, come to believe they are actually talented, and that their talent is the reason for their popularity. When their popularity vanishes—often overnight—they blame producers, the media, politicians, agents, organized religion and organized crime, and in one instance, the flouride in the drinking water. In truth they are simply following the immutable trail described a half century ago by Marat Secord, who analyzed the repression and attendant promiscuity of American girls.

On the screen Fang, in the character of John Twelve, roars away from the gas station leaving a trail of dust. In this trail of dust an Ethiopian boy examines the shoes he has stolen. There is a bubo on his neck the size of a toad. He turns towards the camera and smiles sweetly.

"Will I meet him?"

"Fang? You will play one scene with him."

"One?"

"Just one. But it is a crucial one. Now watch this."

Prester John has threaded new film into the projector. Dominique appears. She turns, and turns, illuminated by the spotlight.

"Beautiful," Ahmed says.

Dominique looks at him out of the corner of her eye.

8. ...*a woman descends*. It was not a woman but a *gajjin*, or transvestite, in this case a young man named Julio Abril. Julio, expecting a busy afternoon, was dressed in his latest finery: French stockings and garter belt, shoes by Charles Jourdan, and brassiere and panties by Christian Dior. Beneath his white djellaba he wore a slick mauve cocktail dress, in the current mode, made by his mother. His breasts had been pumped up and his figure feminized by injections of lamb placenta. He was one of the stars of Le Club Mediteranee, a private organization frequented by politicians and wealthier businessmen. These gajjin are a recognized class in Ethiopia. They are trained to treat men in the way men treat each other, with flattery, lies, and petty deceits. Gajjin are famous for their skills at fellatio. Julio has been heard to brag that he ate so much sperm that he no longer took food. We cannot be certain that this is true.

Women plied the trade of prostitution too, but they were fewer in number and more atavistic in appearance. When John Twelve—or Fang, playing John Twelve—rode past the electric generation plant and along the lagoon, he passed three of these women. Each had her own tree. Shift workers from the plant lined up at these trees. John saw the lines of men, but did not notice the woman at the head of each line. Prester John's camera noticed, however. After each customer finished, the women bathed quickly in the lagoon, thus absorbing through their orifices lead, zinc, mercury, fecal matter, and other pollutants. Each charged half a Maria Theresa dollar, or about 25 cents in U.S. currency. By the end of a shift, this amounted to a goodly sum by Ethiopian standards. The women, however, seldom lived more than a year or two, usually dying of some form of cancer induced by the mercury or lead or other carcinogen in the lagoon. Of the three women at work on the day

59

John Twelve passed, one was already near death. A tumor pressed visibly at her abdomen. Another's body was criss-crossed by surgical scars—a hysterectomy, an appendectomy, a colostomy, plus an exploratory incision which had exposed benign tumors in her viscera. The third girl was only thirteen, recently sold into service just as her sisters before her: their father considered daughters a harvestable crop. Just before the camera approached, this girl was seen applying lipstick and patting at her hair. As a man grunted over her, she turned toward the camera and smiled. The camera lingered for a moment on the happy face. When the man ejaculated she slapped him playfully on his rump. Rather coquettishly she stepped into the water, her back turned to us, hands covering her breasts. Then she squatted, rinsed, and returned to work. The camera moved on. John, meanwhile, in the blazing sun, stares at Julio Abril. Dominique, at the same moment, sits at her dressing table. The room is cool and dusky. A lace garter belt encircles her tiny waist. Ahmed watches as she leans into the mirror to attach diamond earrings. They hang from the lobes of her ears like miniature chandeliers. In the mirror she sees Ahmed approach. Not now, she murmurs as he bends over her. Yet even as these words leave her mouth the figure in the mirror rises to meet Ahmed. Dominique's eyes widen, perhaps in momentary alarm, and then half close into their habitual expression. The mirror is like a movie screen: she sees black hands enclosing pale breasts. She watches as the woman in the mirror exposes her neck to the black man's mouth. There is a genuine grace to her movements, and to his. Perhaps the scene will be accompanied by music. Doubtless the music will be sinuous. As white legs encased in black rise into the air—the tips of the shoes are irridescent—Dominique sees hands, perhaps her own hands, a diamond on one finger and a sapphire on another, pull at the tops of the stockings. Each stocking, stretched tautly, shimmers. The creature in the mirror throws back her head. Dominique can hear—everyone in the room can surely hear— the air sucking into her mouth. Ahmed's weapon—he is a murderer, after all—has penetrated the woman's body. Orgasm and death, in the mirror, are simultaneous. Perhaps they are identical. The music continues as the scene fades out.

9. Only the slaves...remain overseas.... Many commentators have mentioned hearing Amharic spoken in the kitchens of Europe's finest restaurants. It is apparently difficult for those restaurants to hire native people to work the scullery. Ethiopian slaves, who are used to long hours at no pay at all, doubtless find the work easy.

Slavery is a venerable institution in Ethiopia. Prester John, when he was Lebna Dengal, King of Ethiopia, owned more than 10,000 slaves. He also had 1,000 concubines and a hundred wives. He had a hawkish nose, a barrel chest, and a virile member. He sired so many sons and daughters that people often refer to Lebna Dengal as the true father of Ethiopia. Today even beggars in Ethiopia claim to be descended from this prolific man. When he was forty years of age, he was converted to Christianity by a Jesuit. This was not as difficult as one might think. Christianity has had a long history in Ethiopia, and Judaism even longer. Lebna Dengal suffered from one severe flaw: he was an honest man. This was a great liability in his dealings with his own people, and an even greater liability when he began to reflect, as people often do at age 40, on the meaning of his life. He was also a man of great directness. He had used this trait to power himself into the kingship, to hew and hack and slice his way through all opposition. When he became a Christian he put himself into the hands of Jesus. He was too honest, and too direct, to do otherwise. He released his 10,000 slaves into a labor market that was always uncertain. Freedom holds little meaning to most people, and none to most slaves, who found themselves begging on the streets and turning to thievery to sustain themselves. When provinces rebelled, Lebna Dengal, who now called himself Prester John, crossed himself and said he had faith in Jesus;

Jesus was testing him. Prester John smiled at his advisers, and took to wearing simple white clothes. He went for walks, blessing his subjects. Jesus will look after us, he said. We must put our faith in Him. At this moment in history, Islam began one of its periodic expansions. A Musselman named Mohammed Gran led an army across the Red Sea. Prester John laughed at his advisors' fears.

"Jesus is more powerful than an army of Musselmen," he said.

Prester John waited for miracles. The Ethiopian armies, lacking leadership, splintered into ineffective groups. The Moslems slaughtered, raped, and burned their way towards the capital. "We must put our faith in Jesus," Prester John declared again and again. Jesus would not allow the one Christian nation in Africa to be destroyed. Prester John fasted and prayed. He drank only water for fifteen days. He smiled peacefully at all who approached him. "Jesus told me not to worry," he said. "Jesus spoke to me. I feel certain He has great plans for all of us." Such was the force of Prester John's personality that people often believed him. He was an island of peace in a city torn with fear. He walked the streets, beaming at the panic-stricken people, blessing babies, calming mothers. He was in the streets when the army of Mohammed Gran burst into the city. They raced right past him. None of the Musselmen imagined this simple figure, heavily bearded, grinning, might be the King of Ethiopia. As his palace burned, Prester John stumbled from the city. His beard now was singed. There was blood on his hands, up his arms, and over his white clothing, from his ministering to the dying. He slipped and fell into a ravine full of thorn bushes. His clothes, his face, his body were sliced by the sharp thorns. He huddled against the cold. He could see in the sky the ruddy glow of his burning capital. He prayed all night. In the morning ashes floated through the air, like snow. The only visions that filled his head were visions of burning buildings, screaming children, horses rearing in panic, and corpses, piles of corpses, all leaking blood which ran in torrents down his streets. Prester John staggered off into the wilds of his country. For five years Mohammed Gran pursued him. Villagers hid him. He slept in caves. He ate bark and leather from his own boots.

A Portuguese army led by Dom Christoforo de Gama landed in

Massowa, and allied itself with various Abyssinian chiefs. Da Gama was soon killed, but the Abyssinians and Portuguese, united under the new King Galaoudeous, took revenge against Mohammed Gran and at last drove the Musselmen from Ethiopia. Prester John was forgotten. He crawled down the escarpment near Dankaliland, subsisting on wild berries and competing with jackals for the rank carcasses of dead animals. He bathed in the Red Sea. Looking out over that great body of water he swore an oath. Since his words had brought such suffering to his people he would never speak again. To this day, alive and dead, bearded, face burnt and creased by the sun, flesh going slack on his arms and legs, eyes bright with anger, he has been faithful to his oath.

10. There is a face at a window. Ahmed's face was often at a window too. As a murderer it was his nature to be an observer. There was a voyeuristic quality to his life. Because of this it was easy for him to become a film director.

The film, like this book, is called *The Ethiopian Exhibition.* It is a series of images. It is entirely appropriate that the cameraman, Prester John, does not speak. In the late twentieth century only images speak. Words are dead. "In the beginning," says the Gospel of John, "was the Word." In the beginning words had power. They were mysterious. No one understood how words came into being or how they worked their magic. When bards like the blind Homer—he could not see, but he could speak—used their words to relate tales of adventure and mystery, people listened enthralled. They understood such words came from the gods. They understood words were sacred. Only people were blessed with the ability to say and understand words. Words remained sacred even when they were written down. Few people could read or write these words. During the dark ages in Europe, we understand that only monks retained the ability to read and write. This was entirely appropriate. But in the twentieth century, in Europe and the Americas and even parts of Asia, vast numbers of people were trained in this skill. Mass communication became feasible. This did not happen in Ethiopia, of course, where the true nature of words was always recognized. But in the rest of the world, when the mass of people began to read and write, words were quickly destroyed. Political leaders soon recognized that if a lie was repeated often enough, adamantly enough, widely enough, and in sufficient forms—in newspapers, in magazines, over radios and later television—people would accept it even if they knew it was false. Within a few decades words were debased everywhere. War Ministries became Departments of Defense. Invasions became incursions. Weapons designed to maim and kill were called Peacemakers. War was described as an action to protect the rights of the people it killed. Programs of assassination in occupied countries were said to be attempts to reach the hearts and minds of the inhabitants. Words were so debased that they ceased to mean anything. They were used finally only to sell cars, televisions, detergents, political platforms, tax plans, and as justifications for massacres. They were used only to avoid truth.

John Twelve explained all this to Ahmed. Ahmed, as a voyeur, as a murderer, recognized the debasement of words entering his country along with Coca Cola, electricity, and foreign ideologies. "The Ethiopian Exhibition," John Twelve explained, would have to be a series of images. The book itself would use words only to create images. It would be an attempt to purify language of all deception. The movie would be the book in its purest form. No words would be spoken. Even the cameraman must not speak. The purity had to be rigorous.

They sat in a cafe overlooking a broad avenue in Addis Ababba. Gum trees lined the street. A Cord Cabriolet purred past, followed by a huge Packard with a veiled face at a rear window.

"I myself," said John Twelve, "will play the part of Fang, playing me. And to add verisimilitude, I have imported a four-cylinder Indian motorcycle. It is on the docks right now."

Ahmed nodded. He suggested Prester John as cameraman.

"Excellent," said John Twelve. "Are we agreed?"

"We are agreed."

They shook hands. They ordered another round of *cafe a lait* and looked contentedly over the avenue.

11. When the air is very still...this weight may be tangible. Perhaps John Twelve, standing on the parapet of Haile Selassie's summer palace, can feel this weight. If so he gives no indication of it. Instead he gazes down over the Valley of Shoa. The steep sides of this valley are so barren, so gaunt, that they could themselves be the symbol of despair. Yet John Twelve does not appear despairing. He appears satisfied, perhaps even smug. We ourselves acknowledge his accomplishments. He has traveled many thousands of miles. He has overcome great difficulties. Perhaps he has a right to be smug. He stands on the parapet of Haile Selassie's summer palace, dressed in a silk robe, a cup of coffee in his hand, listening to the sounds of construction rising, along with the morning mist, from the valley below.

The cries of the workmen are as harsh as the cries of Ethiopian birds. For six weeks these men have been at work. Night after night trucks howled and snarled up the mountainous road to disgorge lumber, bricks, slabs of concrete, fixtures, and corrugated tin for roofs. Cobbled streets were laid out. Houses rose up the hill, built one on top of another. Although it all looked helter-skelter, it was carefully planned. Engineers stood about with large maps and tape measures. Surveyors shouted instructions. Foremen grumbled. No angle was square, no line vertical or horizontal. Everything was askew, except for the rails on which the cameras would run. These rails were laid with great care. To save construction costs many of the buildings were no more than false fronts. They were incomplete shells. How complete a building was—whether or not it had a roof or a third or fourth wall—was determined by the angle at which the camera caught it. This was all plotted on graphs, which the engineers carried. Windows that faced the cameras had shutters attached. Curtains were hung, and lanterns placed on rude tables. The nighttime trucks also brought loads of shrubs, bushes, and trees, which were placed around these buildings. The plaza itself took seven mature banyan trees, thirteen acacias, and twenty-nine flowering magnolias, plus hundreds of smaller plants. As John Twelve stood on the parapet of Haile Selassie's summer palace, workmen were putting the finishing touches—the last nails, the last sod—into place in this Ethiopian village.

12. ...the refuse pits that encircle even the smallest village. By two o'clock these refuse pits began appearing around the village below Haile Selassie's summer palace. An hour later, when the caravan of vehicles passes, children are already picking through the refuse. Thin gray smoke rises into the air. Pariah dogs loiter in the shadows surrounding the refuse pits.

Zebanias carrying muskets trot in front of the cars.

"*Zourban!*" they shout. "*Zourban!*"

In the second car—a 1936 Hudson Terraplane—Dominique turns to Ahmed.

"What are they saying?"

"They are telling people to get out of the way."

She peers through the window. One of her fine hands fingers the mink pelt draped over her shoulder. She sees children lining the street. Their dark faces smile. They hold little flags which they wave in the air. Behind them are schoolteachers, parents, and the shopkeepers who have come out to wave also. The plaza in the center of town is filled with people standing under the fine old banyon and acacia and magnolia trees. A brass band plays in the bandstand. A tuba goes *oompah, oom-pah-pah.* Policemen in pale green uniforms and polished boots march back and forth. Other policemen, fat ones, squat on Harley-Davidson motorcycles. They wear black leather jackets and sunglasses and stare stonily at the crowds. Everyone else smiles, except perhaps for a few beggar women, who sit in doorways counting their beads, and slaves, thin, dark men who stand rather like storks on one leg. In the car ahead of Dominique and Ahmed—it is a fine old Dusenberg—Haile Selassie himself touches a hand to his braided cap.

Otherwise he does not acknowledge the presence of his subjects. Seated next to him is Sheba. She periodically reaches into her purse, extracts a handful of pearls, and throws them out the window. Children scramble for these pearls as they bounce over the cobblestones.

Dominique stares out the window. There is a secret smile hovering about her lips, which are turned away from Ahmed.

"It's like a parade," she says.

"Isnt it?"

"Have they all turned out to see us?"

"They have come to see the Emperor."

Dominique turns slightly. Ahmed, in the gloomy interior of the Hudson Terraplane, is leaning back into the cushions. Dominique's eyes look cautiously in his direction. The light through the window illuminates half of her face, but none of his.

"The Emperor?"

"Haile Selassie. He was once Emperor of Ethiopia."

After a moment she says:

"Haile Selassie?"

"Yes. In those days he was called the Conquering Lion of Judah. He was deposed—oh, many years ago—in a revolution. But the people have never forgotten him."

The Hudson Terraplane purrs over the cobblestones. Children continue to wave their little flags. Dominique's eyes slip back towards Ahmed.

"Mr. Selassie was an Emperor?"

"The man you see, of course, is actually George Smithers, an actor from Pasadena. But he looks precisely like Haile Selassie. I doubt their mothers could tell them apart. He has the same tiny hands—and even the same taste for young girls."

"He's an actor?"

"Exactly."

"I thought he was the producer."

"That is true also. It is a multiple role, shall we say?"

He leans forward and taps the chauffeur on the shoulder.

"Come," Ahmed says. "Let me show you our village."

Everything has been laid out as planned. Ahmed inspects the rails, which are like the rails of a miniature railroad. The camera, he explains, will run in a special carriage along these rails. He shows Dominique a chalk mark on the rail.

"It is here," he says, "that the camera will begin to rise. It will swoop into the air like a bird. All done hydraulically, of course. John Twelve—or Fang—will be across the street, half in the shadow of that building. This scene must be done at five o'clock, when the sun is precisely in position. As the camera rises, the rooftops become visible. That is why the rooftops, over there, are finished. You will notice that these buildings, on this side, possess only eaves. They have no backs as well. They are what we call false fronts."

Dominique stands a few paces from him. Her shadow falls obliquely to the ground. Her eyes are mere slits.

"You built this village?"

"A month ago it did not exist."

"Who were all the people in the street?"

"Extras, hired for the film."

When she follows Ahmed she remains the same few paces behind him. He sticks his head through a doorway.

"Empty," he says. "No back. Only rudimentary walls. While over there"—he nods across the street—"over there are shelves filled with canned goods. A kerosene lamp that actually works hangs from the ceiling. An ancient cash register with brass keys will be on the counter. A man could open that store—tomorrow. Would you like to see?"

She shakes her head.

"Ah," says Ahmed. "And here is the Indian motorcycle."

It is in a dark shed-like building. A near-naked man squats at its side with a glowing torch in his hand.

"This is the machine," Ahmed says, "that Fang will ride as he portrays John Twelve. Unfortunately the pistons are rusted. The whole engine is quite frozen. The motorcycle, you understand, is rare, and it has not been possible to obtain parts for it. So this man is attaching another engine, a small gasoline engine, to the right side of the motorcycle. The camera will always be on the left, so this engine will not be visible. A simple solution, yes? Of course the machine will not be able to go very fast, but speed wont be necessary. And the sound of the engine—well, these modern engines make noises like yapping dogs. But it will be a simple matter, in the studio, to dub in the deeper pounding of the original, four-cylinder engine."

Sparks fly as the torch burns into metal.

"Ah. And there you see another pail of rails. These will carry the camera into an alley behind the Hotel Savoy, where a murder will take place."

"A murder?" says Dominique behind him.

"One must have drama in a film, mustnt one?"

He turns to her and holds out his hand.

"Come. Let us take some coffee, eh?"

The cafe has rude wooden tables and chairs. A gnomish woman, dressed in black, waddles up. Ahmed orders two coffees with milk. Deeper in the shadows three men—perhaps they are construction workers—stare at Dominique. Their faces have the slackness of habitual drinkers, although they do not seem yet to be drunk. They murmur to each other but make no move to interfere with the scene that now unfolds.

Dominique sits upright in her chair, lips pursed together, toying with her chipped cup. A sensitive observer—Ahmed, for instance— would recognize in her expression anger, uncertainty, and a trace of fear. It may be—it is probable—that she feels she has been taken advantage of in some obscure way. It would seem she has not been told everything relevant about this film. She has been allowed to assume things that were not, in fact, the case. Whatever secret pleasure she felt earlier, driven like a movie star, or a lady of state, past crowds of cheering children, has vanished. Perhaps in the aftermath of this elation she feels foolish. She is far from home, far from her family. She

71

has put her faith in a man she hardly knows. The sun, falling towards the horizon, illuminates this man's face. It may be a sly face. The age of this face is indeterminate. The eyes are dark and seem to reveal nothing. He talks smoothly, perhaps in several languages. Perhaps he lies smoothly in several languages. It is probable that a movie is being produced, or at least contemplated; that much can be deduced from all the preparations. But the movie may not be what she was led to expect. Nothing is clear. Dominique was raised in a culture in which uncertainty is unacceptable. Americans, in fact, will accept the most blatant fabrication as an alternative to uncertainty. The easiest fabrication, as American politicians know, is xenophobia. Since it is her nature to be secretive, especially when filled with mistrust, she will say nothing, ask nothing, to clarify her position. She will watch through her slitted eyelids while people try to take advantage of her.

Ahmed sips with apparent pleasure at his coffee.

"My dear Dominique," he says. He spreads his black fingers and stares at them. "It is a great pleasure to work with you on this film. You must understand that as an artist I worship beauty. Beauty is my sole source of pleasure. That is why I create films. I am allowed—even paid—to take disparate elements, to take confusion and incoherence, and bring them to the highest order possible, the order of beauty. But such order, such beauty, is like a pearl. It requires a grain of sand around which to coalesce. In my art I think of this grain of sand as the Central Metaphor. It is the metaphor around which everything else gathers. In this film, my dear, and perhaps in my life—if you will allow me a deeply personal observation—you, Dominique, are the Central Metaphor."

Outside, children climb on board a bus. Flags litter the roadside. Black smoke puffs from exhaust pipes.

Someone—perhaps Dominique—utters a word:

"What?"

"I understood that, of course, the moment I saw you. As an artist I am trained to recognize metaphor." He gestures, open-palmed. "The film was dying. We were assembling elements, but nothing would fit together. You must understand my despair. I knew I had something truly exceptional here. This film—the possibilities of this film—were enormous. Money was invested, people were gathering from all over the world, equipment ordered, all was coming together—except in my own mind, where it all fell apart. Nothing would hold. We were in Puerto Vallarta, having a story conference. Everyone looked to me to explain what we were doing. I was speechless. Halfway through the conference, I could stand it no longer. I rushed outside. It was almost dark. I stalked the streets of Puerto Vallarta in absolute confusion. No, Dominique, in terror. If I could not create, out of all the resources given to me, I was lost. I had fallen into perdition. And then, my dear, I saw you."

13. It is dark. Actually it is twilight in the cafe. Ahmed chooses this moment to lean forward. He puts his hand on Dominique's leg. It is a gesture which can be interpreted many ways. For a moment Dominique struggles with her interpretation. Then her legs part, slightly.

Outside the cafe the Hudson Terraplane awaits them. The last bus has long vanished down the road, carrying the last child to the barracks—four barracks exactly four miles away—that house all the extras. As the darkness deepens pale globes begin to glow above the street. Eventually two people emerge from the cafe. Dominique has her hand in the crook of Ahmed's arm. They stroll along the sidewalk. The Hudson Terraplane demurely follows.

All this time Ahmed has been talking. His exact words are not important. He has mentioned truth and beauty. He has discussed film as a higher order of reality. All realities, he argued, were creations. What was left out was just as important as what was included. This was as true in life, he said, as it was in film. He called attention to the small engine attached, like a succubus, to the right side of the Indian motorcycle. On the screen this engine would never be seen; hence one could say it did not exist. But wasnt the absence of the engine, which at least worked, as significant as the presence of the engine which didnt? Wasnt the *unseen* as real as the *seen?* His dark hands waved in the air. Occasionally they dipped to Dominique's leg. Like her legs, her lips were slightly parted. The lips seemed fuller than before. Perhaps she has added lipstick. She wore, and continues to wear, her twilight dress. She will wear it, or a copy of it—three have been made for her—for the rest of the film, and the rest of this book. She will also wear her patent leather shoes, iridescent in this dim light. The shoes have very high, stiletto heels. Her black nylon stockings—perhaps they are silk—have seams down their backs. All during the rest of this book, and the movie, her thighs above these stockings will be soft and faintly moist. When opportunities arise Ahmed will slide his hands up these legs, along the slick nylon encasing them, to the moist thighs. These opportunities will be described as they occur.

She walks, her hand in the crook of Ahmed's arm, with the same liquid grace as Ahmed. This liquid grace is admirable. We admire it, just as we admire the purring Hudson Terraplane that follows them down this Ethiopian street.

14. It is dark, perhaps very dark. But the darkness is ameliorated by the lamps set around the courtyard of Haile Selassie's summer palace. The Hudson Terraplane has come to a halt in this courtyard. The chauffeur—portrayed by Dar bin Saleh, who was, or will be, murdered behind the Hotel Savoy—opens the door for Dominique, who slides her legs out, and then for Ahmed, whose face gives no sign of recognition. Dominique and Ahmed walk through aromatic air, past blossoming citrus and night-blooming jasmine, and enter the palace. Their walk continues inside the palace. It is not our intention to describe this walk in great detail. It takes the two of them, at their stately pace, a considerable length of time to reach our next scene. The palace, built in the grand days of Haile Selassie's reign, is gigantic. Each hallway runs in a cardinal direction. Slaves stand, rather like storks, at regular intervals, holding hyena-tail fans. The floors are marble, quarried from the Rift Valley. Dominique's heels tap on these floors. During the course of this walk they pass two black panthers attended by boys in white caftans, and three lion cubs playing in the intersection of two hallways. One of these hallways is hung with copies—we imagine they are copies—of the Black Paintings by Francisco Goya. *Saturn Devouring His Son* is prominently displayed. The stately walk of Dominique and Ahmed does not falter—her right hand in the crook of his left arm—as they pass this gruesome work. There is no need to continue this description. Tapestries cover many of the walls, illustrating scenes of Ethiopian life. Artists like Mali, Cheboya, and Keto spent their lives in this palace, designing these tapestries. Looms hummed day and night. Artisans created the bejeweled chandeliers, using gold originally mined from Ophir, whose location is now forgotten. Court painters filled entire rooms with masterpieces never seen outside Ethiopia. Many of these resemble the Black Paintings of Goya in their morbidity. Others are frankly erotic. Only a few are playful—Ethiopian artists are seldom playful. The walk of Dominique and Ahmed besides these works of art is just as striking, in its own way, as the art itself. Perhaps they are themselves works of art.

They come at last to a large room. The room is large enough so it could be used—in a film, for instance—as the setting for a nightclub, or restaurant. A giant Panavision camera stands to one side. Prester John waits next to it. Elsewhere in the room the Queen of Sheba, as low to the ground as a hyena, examines a jewel-encrusted icon. In one corner, surrounded by the six Princesses of the Court, is Haile Selassie, or George Smithers. On a dais is an old lion. His pelt suffers from mange. Flies circle him, landing occasionally in his eyes, which then blink. Standing outside—he is visible through the open doors—is John Twelve. He is at the parapet, looking down over the Valley of Shoa. He wears his black silk robe. There is a lion embroidered in gold thread on the back of this robe. This lion looks healthier than the lion on the dais.

A discussion takes place at dinner. All sit at a long table. The first topic of conversation is The Agony of Ethiopia. Following this is The Disequilibrium of the West, The Corruption of Beauty, The Desolation of the Human Spirit, and The Apotheosis of John Twelve.

The behavior of the twelve people at the table during these discussions is worth noting. Haile Selassie and his six Princesses of the Court are to our left. The six Princesses are all between the ages of ten and twelve. Each has budding breasts and has experienced the menses at least once. They wear tight black skirts and black patent shoes with high heels. Sometimes they sit. More often, as the conversation progresses, they cluster around Haile Selassie. Selassie's tiny hands— like silver fish—dart into their clothing. The girls giggle and jump. He puts morsels into their mouths. They put their hands over his eyes and whisper into his ear. Haile Selassie pays no attention to the conversation at the table. Haile Selassie has become senile. This was apparent during the last years of his reign. He spent more time putting his hands up the skirts of his Princesses than he did on affairs of state. The

Princesses did not seem to mind this—they competed amongst themselves for his attention—but the country fell on harsh times. Rivers dried up. The desert spread. The famous gum trees of Addis Ababba, which Selassie himself had caused to be planted, were chopped down for firewood. With no one keeping an eye on the treasury, greed became unchecked. Government officials drove increasingly huge cars and began keeping many mistresses. Selassie's edicts became erratic. He only wanted to play with his Princesses, who loved him so, and he resented the questions his ministers kept bringing him. The Princesses entertained him even after he was deposed, although by then they existed only in his imagination. He loved their satiny little breasts with the hard little nubbins at their tips. He loved the way they squealed when his tiny fingers nibbled, like fish, at their orifices. He grinned happily. He wore splendid uniforms with lots of gold braid and he had never felt so loved.

While Haile Selassie plays with his Princesses, Prester John, on the far right, gets up to check his Panavision camera.

Crab meat, piles of yeasty bread, and asparagus soup steam on the table. The camera, guided by Prester John, records all of it. In preparation for the Ethiopian Exhibition, Prester John studied cinematography for a year at a university in Southern California. Since he lost his faith in Jesus nothing else has so excited him. Although he does not talk about it—he still will not speak—he understands film is the perfect metaphor for the modern world. Everything had become superficial— a micromillimeter deep. Television, of course, was even better in this respect than film, but Prester John could not stand the blown-dry hairdos and the rictus-smiles of the men and women who worked in television. Film was more ambiguous, because, although it could be as superficial as television, it could also strip layer after layer off the modern life he despised. He saw modern life as being composed of layers of falsehoods. When you stripped off one lie you discovered one more below it. Below this lie was yet another. If all the layers were stripped away, what would be left? Nothing? The truth? Or the biggest, most grotesque lie of all? The pursuit of this engrossed him. Perhaps, he sometimes imagined, the central lie was Jesus. Or God. He grinned secretly at this possibility.

The university where he studied cinematography was very expensive. Nevertheless it was surrounded on three sides by a black ghetto. Twelve times Prester John strolled through this ghetto. On seven of these occasions he was mugged. Sometimes he gave his muggers money—he always kept a few dollars on him—and his wrist watch, which didnt work anyway. Sometimes he merely smiled at the muggers, and continued on his way. What could muggers do to a dead Ethiopian king? Other times, when he felt irritable, he drove them off. He boxed their ears. He kicked them. If he'd had his sword—how he missed his sword!—he'd have chopped them to pieces. But his rage dissipated quickly. Mostly he was amused. He was amused that the female students at this university, after paying their expensive tuition, had to be escorted by burly male guards to their dorms and the parking lots. This was an effort to keep them from being raped. The notion of raping one of these pale, insipid creatures was amusing also. Sometimes he wondered if he himself should rape one of them. Would the experience be as superficial as he imagined? In his mind he created the camerawork necessary for such a scene. He also panned over the jewel-like campus, past the keen-faced engineering students planning the future of the world, and slipped into the dark streets surrounding where no future existed. The camera is his head was forever busy. Since he eschewed words he thought in images. He saw faces that looked like BMWs. He saw faces that looked as raw as uncooked heroin. He saw eyes that looked like the barrels of rifles. He saw a whole city dissolving in its own acid. He thought these images were lovely.

Sheba sits next to Prester John. It is said—although perhaps this is legend, and not truth—that once she was beautiful. Certainly she had

79

courage. As a young Queen she made the arduous journey from Ethiopia to Israel: she had heard of the great King Solomon, and wanted to know him. She was already tired of Ethiopian men. She was tired of men who lied. She was tired of men who were stupid. She was tired of flatulent men, and vain men, and men who wore out before she did. There was already something feral about her. Her lower jaw was slung forward, so her teeth always showed. Just by staring at a man who displeased her she could make his legs collapse. But perhaps she was beautiful. She journeyed to Israel, beautiful or not, with camels weighted down with gold and spices and jewels. She carried jasper and sapphire, chalcedony and emerald, sardonyx, sardus, and chrysolite, fine beryl and topaz, chests of chrysoprase, jacinth, and amethyst, and, of course, the finest jewel of all—herself. Solomon had never seen such riches.

"Solomon!" she brayed once to Ahmed. "What an asshole!"

What a disappointment. His buttocks, she claimed, were wider than her own, which were wide enough, even then. A paunch drooped over his penis, which was indiscriminate in its attentions. His famous wisdom was nothing but primitive shrewdness laced with sadism. Perhaps Sheba's memory is faulty. This was three thousand years ago. Her hips now are like the haunches of a hyena. Her head hangs forward, like the head of a hyena. Solomon had praised her pomegranate cheeks, but her cheeks now are hairy and mottled. All that honey and cream! she cries. God, was I sick of myrrh and aloe! Was her navel a goblet filled with wine? Were her breasts like fawns? Perhaps. But *his* kisses were not sweet as wine, they were sour like yesterday's arak. His famous temple was shabby—his palace even worse. The Israelites themselves were a flatulent lot, perhaps because of their strange diet. And their god! He condemned this, he condemned that, just like a man! When she menstruated she had to go into a special room in Solomon's palace and stay there for seven days. That was humiliating for a woman who considered her body's blood as valuable as rubies, her effluvium as rich as diamonds. "What an asshole!" she brays.

She returned to Ethiopia and took solace in sardonyx and chalcedony. She spent hours examining rubies. Amethyst and topaz were woven into her hair. When she needed a man, which became less and less frequently, she bought one with a gem. In recent centuries she particularly liked poor Spanish boys. There seemed an unending supply of them. They would do anything for her gems. They were pretty to look at, too. They were as pretty as jasper, although they didnt last as long. They had pretty eyes, pretty hands, pretty feet. Sometimes this roused her envy. Her own feet were yellowed and callused. Her hands had fat, yellow fingers. Her eyes were yellow too. Once to see what a pretty Spanish boy would take from her, she inserted twenty-four large rubies into his rectum. His smile grew wider with each gem. At the twenty-fourth his face suddenly paled. Blood poured from between his pomegranate buttocks. Nevertheless he continued to smile. When she left him he was all white and red and still, but the smile remained on his face. She was grinning too, lips drawn back from her yellow stubs of teeth.

On the dais the lion stirs. He snaps at a fly, yawns, and settles his head again between his paws. Ahmed nods towards him.

"Once," he tells Dominique, "lions were plentiful in Ethiopia. Great lions, virile lions."

"What happened?"

"They were hunted to extinction, of course."

All conversations take place on two or more levels. This one is no exception. Ahmed was also saying—although these words were never uttered, but lay beneath the surface—that only man was crueler than the great cats. But everyone knew that. Everyone acknowledged, for instance, Ahmed said beneath the surface, the horror of war. Yet wars occurred with great regularity. Increasingly efficient weapons killed increasingly large numbers of people. Great multitudes of men and women worked for living wages producing bombs, bullets, missiles, barrels, breechlocks, stocks, mortars, gunsights, tank turrets, cannons, troop carriers, shells and shell casings, poison gases, revolvers, carbines, automatics, and innumerable other instruments of destruction.

More people yet paid money—pennies, nickels, dimes, dollars, rupees, shekels, rubles, pesos, pesetas, lire, dirhams, rials, zlotys, francs, balboas, rands—into the coffers of governments which converted that money into acts and instruments of destruction. All this was done daily, hourly, by the minute, by night as well as by day, on weekends and on holidays. That in itself was horrible. What was even more horrible, Ahmed said, or implied, was that all of us were capable of such acts of destruction. It was in our nature. All of us, he said, are murderers. There is no cruel or despicable act ever done by any human being, anywhere, that I am incapable of doing myself. And you.

No, not I, protested Dominique.

Yes, you. Me. All of us. It is our nature.

That would be too horrible—

We do not judge nature, my dear. Nature is the standard by which we are judged. And nature has decreed our cruelty. There can be no other explanation for the history of our race. I myself have felt every stirring of greed, every perversion, every hatred. It is impossible to be a human being and not be cruel. To claim otherwise is a contradiction of terms.

I dont believe—

Only one thing makes this bearable, Ahmed continues beneath their other conversation. Humans are also the most creative creatures on earth. No other creature has this power to the same degree. There are only three events of importance in human existence, Dominique, and these events repeat themselves, metaphorically, throughout our lives. There is birth, which is creation in its purest form. There is death, which is the ultimate destruction. And there is sex, which combines both creation and destruction into a single act. Can this be doubted? A man's organ penetrates into a woman's womb in exactly the same way a spear penetrates the thorax. There is thrusting, and more thrusting. The weapon twists, cruelly. It withdraws, dripping blood—or semen. All the words which describe an act of sex may be used to describe an act of violence. An orgasm is like death. Yet such is the alchemical nature of sex that this act of violence is turned into creation. Only a woman can do this for a man. Her body absorbs his. His weapon is taken. His thrusting is accepted. The agony of destruction is joined immutably to the agony of creation. It is alchemy. It is the alchemy of art. It is the same transmutation that the artist achieves in his work. Death and creation become one. They become transcendent. Only this, Dominique, allows a man and a woman to truly live. Without this a man walks in desolation. He is a warrior dying in the desert. Without this a civilization can only destroy. That is the desolation of our modern world. We are out of balance, Dominique. We are warriors dying in a desert. We are warriors walking in desolation, dying in the desert.

Dominique's face has gone pale. With his fingers Ahmed touches her face as gently as the wing of a bird touches the wind.

"That is why," he says, "you are my love. My salvation. My hope."

At the center of the table John Twelve lifts his head. His face is pale, too. There is sweat on his skin.

"Listen," he says. "They are coming."

His face is pale with fear. Fear is visible in every line. Yet there is something else. There is something else in his face. It is glory. This glory illuminates him. As the light in the room grows dim, this glory in John Twelve's face seems almost luminescent.

15. *It is dark.* Below them, however—below the summer palace of Haile Selassie—there is light. Everyone except Haile Selassie and his Princesses gathers at the parapet. They watch the lights moving below. They listen to the songs rising from below.

In the darkness the town is not visible below the summer palace of Haile Selassie. Even we cannot see it. If we were an Ethiopian bird, however—or the camera in the head of Prester John—we could rise off the parapet of the palace and swoop down through the black air. We could glide to the square far below. In this square people are milling. They carry torches. It is these torches which the people above can see. These torches circle right and left. More torches emerge from the darkness, from the dark streets which have been created around the central square. Some of these torches are carried by blind children. Translucent skin has grown over their eye sockets. They are led by children who have single eyes and as many as fifteen fingers. All are dressed in black. Children with no legs and mere fins for arms are carried by children with hydroencephalic heads. Julio Abril, in his mauve dress and his Charles Jourdan shoes, mingles with them. His pointed tongue flicks at his painted lips. He has just received a new injection of lamb embryo, and has never felt so feminine. A Nazi, or someone playing a Nazi in jackboots and peaked cap, eyes him invitingly. The shadows thrown by his torch linger over the bodies of Dankalis, thin savages, nearly naked, who dance at the edges of the group.

The murdered Dar bin Saleh, in his chauffeur's uniform, raises his torch and cries out. He starts up the road which leads from the plaza to the summer palace of Haile Selassie. The engineers and surveyors who

84

helped build this road saunter along the side, carrying their clipboards. They comment caustically on the quality of work and material that were used on the road. The laborers themselves follow behind, many of them drunk. Tourists are clustered in the center of the road. Each carries a camera and traveler's checks. They are tall, somewhat fleshy people, wearing flowered shirts. They have slack jaws and eyes that are withdrawn, protectively. At the tail end of this group are teenaged American girls, many of them bloodstained. Black children pluck at the tourists.

"Money!" they cry.

"Money!"

"Money!"

Their thin black hands dart into pockets. They wave wallets, keyrings, coins, and traveler's checks in the air like trophies. The tourists slap at their clothes, slap at the boys, and mill protectively together. All of them move up the road, illuminated by torches which burn like hot red eyes in the darkness.

John Twelve moves closer to the edge of the parapet. For a moment his black robe billows behind him. Then he pulls it closed.

"Wont someone help me?" he whispers.

Prester John turns busily to his camera. Sheba inspects the rings on one of her hands. In the other room, though visible through the open door, the lion on his dais yawns and shakes his head. Dominique turns to Ahmed, who puts up a hand. There is no one to help John Twelve. His face is waxen. With an effort he steadies himself. In the other room a Princess giggles, loudly, as Haile Selassie's fingers, like fish, nibble at one of her apertures.

"I'm sorry," John Twelve says. "I'm all right now."

His gaze falls to the scene below. Outside the camera's range, Ahmed watches.

The same wind that whips John Twelve's robe around his bare ankles now makes the flames of the torches roar and sputter.

These torches cast their glow beyond the road's edge. Visible beyond the road's edge are oil cans, a dead dog, plastic bags and cups, leather shoes whose soles hang open like mouths, broken glass which sparkles in the light, soiled disposable diapers and menstrual pads, scraps of toilet paper fluttering in the wind, red and white milk cartons, and at least one empty box of texturized soya protein. The hooves of a white pony—ridden by a black Abyssinian—dance among this detritus. Pariah dogs, running at the outskirts of the crowd, stick their noses into the plastic, paper, and leather oddments. An Ethiopian poet, skinny and effete, sneers at this and composes in his head an ironic couplet. We will spare our readers.

The cameras, mounted on giant hydraulic devices, swirl overhead. Fat policemen on Harley-Davidson motorcycles—cleaned and polished for the occasion—glance up at them and straighten their leather jackets. Other policemen in pale green uniforms march up the road. They pass a kneeling Julio Abril, practicing his craft on the ersatz Nazi, and the old women beggars who squat in the shadows, counting beads. These women wear t-shirts with the names of rock groups printed on them. We can see REO Speedwagon, The Boss, Beatlemania, Stones In Concert, and even Fang, his incisors dripping blood. Just beyond them a whore wears a Mickey Mouse t-shirt. It is all she wears. Her breasts flap within this t-shirt and her belly, round and scarred, rises below it. Three drunken Ethiopians, holding each other up, stagger towards her, grinning. They leave behind them a trail of beer cans. A single camera swoops down to focus tightly on the whore's face. There is something beatific about her. Her eyes look beyond the drunk Ethiopians descending on her. She feels something more than their hands groping at her thighs. Perhaps she feels the tumors growing and pulsing within her abdomen. A great warmth spreads outward from her. Her eyes seem focused on something far, far distant, perhaps so far distant that no one else can see it. The camera lingers as she assumes the position of her trade, and the first drunk Ethiopian settles over her.

From above, the road seems a river of fire. From this river of fire a song emerges. It is sung by children waving flags. It is sung by children crawling on the pavement. A band plays, drums thumping, wind instruments wailing. By the time the song travels upward to the parapet where John Twelve is poised, the song is as soft as the breast of an Ethiopian bird. As the river of fire curls left, then right, mounting the hill to the summer palace of Haile Selassie, the song becomes stronger—though no less soft—and then weaker, though still beautiful. Everyone can hear it. A sound technician—perhaps he has been here all this time—sits at a bank of toggle switches and dials. Earphones are on his head. He leans forward and moves a switch, slides a lever, and taps thoughtfully at a dial. The lion walks through the doorway and onto the parapet, where he sits, licking at his mangy fur. The sound technician ignores him.

"How much longer?" says John Twelve.

"Minutes," says Ahmed.

Dominique stares from one to the other. She sees John Twelve's robe flapping at his bare ankles. She sees Ahmed standing to one side, his face immobile. She edges away from the lion and puts a hand between her breasts. From the other room comes a burst of laughter. The sound technician raises an eyebrow. He scowls into his bank of instruments.

16. It is dark. It is very dark. The full moon is behind dark clouds. Yet in spite of this, the glory on the face of John Twelve is visible. The glory is just as visible as the fear. The fear is just as visible as the sweat dripping down his face. His arms are raised. The wind whips his black robe away from his nude body. The robe flaps like a cape. It flaps like black wings from his shoulders.

The others on this parapet are visible also, although they are not lit from within. Dominique stands roughly equidistant between Ahmed and John Twelve, that is, about five paces from each. Her makeup is immaculate, as though applied specifically for this occasion. There is a gloss to her scarlet lips. There is a gloss, in fact, to her face, which turns one way—towards Ahmed—and then the other, towards John Twelve. The lips of Dominique are slightly parted, although at this moment the expression is not seductive but anguished. They are nonetheless tender. Even at this moment one might imagine—Ahmed, for instance, might imagine—kissing them with one's own lips. Like all American girls she has small, fine teeth, though whether or not this is the result of expensive orthodontics is unclear. Her legs, sheathed in taut nylon, are as beautiful as ever. Like her eyes, they turn nervously—first towards Ahmed, then towards John Twelve. All her movements are indecisive.

The clouds part. Prester John, taking advantage of the moon's illumination, steps to his camera and makes last minute adjustments. It may be that his face, normally fierce, is softened by the moonlight. Beyond him, nearly obscured by a shadow, stands Sheba. Her head is lowered. Her yellow eyes stare, like the expressionless eyes of a scavenger, at John Twelve. Near her the lion moves restlessly. His tail switches from side to side. The bones and muscles move under his skin. The sound man, at his bank of instruments, seems bored. He listens through his instruments to the sounds of arc lights turning on in the distant rooms of Haile Selassie's summer palace.

❖

These arc lights turn on with a *clang!* The lights are so powerful the people in these rooms stop. For a moment they mill about. Even the blind children seem pained by the light. Another light *clangs* on. Cameras are whirring overhead. Pressed from behind, by the great mass of people behind, the children, led by Dar bin Saleh, spill forward.

We have already described the rooms through which they pass, and the slaves, who stand one-legged, like storks, at regular intervals. None of this has changed. Some of the tourists stop to admire the paintings in one hallway. A construction worker, elsewhere, tries to pry loose jewels encrusted to a statue. The hooves of a delicate Abyssinian pony rattle on the marble floor, rather like the stiletto heels of Julio Abril. Each time the children enter a room or pass into a new hallway, the giant arc lights come on with a *clang!* A new camera begins to whir. Cameras swoop down from the ceiling. Cameras on rails race past the hurrying figures. Black children chanting "Money! money! money!" swing off to the right, down an empty corridor, searching for items to steal. Others, men and women, old and young, including a slow moving beggar woman who counts her beads with each step, go astray by accident. Some of them will be in the palace, still lost, for years to come. The palace is huge. Some rooms are designed as mazes. People circle there, endlessly. Odalisques from another era lie on mats, their flesh as opalescent as pearls. There are thousands of slaves, stables filled with black and white horses, and lions who roam free in the deepest passages. All this still exists. The cameras, and the arc lights, do not go to these parts of Haile Selassie's summer palace.

Dar bin Saleh and the deformed children burst into a room large enough to be used as a nightclub. Arc lights—three of them—*clang!*

89

clang! clang! White light bounces off the walls. Haile Selassie, or George Smithers, looks up, bewildered. One of his hands is in the skirt of a Princess. Her hands are at her face, hiding her mouth, which is giggling.

On the parapet Ahmed nods.

"Theyre here," he says.

"Theyre here," says John Twelve.

His lips are drawn back, revealing incisors that look like fangs.

A bird floats high overhead. His beak is hooked. He is an Ethiopian bird of prey. His talons lay flat against his feathers. As he banks to one side—he is circling above Haile Selassie's summer palace—he sees arc lights spring to life. He even hears them: *clang! clang! clang!* This does not disturb his slow circling high overhead.

From this vantage Prester John's camera can be seen to be in constant motion. It moves forward as children—blind, deformed—burst onto the parapet of Haile Selassie's summer palace. Then the camera swoops into the air, imitating—but not equaling—the flight of an Ethiopian bird. At the very edge of the parapet stands a figure in a black flapping robe. Five paces from him is a woman in a twilight-colored dress. Five paces further stands a dark, wiry Abyssinian. These three people are quite still. Then, pushed by those crowding behind, the children spill forward. They can be seen spreading out, in a fan shape, over the parapet. Yet even then the three figures we have mentioned do not move. Seconds pass, perhaps several seconds. The wind, which has been plucking, plucking at the robe of the man at the edge of the parapet, at last pulls it free. It slips from the man's shoulders. From our vantage high above, it looks like a bird suddenly released. The black wings of this bird-like robe flap over the heads of the advancing children, over Dar bin Saleh, over beggars and drunkards and thieves and liars, past a preening Julio Abril, past fat policemen sweating on their motorcycles, past a whore who limps, her eyes focused on eternity, and into the throat of a giant tuba which falls abruptly silent. The thin man, red and bony, stands naked at the edge of the parapet.

Perhaps he moves back. From above he seems to falter—to collapse a little. Perhaps his weight shifts backwards. At that moment the dark Abyssinian appears to make a gesture. This gesture is not seen clearly from our position. The woman, whether in response to this gesture or not, takes three steps towards the man at the parapet. The light must be blinding. Her hand goes up. The man at the edge of the parapet spreads his arms and dives off the edge.

Prester John's camera sees the same things as our Ethiopian bird of prey, but adds a few details. When the lights *clang! clang! clang!* Sheba becomes visible in a corner, hissing between her yellowed teeth. Her face itself is yellow, hairy, and mottled. Other faces are also seen more clearly. We see the faces of the deformed children, many of them confused. We see the face of Dar bin Salah, revengeful. We see the faces of thieves and drunks. The shadows of all these people race over the parapet and over each other, cast in three directions by the three arc lights. This adds more confusion to the scene.

The black robe flaps, and like a shadow frees itself from the man at the edge of the parapet. It sails over heads, through doors, and into the next room. The man at the edge of the parapet, now naked, is back-lit. A halo of light glows around his thin red body. Yet he now seems to falter. His shoulders hunch together. One foot gropes back from the edge of the precipice. At that point Ahmed—we see it clearly—lifts his hand. Dominique sees this, too. The lights blind her as she turns back towards John Twelve. Her eyes—tearful—flash as the light strikes her face. There are thousands of watts directed at her. Her eyes in this light are iridescent. Even her mouth, partly open, glows. Her dress lumi-nesces. She cannot see John Twelve's eyes. We can. The glory has drained away, replaced with fear. But when he sees this glowing woman, one hand raised, his features lose their tension. The glory returns. His head lifts. Dominique, blinded, cannot see the effect she has on him. Her eyes are flashing like diamonds. Her mouth is like a ruby. Her dress glows like a sapphire. John Twelve, or Fang, raises his arms from his naked body. The edge of the parapet seems to crumble. He leans forward into the darkness.

The lights *clang! clang! clang!* Shadows race everywhere. The woman, in response to her cue, steps forward three paces. Her beauty and mystery are unmistakable. Her entire body is radiant. John Twelve, or Fang, who has dreamed forever of this radiance, steps to the edge of the precipice. His robe has already flown from his shoulders and over the heads of the deformed, the cruel, the terrible creatures who press towards him. He leans into a darkness made radiant by beauty. He leans, naked, into a darkness made beautiful by radiance. The precipice crumbles beneath him.

The lights hiss as they cool. People talk, complaining about the food, the weather, the long hours. Their heels tap on the marble floors. More lights turn off, and begin to hiss. We hiss, too, as the summer palace of Haile Selassie is emptied.

17. It is dark, perhaps very dark. Yet in this darkness is visible a woman. She sits on the edge of a bed. Her hair seems thicker and longer than when last we saw her. Her eyes, though still hooded, are deeper. Over her shoulders is a black silk robe. Her slender legs are placed carefully before her. All this is barely visible in the black, black air.

Morning comes. A sea, to the east, reddens. The streets of the town fill with murderers and thieves, with petty cheats and foolish liars. Garbage litters the gutters, where dogs slink from shadow to shadow. Men drop their feces in alleys. Cracks spread across concrete walls. Pavement buckles, as though the earth itself heaved. The sun blazes down on all of it. It blazes through the window and into the room where the woman sits. At last she moves. She moves wearily, but with exquisite grace, to the window. Her robe is open, thus revealing to us her long thighs, the little patch of hair between them, her flat stomach, the still young breasts. At the window she stares down into a daytime world in which everything is visible. There are no mysteries in the harsh shadows. There is no radiance in this harsh glare. In the harsh light nothing luminesces. The woman turns away. She moves with her weary grace across the room. With her eyes lowered she examines her face in a mirror. She touches one breast. Then she goes to her purse, which lies open on the bed.

Within this purse are tickets. It is not clear how they came to be there. There are bus tickets, first, second, and third class train tickets, tickets good for journeys on coastal steamers, and airplane tickets to destinations throughout the world. Some of these tickets would return her to the country and the city from whence she came. Many would take her to places she has never been. Some of them—we are not certain how many—would take her to Ahmed. He is waiting, in another place. None of the tickets include return journeys. They are all one way. That is one of the peculiarities of Ethiopia. In Ethiopia, a journey, once taken, can never be undone, just as the Ethiopian night, once glimpsed, can never be forgotten. Restlessly, restlessly, the woman moves from the bed to the window to the mirror, while outside the sun blazes across the sky. As it dips towards the horizon we can see the shadows lengthen. Perhaps there is a distant murmur. Perhaps there is a suggestion of luminesence—of radiance—to the air. It cannot quite be seen. Nevertheless we have faith it is there. We have faith she will see it. Night will come. In Ethiopia, night will always come. We will wait for it, just as we wait for her, faithfully.

MAYA

Mä´ya, n. A member of a race of Indians who formerly lived in southeastern Mexico and Central America and are still found in Yucatan.

Mä´ya, n. In Hindu philosophy, illusion, often personified as a woman.

—Webster's New Twentieth Century Dictionary of the English Language, Unabridged

The quotations in Part Three are from *The Book of chilam Balam of Chumayel*, translated by Ralph L Roys and published by the Carnegie Institution of Washington in November 1993.

PART ONE

I.

The white plumerias are at the window, as expected. The woman withdraws her head. The man is in the bathroom to our left. He is shaving. He becomes visible to us only as the camera draws back and turns, slightly. The razor scrapes at his cheek. This scraping is the only sound audible, other than the slight hiss—it sounds like a hiss—made by the film moving through the camera. The camera continues to retreat. It drops lower and *pulls away*. A wide angle lens is used. Our perspective, as viewers, is thus altered in a predictable way. The man recedes to our left, *diminishing* to our left, the woman somewhat less so to our right. *Without moving they draw further apart*. That is the effect we are after. She is lit through the window. The massed plumerias glow in this light. Her shadow crosses to our left, as black as pitch, as black as night, as black—

Only at the very end, with the camera almost on the floor, is the third person visible. It is the priest. He sits at our left foreground, his swollen leg propped up before him. As the scene ends he claps, politely.

2.

Her face is at the window. She withdraws her head. *It is the same movement which began the previous scene.* Each scene is thus *a palimpsest.* This cannot be emphasized too much. The white plumerias glow in this light. The camera moves past them, out the window. The outer world is visible below. It consists of green jungle. There are low hills on all sides. Within view is a large, cross-shaped building. This appears to be a church. One side rises into twin towers, or steeples. We are some distance above the ground, perhaps at the second floor of a hotel. The camera drops. Its movements must be fluid. It descends through trees. It descends through giant ceibas, or the yax-cheel-cab, known as the first tree of the world. It descends through red zapotes. It descends through red bullet trees. Other trees will be examined later. Closer to the ground, as we move forward, are the black laurel and the white *Callisi repens.* The camera *fluidly* continues past the ix-batun, the chimchin-chay—it can be boiled, then eaten like cabbages—and the jicama cimarrona, which is eaten only in times of famine. Everywhere are the white plumerias. All throw their shadows directly at the camera: we are moving *into* the shadows, *into* the light. Each species mentioned must be seen briefly: the balche tree, whose bark is fermented with honey; maguey and calabash and chulul trees; the yaxum tree; the num; the chacah, or palo mulato; the white guaje; the chaya, whose leaves are edible. Hanging from the leaves of the chaya tree are pupae, spun by larvae, which will burst, in their season, into blue-veined moths. Visible also—although they remain at the edges of the screen— are the insects and animals. These include the Quetzal bird, or yax-um, in the limbs of the ceiba; the monkey known as maax; the sun-eyed fire macaw; the balam, or jaguar, whose eyes are glowing ochre in this light; the hanging bats which suck honey from flowers; the mut-bird; the long-toed grouse; the opossum; the kinkajou; the fox; the slow moving turtle; the ppuppulni-huh, or swollen iguana, whose eyes are hooded, exophthalmic; two snakes, the nahuyaca, which has four nostrils, and the tepolcua, which will embed itself in a man's anus; and finally the insects: the xulab, or stinging ant; the chac uayah-cab, the stinging ant who lives underground; the cicada and locust; the scorpions, their stingers erect like the organs of importunate lovers; and the false scorpions and the whip scorpions who scurry quickly, from right to left.

The camera moves to the northern doorway of the cross-shaped building just as the man and the woman duck their heads beneath the lintel. They enter from the north. She leads; he follows. Later this order will become important. Within the room—he comes erect as the others enter—is the priest, standing at a display case.

Movement stops for a full beat as the scene ends.

3.

The film hisses through the camera. The camera hisses through the room, past terracotta figures, jade masks, carved limestone. The shadows are thrown forward. Her shadow is thrown forward, across us. One can almost feel it: a coolness passing visibly on the screen.

4.

His belly slaps against hers. Her shadow is thrown forward. The film hisses.

5.

Because of the shadows it takes a moment for the viewer to recognize what is happening. *This disorientation is deliberate.* His belly slaps against hers. When her face turns towards us we can see the bruise at her eye. A breast is momentarily visible as she turns. The moon is called pach caae. It is the source of light and thus, paradoxically, the source of the shadows. The plumerias at the window are waxy, succulent. Their leaves are pinnately veined. It is known that the sap of these flowers is poisonous. The flowers are visible beyond the visibly slapping bellies.

6.

The woman walks along a path. She wears a white dress. She wears red shoes with high heels. *The camera follows on a parallel at some distance.* She is glimpsed through apertures in the foliage of the yax-cheel-cab, the white guaje, etc. She is seen at the same time as, in the foreground, the kinkajou, the opossum, the slow moving turtle, etc. The ppuppulni-huh rises on its forelegs. Immediately the camera lifts into the air. It rises as the woman hesitates at a red-painted door. Soon we see the cross-shaped building in its entirety. We have risen high above it. The walls of the northern arm of this cross-shaped building are white-painted adobe. The eastern walls are red brick. There is a red ceiba tree next to this eastern wall. The western walls are black, and there are rows of black-speckled corn beyond them. Lintels are of stone, many of them carved. The massive façade of the south is yellow stone. Two towers rise from this façade. In the courtyard below are yellow ceiba trees and yellow bullet trees. The center of the building is a dome made from red brick. It is circular, of course, set into the rectangular belly of the building. The woman is at the western end of the building. She is tiny. She is scarcely visible. Then she is gone.

7.

The hissing camera moves through the darkened room.

8.

They have gone to the doorway. The light is behind them. We are behind them. *They stare forward as their shadows are thrown forward*, away from us, to the edge of the cenote.

The cenote is in the center of the building. It is beneath the dome. Its edges are rugose, but roughly circular. The only light comes from the doorway, *cast forward*, to the edge of this cenote. The husband stands there. He is broad and flat, except for his belly, which falls over the belt of his pants. He seems to have no fear of the darkness. The shadows of the woman and the priest end at his feet. The light comes from the electric bulbs, whose filaments glow like the ochre eyes of the balam. The woman's hair glows, as yellow as the yellow can-lol. She may be perceived as a simulacrum, illuminated, effulgent. The priest is a gnarled figure to her left. Only once does he look toward us, and his eyes are stricken. The woman's lips are glossy, as though waxed. Beyond her the husband is a distant tiny figure, as tiny as a homunculus. His shadow, if he has one, falls into the cenote. Outside—this may be seen, or perhaps inferred—rain has begun. The plumerias open wider. The earth swells like a sponge. The eyes of the balam, or jaguar, glow. They are ochre, like the ochre filaments of the electric light bulbs. "Each bruise is an orgasm." "A virgin death." "Yes, priest, a virgin death." These lines are not spoken. More shadows—that is, the shadow of the priest, who is diminished, and the shadow of the woman, who is enlarged—end at the feet of the husband, whose own shadow, if it exists at all, is cast, and lost, into the cenote.

9.

The husband stands at the edge of the cenote. It may be that he has no fear of the darkness. He is broad and flat, except for his belly, which protrudes over the belt of his pants. His hands are thrust into his pockets. He is facing the light that emerges from the room with the red door. The light comes from electric bulbs, whose filaments glow like the ochre eyes of the balam. This light does not reach into the depths of the cenote, which, though irregular, is shaped like a circle. The ceiling is a dome and is set—as we have stated—into the belly of the building. The building itself is shaped like a fat cross. The earth outside—we may infer this—swells in the way a dried sponge will swell when dipped into sea water. Steam rises from the earth. This steam is composed of fetid humors. This rich effluvium is visible. It is as pungent as the farts of old men, as acrid as the scut of the balam. The red plumerias, the scarlet plumerias, the white-petalled plumerias exude odors as dense as oil. The air itself is dense as oil. A swollen iguana moves slowly through this air. A scorpion raises its stinger, from which emerges a drop of poison. This drop of poison is milky white, like the semen of a lover. Hanging from the leaves of the chaya trees are pupae, spun by larvae, which will burst, in their season, into blue-veined moths. Through all of this treads the balam, fur shining with oil, past the ppuppulni-huh, past the erect scorpion, past the maax and the kinkajou, past the opossum and the slow moving turtle, the xulab and the sun-eyed fire macaw. The balam's movements are themselves slow through this turgid air, air dense as oil. In the darkness he casts no shadow.

The woman and the priest cast shadows. Their shadows end at the edge of the cenote, and thus at the feet of the homunculus we call the husband. His hands are thrust into his pockets. He seems to have no fear of darkness. He stares towards the light. "A perfect virgin." "A perfect death." "Yes, priest, a perfect death." The film hisses, audibly, as it speeds through the camera.

"What are you staring at?"

The film hisses—audibly—as it speeds through the camera.

"What are you staring at?"

The film hisses—audibly—

"What are you staring at?"

"Nothing."

PART TWO

I.

One lizard eye stares up at her. She lies on a sack bed—burlap stretched over a wooden frame—in a dark corner of the room. There seems to be a lizard at her breast—specifically, a swollen iguana, or ppuppulni-huh, its chitinous teeth fastened at her teat. One exophthalmic eye, with its translucent lid, stares up at her face. Her face sweats, and sweats. Her lips are swollen, bruised. A gecko runs up the wall beyond her. Elsewhere in the room the priest—the man who plays the priest—sits with his face in his hands. The "husband" sits in another corner, a cigarette glowing between his lips. A twist of blond hair lies lankly on his forehead. There is an oily sheen to his face. All of them—all three of the people in the room—are illuminated by the ochre glow of the napalm that flows softly over the hills outside. This glow pulses as each canister of gelatinous petroleum splits open and ignites, one after another. An F-4 Phantom—the smiling pilot is visible through the plexiglass cockpit—banks away from the line of horsemen descending the defoliated hillside. We marvel at the beauty of the scene: the sky to the east a deep purple, the sun rising through the smoke that rises from the ruins of Saigon. Or is it Quang Tri? Or Hue, that ancient city? In any case the horizon is swirling with a smoky, purple glow. Another plane banks away. The pilot, goggled and masked behind his plexiglass, makes a gesture: thumbs up. We watch the line of horsemen descend the blackened slope, threading their way, wearily, between the ochre blossoms of napalm.

The woman pushes the swollen iguana from her breast.

"Are we going to breakfast?"

"We're going to the museum."
"I could use some tea."
"The tea here is terrible."
"So is the coffee."
"At least it's drinkable."
"Just a cup—first—"
"First?"
"Before the museum."
"What difference does it make?"
"I'd like just a cup—"
"The coffee is bad enough, but at least it's drinkable."
"Coffee, then."
"We'll go to the museum first. If you need to drink—"
"Then afterwards—"
"We'll see."
The swollen iguana crawls back to her breast.

2.

Along the tiled floor of the building scutter scorpions. Occasionally the man who plays the husband takes off a shoe and slaps at one. He swears using short, guttural words. Perhaps he is German, or Dutch. We cant be certain. There is no discernible accent when he speaks his lines in English. A good actor, of course, is a good mime. He may be a German actor mimicking American speech patterns, or, equally, an American mimicking a German's profanity. He is blond enough to be a northern European—or an American of northern European descent. His lips are thin, but fleshy. That is, they are not thick lips, but they protrude from his face. They are red and slick, as though perpetually wet. This may be more a characteristic of Germans than Americans. He wears a white T-shirt, as many Americans do. His belly seems soft. It falls over the belt of his pants. His shoes are supple brown leather, moccasin-type. He smokes Gauloises—the pack is in the rolled-up sleeve of his T-shirt—but this may be an affectation. The Gauloises are not necessarily an indication of his nationality.

The scorpions enter the room from the cenote, along with other animals and insects which will be named. The actor lights another Gauloise and blows the smoke toward the woman.

"Let's run through it again."

"No, it's too hot."

"I want it to be perfect."

"I cant concentrate—"

"Just start. Are we going—"

"Are we going—to breakfast?"

"We're going to the museum."

"I could use some tea."

"The tea here is terrible."

"So is the coffee. God, I could use some iced coffee."

"You have no discipline, do you?"

"It's so hot—"

He roughly stubs out his Gauloise. He turns to the window as napalm bursts nearby. For a moment his eyes glow orange.

"Discipline. That's what you lack—what all of you lack."

"All of us?"

"You are too soft."

"It's this heat—"

"The heat has nothing to do with it."

There is a scorpion on the sill. The actor takes off one shoe. He fondles it. He runs his fingers into the shoe, where his toes would go. Then he turns the shoe around and slaps the heel onto the scorpion. He scrapes the carcass off the sill and pushes it along the floor to the foot of his bed. He pushes it into a pile of other dead scorpions.

"The heat," he says, "has nothing to do with it."

He unrolls his pack of Gauloises from his sleeve. He shakes one into his hand. After a moment he puts it between his thin, wet lips. He doesnt light it, however. He continues to sit there. Finally he leans back against the wall, and shuts his eyes.

3.

A single eye glares at her. He has, of course—the man who plays her husband—two eyes. But it is his affectation to lower the lid of his right eye while staring at the woman. We believe this is a conscious act. He must be aware of the unsettling effect this stare has on her, and on others. His left eye is stern, even mad. It seems paler, a paler blue, than his right eye. Is that possible? The woman turns away from this stare. The iguana, the ppuppulni-huh, crouches on her belly, which is otherwise bare. His tail switches once, twice between her legs. With each switch she gasps, and her face turns further away. Her face is so oily with sweat we are not sorry to have it thus averted. When she speaks, her words are muffled. The husband has to lean forward to hear her.

"I heard screams last night," she says.

"Screams?"

"I'm certain of it."

"I heard nothing."

"I was awakened—they awakened me—"

"Awakened?"

"I dont know the time."

"You were possibly dreaming."

The priest, until now silent in his corner, lifts his head.

"I heard them too," he says.

"You?"

"Distinctly. Quite—quite distinctly—"

"Sound effects."

"What?" says the woman.

"Sound effects," repeats the husband. "If you heard anything at all."

The sun glows through the window to his left. There is a softness to the air that occurs only in the tropics. In this light—especially when augmented by the bursts of napalm—the man seems recognizable. That is, we imagine we have seen him before, perhaps similarly illuminated. He bears a certain resemblance to the film noir actors of another time—Dan Duryea, perhaps, or even Alan Ladd. But their time has gone. If this man is an actor like them, he is an anachronism. It may be he actually appeared in films during the dying days of film noir, or perhaps in the later European films influenced by film noir. If so he must be older than he looks—at least fifty. He would be out of place in modern American comedies about adolescent boys or horror movies filled with plasticized faces and rubbery monsters. Nor would there be a place for him, or for his rapacious glare, in the cineplex boxes which have replaced the grand movie palaces across the American landscape. Perhaps he is aware of this. His soft belly and sallow skin suggest the dissolution of dreams. His thin, wet lips curve into a sardonic grin. Even his presence here, in what must be the lowest of low-budget movie making, is an admission of dispossession. He is dispossessed. He grins, sour, sardonic, sallow, at the sweat-stained body of the woman who plays his wife.

She seems familiar also. We have seen a poster which may be a portrait of her. It achieved some fame during the American-Vietnam War. If it is her, she was both younger and happier then: the skin of her face, in the poster, is tauter, the eyes livelier. Her arms are raised above her head in an attitude of triumph. From her waist to her ankles she is sheathed in white latex pants. Clearly outlined at her crotch are the swelling shapes of her labia major. Because the pelvis is thrust forward, these labia are not only clearly defined by the thin, tight latex, but seemingly *offered*—thrust forward, presented, exposed, delivered to the hungry men of the 9th Marine Expeditionary Brigade and the 173rd Airborne and the 1st Air Cavalry who, at that time, slid through the jungled valleys and denuded back alleys of Vietnam, M-16s cocked, M-60s shouldered, grenades hanging, pockets stuffed with K-bars, C-rations, infrared night sights, packets of C-4, phosphorus bombs and 9mm pistols. How many of these teen-aged lips—most of the American soldiers seemed to be teen-agers—how many pressed hungrily against those printed, proffered labia limned there in those white latex pants? Men jerked off in ditches and foxholes, behind crates of ammunition and in flapping tents. Semen flew through the air like shrapnel, precious seed spilled like blood, bodily fluids exulted, whooshed, blasted like rockets into the thick Vietnamese air. During her tour of Vietnam—it was her apogee as a starlet—she wore the white pants at every stop. She wore them at Da Nang, she wore them at Cam Ranh Bay, she wore them—or a pair exactly like them—at Bien Hoa and An Khe and Phu Bai, even at Bong Son and Nha Trang and, one famous night, at Phuoc Binh. At Phuoc Binh, cheered on by GIs still glassy-eyed from a mortar attack and a fire fight, she—according to rumor—took off the white latex pants: *peeled* them off, peeled them down her hips, peeled them down her thighs, peeled them down her calves, removing and re-tieing her high-heeled, black patent, ankle-strapped shoes, and danced—perhaps for an hour, perhaps *all night*— on a raised platform in front of these desperately hungry men, some still bloody, heads and arms wrapped in mud-stained gauze, uniforms stained, faces stained, bodies thickened and stained with lust, blood, sweat and tears. Is this true? Which battalion, which company, which platoon witnessed this event, which became famous throughout Vietnam? The story, the rumor—true or not—preceded and followed her everywhere she went in that dark, blasted country, like a miraculous vision: labia glossy, engorged with blood, red and slick and swollen— the night brazen, unleashed, still smelling of cordite and death, swollen with the odors of crushed flowers and rotting fruit, swollen with her perfume soured with their sweat, swollen with musky semen, swollen with her dark, effulgent secretions, her black shoes brilliant, beating on tables, beating on counters, beating on platforms, beating on backs, beating in the air, beating while raised high above her head while her white legs flashed in the black, swollen, thick night, the black night which gave way to a thin red dawn, to thin roosters crowing, thin children crying, thin faces emerging, sallow, yellow, exhausted, from bamboo huts, from tin shacks, from holes in blasted walls, from craters in the blasted ground, the ground turned red by the thin, silent sun, and black by the thick, silent, drying blood which stained the earth from border to border to border.

4.

The building is shaped like a fat cross. It has been, we are given to understand, constructed—at some expense—as a duplicate of the original building, which is somewhere on the Yucatan Peninsula of Mexico. There is a cenote there, which is a kind of natural well, formed when the peninsula's limestone shelf—a limestone shelf covered by mere inches of soil, a scant country, earth pungent but flimsy, as easy to rip apart as tissue paper—formed, we say, when this limestone shelf is undermined by an underground stream. This limestone then collapses, exposing the water underneath. At the site with which we are concerned, and at many others in Yucatan, the cenote is considered sacred. The most famous example of this, at least to foreigners, is the cenote at Chichen Itza. In some cases—in our case—a temple was built around the cenote. When Francisco de Montejo swept through Yucatan in the service of the Spanish king, this Mayan temple, like many others, was torn down. The limestone blocks, plus additional stones and adobe, were then used to construct a Catholic church on the same spot. This was not seen by de Montejo and the other Spaniards as a desecration, but as proof of the power and rightness of their religion. During the Mexican Revolution, and particularly during the regime of Plutarco Elias Calles, Catholics were persecuted and many of their churches—including the one of which we speak—were closed. It was not confiscated, but neither was it allowed to reopen. Over the years artifacts were brought to it, including some which had adorned the original temple. It thus became, by default, a kind of museum, and remained one until well into the present century, though largely ignored: it was too far from Merida for convenient day trips, and not close enough to any major sites to attract tourists. A hotel was built in the 1930s in a nearby village, but it drew few guests and by the time of our story was largely inhabited, on the upper floors, by relatives of the original owner—primos and tíos, hijos and hijas, abuelitos and cuñados—and on the lower floor by chickens and goats. This hotel has not been reconstructed for this film.

It was a long journey for the three actors to reach this site. They met for the first time in the Hotel Don Jesús. They flew in separately. The woman was disoriented. She staggered down the hotel corridor. "Where am I? Where am I?" Her room was anonymous. It told her nothing. Her luggage was piled all around her. Outside, buses without mufflers snarled past like angry beetles. Everything was hot. Even her air-conditioned room seemed hot. The airplanes, however, had been cool. The airplanes, like the hotel room, had been anonymous. She got on the first one in Iowa. The ticket specified dates and times but said nothing about weather. In Iowa it was always cold, except for the summers, which sweltered. In the airplane the air was thin and chilled. She flew for hours, for perhaps thousands of miles. Clouds passed beneath her at incredible speeds. Yet she sat still. She exerted no energy. When she changed planes she felt expelled—expelled down one chute, into another chute, jostled by strangers who tugged at her purse, who plucked at the sleeves of her mohair coat, whose hands—fleetingly, anonymously—brushed her hips, her fanny, and even her breasts. The caresses were casual, and vanished as soon as she experienced them. Soon she entered another plastic compartment. The seat was comfortable. There was a strange rumble, a kind of pressure, and then silence. People murmured softly around her, as though they were in church. Finally a child began to cry. It cried, perhaps for hours, for thousands of miles, across frontiers, across continents, past ruined civilizations, past third world countries and second world countries and first world countries in the throes of insurgencies and bankruptcies. On the earth far below muggers mugged, judges judged, coups couped, cars lurched off assembly lines, and giant machines stamped out millions of plastic cups. Yet within the plane was audible only a slight

122

hiss, perhaps a faulty air-conditioning vent, and the lonely cry of a single child.

At the hotel she asked the blond man where he was from. He grunted something incomprehensible in reply. It did not sound like the name of a place. They were in the room of the man who looked like a priest. He had instructions, vouchers, tickets spread over a table, but he seemed confused by the whole display. The blond man pouted, and kept muttering his incomprehensible words. A map was spread on the table also, but nothing on it was recognizable.

"Wow," she said. "Did you see those men? At the airport?"

They turned their faces towards her.

"In the blue uniforms. They were cute. You know, sexy. But they had these funny guns—all black, like pistols, but big—"

"MAC-10s."

"What?"

"MAC-10s." It was the blond man, whose single eye now transfixed her. "Machine pistols, my dear. A slight pressure on the trigger—and you are cut in half. Verstehen sie? But you are right. Very sexy."

"Ugh," she said—to herself; the two men had turned back to the map. "No one told me they were real."

5.

She enters the train station from the south, preceded by the man.

This order is exactly the opposite of what will occur later, at the cross-shaped building. It is thus a *mirror symmetry*. All symmetries are disturbing, but most disturbing of all are the mirror symmetries. Catching a glimpse of a symmetry in the course of our daily lives is like seeing the bare bones of a man passing us in the street. Bones are supposed to be hidden by flesh, flesh hidden by clothes. Bones are exposed only at times of trauma and death. To see them at other times—to see a man's pelvis swinging with his walk, a woman's white scapula poking out of a silk blouse—is to be made aware of our skeletal understructure, of what supports and moves us beneath our surfaces. The same is true of symmetries. When a symmetry is exposed we are seeing something not vouchsafed to most people. Such a symmetry rouses unease, and when it is a mirror symmetry one may rightly pause, and gather one's defenses. The woman and the two men are unaware of this. They take two taxis from their hotel. The woman enters the taxi from the north, an irrelevancy. One leg lingers for a moment on the street. It is shapely in a high-heeled pump. The foot is planted firmly on the pavement, thus exaggerating the arch of her instep. Motorcycles, mopeds, other taxis, sedans, and finally a bus roar past. The leg lifts slightly and follows the rest of the body into the taxi. Its door shuts. The driver looks over his shoulder. Everyone, all three of them, are in. The second taxi, filled with luggage, idles behind them. At the railroad station—white concrete, uninspiring—the woman enters from the south, as we have said. The man precedes her. The priest trails behind the two drivers, helping with the luggage, unaware of what he has witnessed.

"It's raining," the woman says.

"What?"

"Isnt that rain? Look—outside."

A white arm points. The priest has almost bumped into her. Outside a deluge of water roars over the street they have just left. The husband is in an office—he can be seen, bent over a table, while sheets of paper are examined, stamped, signed. The priest blinks his eyes. He runs a hand through his graying hair. Sweat has already darkened his shirt. Luggage—expensive Vuitton, heavy duffles—are around him. He stares at the woman, and then looks outside.

"Ah," he says. "The rain. Have you been in the tropics before?"

"Is that where we are?"

"It must be the rainy season."

The rain eases, and for a moment there is a breeze, almost cool.

"Nice," he says.

"What?"

"This breeze. Though you seem cool enough."

"It's hot though, isnt it. Sticky. Will it be cool where we're going?"

"Cool? I doubt it."

"But air-conditioned, at least?"

"Yes. Well, one can hope, can't one?"

6.

There is a slapping sound. Perhaps it is the wheels on the iron tracks. Or perhaps—although this could occur at this point only in the imagination, if at all—it is the sound of one belly slapping against another. Does she imagine the blond man, or the priest, on top of her, slapping away? Do they imagine, either of the men, penetrating her body, sliding their organ rhythmically within her sleek orifice? She is certainly beautiful. The moonlight—the light from what the Maya call pach caae—is cast through the windows of their railroad car. This glow is golden on her face. She sits with her legs pointed into the aisle, one leg crossed over the other. The two men are opposite her in seats which face each other. The seats are leather, the wood dark. The carriage is small. Their luggage is piled to one side. Within the woman's expensive bags are carefully folded dresses, shoes snugly heel-to-toe, and undergarments so flimsy they would rip apart at the merest caress. Later many of these items will be described, and their uses delineated. Outside is a landscape of cavernous trees. That is, the trees are so thick, so blackly green, they have the appearance of deep caves. The train rattles and sways past this dense landscape.

Attached ahead of them is another train carriage—a second-class carriage overfilled with people. The people can be seen dimly illuminated by overhead lights, packed together. Occasionally they press their faces against the glass pane of the door at the end of their carriage. The faces are brown, small, pointed. Teeth are missing from their mouths, and the teeth that are present are often outlined in gold. The eyes are so dark that their pupils cannot be seen. When these eyes turn, just so, toward the light, they pick up a coppery sheen. The faces press against the window pane, then turn and talk volubly. After a while a new face will appear. The eyes in each of these faces shine like polished copper.

Earlier the woman said:

"Does anyone know where we are going?"

"It's marked," the blond man said.

"Marked?"

"On your map."

"Oh." She pretended to study it. "It doesnt make much sense."

"Let me show you." It was the priest. He stood next to her and with a pencil followed a line on the map. "You see? We arrived here. It's the provincial capital. The train—ah, here it is. This way—this way—to here. A small village, I should think."

"Is it far?"

"Given our speed—or our lack of speed—we should arrive tomorrow. Perhaps late."

"Are you an actor?"

"An actor?" He drummed the pencil against his wrist. "An actor. Well, I suppose I am. For this movie, at least. But what I really am—what I really am, you see—is a playwright."

"A playwright?"

"But not a successful one."

He drummed the pencil some more, then abruptly stuck it in his shirt pocket.

"No," he said. "Not a successful one. If you wish to speak of acting you must talk to Garred."

"Garred?"

"Our companion. He is the only professional amongst us, I'm afraid."

She leaned forward and whispered: "Is he angry with me?"

The priest raised his head and blinked his eyes.

"Well," he said softly. "He does seem—well, he does seem angry. But I'm sure—I'm sure, my dear—you neednt take it personally."

"I neednt?"

"Not personally. No, I dont think so. Neither of us."

"This morning I thought he was going to hit me."

"No, no."

"You dont think so?"

"I cant believe—"

"Well," she said. Then she added: "I'm an actress."

"Yes?"

"I was in two movies. I mean, I was supposed to be. I had lines, and everything."

"What happened?"

"My scenes were cut."

"Ah."

"I was never so disappointed. I told all my friends. Can you imagine? And then I'm not there at all."

"Yes, disappointing. I can see that."

"I hope I wont be cut from this one."

"Yes. Yes. We can hope so."

Beyond them, at the window to the next carriage, a face pressed. It was so flattened and distorted by the glass it was not clear if it was a man's face or a woman's. It stared into the carriage, the eyes picking up coppery glints of light .

"Yes," said the priest, eyes vaguely moving. "We can all hope so."

During the day the train stopped at villages. People got on. No one ever seemed to get off. Men, women, children stood alongside the tracks with huge boxes tied with twine and jute sacks stacked one on top of the other. How did they get in? The carriage was already full. Children wailed, women cried out, men shouted. But once the train was moving the track was empty and the wails and cries disappeared beneath the clack of the iron wheels.

"What did you say your name was?"

"Garred Haus."

"Garred Haus! What a funny name. Have I introduced myself?"

"Yes."

"I'm Virginia White. I toured Vietnam with the USO. That country looked just like this. We're not in Vietnam, are we? I wouldnt want to go there again!"

"Never fear, my dear. We're in no country youve ever heard of."

"I mean, I enjoyed my tour. And it was good for my career. But it was so terrible, what happened to our boys there. So terrible, dont you think? And then just to pull out, as though nothing had happened. It's all politics, isnt it? That's what they told me. All those boys—they were so angry. We didnt let them do their job, did we? I mean our politicians didnt. We could have won that war. Our boys could have won it—that's what they all told me. If we had just turned them loose, to do their job."

"It was a nasty war," says the priest.

"Do you know what this movie is about?"

"Havent you read the script?"

"My agent read it. Do I have a good part?"

"Essential."

"You mean it's important? My agent said it was important."

"That's right."

"They wont cut me out in the editing, will they?"

"Not unless they cut everything."

"Good." She smiled. "What is your name? Did we do this before?"

"We introduced ourselves back at the hotel."

"But I've forgotten."

"Osgood Fetters."

"Osgood Fetters!"

"That's right."

"What a strange name!"

"Isnt it?"

7.

The night is occluded. The moon—pach caae—is obscured. Rain spatters the window. Earlier, the woman—the one who calls herself Virginia White—wondered aloud about lunch. No one had thought to bring food, and there was clearly no restaurant car on this train. The next time the train stopped, Garred Haus—the "husband"—leaned out a window and, via sign language and a display of currency , acquired what looked like corn tortillas or chapatis folded over a smear of gravy. No one else wanted one, however, so Garred ate them all, wolfishly. Water? There was no water. The bathroom at one end of the carriage—they had to brave the faces pressed against the window to approach it—had a broken tap. The toilet itself was merely a hole in the floor open to the track below. There was a lingering odor within the tiny room of ammonia, and no one, especially the woman, spent any more time within its confines than necessary. The next time the train stopped—more people got on; no one got off—Garred Haus again leaned out the window, and moments later brought forth three bottles of Coca Cola, surely the most ubiquitous liquid in existence. They were tepid and sickly sweet, but wet. The woman wrinkled her nose: Was there no Diet Coke? She took pretty little swallows, as though by drinking so slowly she would imbibe fewer calories.

All this time she is dressed in white. While she is dressed in white the train passes shrubs blossoming with the white plumeria. Sometimes these flowers are so close that Garred Haus, had he so desired, could have plucked one and given it to the woman, who herself—as we shall see—resembles the plumeria. Each blossom—we are speaking now of the flower—has a five-parted calyx. There are five stamens. There are five spreading corolla lobes, or petals, that overlap at their bases, rather like propellers. The lobes have a waxy appearance. The flowers, as well as the succulent branches, which possess large leaves pinnately veined, contain an abundant milky sap that is reputed to be caustic, perhaps even poisonous. The flowers are generally fragrant. They are named after Charles Plumier, a French botanist who died in 1704. The plant, in both shrub and tree form, is found throughout tropical America and the West Indies, where they belong to the dogbane family, and in Hawaii, where they are often used in leis for tourists, who do not understand what they are putting around their necks. They are common also throughout Asia, where they are a favored offering to Buddhist temples, and thus often called the temple flower. The woman Virginia White resembles the plumeria, especially the white plumeria, in the following particulars: her pale skin, translucent and waxy with sweat; the blossom between her legs, whose lobes, or lips, are noticeably waxy from their effulgent secretions and tinged with the same pink often found in the heart of the plumeria; her succulent limbs, veined; her abundant sap, which may or may not be caustic; her fragrance. The flower itself is robust; so too is the woman, although this would be more apparent were she naked. Her flesh, like the thick-petaled plumeria, is firm, well-packed, amply curved, swelling. With one exception this robust body is clothed in garments of exceeding delicacy. The exception is her hose: a one-piece garment which pulls up to her hips, covering her from the tips of her toes to her waist, and named Ironweave Pantihose. This garment is available in supermarkets throughout America and offers protection against mosquitoes and sunburn; it repels water and—because of its rough texture—roving hands. In particular it occludes the woman's sex organ, the waxy lobes of which are flattened by the Ironweave and hidden even more completely than the moon overhead is hidden by clouds. If one saw her clad in this garment, one's first impression would be that she had no orifice, that there was no entrance to her body, no exit. Smooth to the eye, rough to the hand, apertureless, the lower half of her body thus resembles a mannikin, one of those window dummies whose only purpose is to display artifacts for sale.

Her breasts, however—we shall continue this description—are sheathed by a brassiere so fine, so delicate, it is a wonder it can contain her swelling flesh. Through the material is visible the roseate glow of each nipple. Over the brassiere a thin slip falls to mid-thigh; then a translucent blouse tucked into a straight white skirt. On her feet are white pumps with spindly heels at least four inches high. The lips on her face are painted pink and covered with a waxy gloss. They are unrestrained, open, exposed, well-rounded, fleshy, and thus inviting, exactly the opposite of the lips between her legs so crushed by the Ironweave fabric of her hose. It is not clear what one can make of this. Perhaps, in the course of this story, or in the course of the film, we will find out.

In the meantime the night is occluded. Rain slaps against the window panes. The air outside is thick with insects. Within the carriage the three actors prepare uneasily for sleep. Faintly perceived above the clack of the iron wheels are the cries and moans from the people pressed together in the second class carriage. These people stand, sit, lie, flesh to flesh, amongst children half crushed, women seemingly in labor, men wild-eyed with hunger, draped over sacks of dried corn, bags of rice, and chickens gasping in bamboo cages. None of them, we are sure, can sleep this night, unless it is the sleep of the mad: the air filled with perfervid images, contorted dreams, thick fevers. In the smaller carriage the three actors themselves sleep fitfully on their leather seats. None has undressed; only shoes have come off. In the morning the three are noticeably awry. Waterless, they can only pat at their faces, rearrange their wrinkled garments, run brush or fingers through hair still damp from the night's sweats. When the train stops, Garred acquires more Cokes, which restore them somewhat. More people climb on board: withered women, crippled men, children with pus dripping from wounds.

As the train lurches through the lush countryside the woman Virginia White walks—cautiously on her four inch heels—to the cubicle at the end. Dark faces stare at her; lips move rapidly in speech that is not audible; their eyes flash, right and left, with coppery glints.

When she emerges the faces are still there. A fist bangs on the glass pane of the door. The faces twist and turn; their lips distort.

"I think theyre trying to get in," she says. "They cant get in, can they?"

"Our door is locked," says Garred. "I checked it yesterday."

"Perhaps," says the priest, "we could let a few of them—the women—"

"If you let one in, they will all come in. Forget it, priest. They are used to their conditions."

"I'm not a priest."

"Of course not."

Garred Haus reclines on his seat; his feet are up on the seat opposite, in twisted beige socks. His shirt is open to the waist. His eyes are closed. His sallow face is shiny with sweat.

"It's hot," says the woman. "It's already hotter than yesterday."

No one responds. After a while the banging on the window ceases.

133

8 .

The northern walls are adobe and painted white. Shortly these walls will come into view. First, however, the train stops at another village. A black limousine is parked there. At its side stands an Oriental man in a visored cap. When the train stops, he comes up to the carriage window.

"Mr Haus? Mr Fetters? Miss White?"

"It seems," says Osgood Fetters, "we have finally arrived."

"Thank God."

The woman's hand, with its pink nails, is at her throat.

"I dont think," she continues, "I could take another minute of this."

They stand by the car. Ragged children drag luggage from the train across the red dirt. These are stacked in the limousine's voluminous trunk; only the last two are tied on top. The Oriental man, who has a round face and a chubby body, opens a door. The three actors fit comfortably in the back seat. As soon as the engine fires, cold air begins to hiss around them. Almost immediately sweat pours down their faces, their torsos, their thighs: their bodies are still producing sweat to cope with the heat experienced outside, but in the cold air the sweat no longer evaporates. Black smears of mascara descend from the woman's eyes. Her thin blouse, already grayish and damp, becomes sopping wet. She gasps, drawing cold air into her lungs. It takes several minutes for their bodies to adjust to this cold. By then they are squirming in their own moisture, the woman especially. It is at this point that Osgood Fetters, perhaps in his role as priest, taps at his window—he is sitting on the right—and says:

"Look!"

"What is it?"

"They're burning something—no, someone—"

Virginia White cranes her neck around, brushing at the sweat in her eyes.

"What is it?" she repeats. "What did you say?"

"That man's on fire!"

The scene the priest refers to is being enacted in an open space surrounded by trees. The limbs of these trees droop low to the ground. Between the ceibas and the red zapotes and the tall balche trees are the plumerias, some of whose blossoms are plum colored, some scarlet, others white. The tallest tree of all is the *Antiaris toxicaria*, or sack tree, whose poisonous sap is often used in punji traps. These trees, within whose cavernous depths roam kinkajous and foxes, swollen iguanas, grouse, even jaguars, form a dense wall around the clearing. Although they possess genuine beauty, they are genuinely foreboding as well. Within the primeval forest are forces which are truly dangerous. The primitive people who live within these forests, and the village people who carve out spaces at their edges, give many names and meanings to these forces. In truth the forces which exist there are embodied in the jungle itself: that is, the plants and animals are themselves those forces exemplified, made visible. They exemplify the urge to life, an urge which is perversely destructive. That is why parasites kill their hosts, why a vine will claw its way over a tree until the tree dies beneath it, why scorpions drip poison, why a spider will kill its mate, why trees exude vile sap and animals devour each other in their mad lust for life. The very fertility of the earth depends upon death: the decomposing carcasses are themselves the humors of life. It is in this context that we must witness the events in the clearing which our three actors are now passing. Plunging from the trees—out of the darkness—is a crane with a giant Panavision camera mounted at its tip. It rises drunkenly from the shadows, and then swoops low over the ground. At its base stand men in jungle fatigue pants and T-shirts. Across the clearing are fifty to sixty people, some of them in the orange robes of Buddhist monks. Several are dancing; their robes swirl around their sandaled feet. In front of them is a gray car, perhaps a French Simca, or an English Hillman, with its hood, or bonnet, raised. To one side is a five gallon can of the type used to carry gasoline. In the center of the clearing is the man himself, the Thich, or Venerable, Quang Duc, or his simile. His hands are in his lap. He sits lotus fashion. Around him swirl—rather like the orange robes of the dancing monks—ochre flames. These flames are deceptively light—insubstantial, translucent, perhaps soundless, although this must be uncertain from within the limousine. Nevertheless they are fierce enough to turn the Venerable Quang Duc's skin—or his simile's skin—black. The skin peels. A darkish smoke, an oily smoke, appears around the flames, whose density perhaps increases. When a wind blows aside the flames, an expression of ineffable pain can be glimpsed on the Venerable's face.

"That man's burning to death!"

"Dont be a fool, Fetters."

"No—the skin peeling—my God, those eyes—"

"Remember where you are, man. This is movieland. Nothing is real."

They have passed the clearing. The way is rutted, and tree limbs occasionally brush the top of the limousine.

"No, that was real—he looked—"

"Looked, Fetters. Seemed. Actors will burn their Equity cards, but not themselves. Not even for a percentage of the gross."

"I swear—"

"Take hold of yourself, man."

"It looked so real!"

"Good. Perhaps this production isnt as half-assed as it seems."

The woman, who sits between the two men, stares from one to the other. Garred Haus has scarcely stirred; it is not clear he even looked at the burning figure. Osgood Fetters at last falls back into his seat, although his face remains pale.

The woman claps her hands together. "My goodness!" she says. "This is exciting!"

Soon the white adobe walls, as we have promised, come into view. The building is surrounded by trees and shrubs. The air is darkish, damp.

Osgood Fetters comments that the building looks like a church. The woman, still on the edge of her seat, agrees. The car stops to the north, where a path begins. Garred Haus watches suspiciously—the lid of his right eye lowered—while the Oriental man unties the two pieces of luggage. He carries these two pieces—quick short steps, as though he were walking in Japanese sandals—ahead of the three actors, down the path, between chacah and chulul, past homa gourds and scorpion trees, yellow kan-lol and hanging pupae, to the white door set between the adobe walls. The oriental man immediately announces—as he pushes the door open—that he speaks no English. Perhaps he has announced this to forestall questions. Nevertheless Garred speaks. German? he suggests. French? Spanish? *Hungarian?* No English, repeats the Oriental man. He puts the two pieces of luggage down inside the door and scurries away. The three actors go inside. They move from display case to display case. What is this? the woman asks. Terra cotta, Osgood answers promptly. There is obsidian and carved limestone, ceramics and jade, both inside the cases and fastened to the walls. Osgood Fetters puts glasses onto the bridge of his nose, and stoops low, sniffing. These look like pustules, he says, smallpox pustules. Although I suppose—and what is this? Pretty, dont you think? What do they call it? Not ceramic—er—mosaic, that's it, a mosaic jade mask. And look at the ruby eyes—well, theyre probably glass—in that jaguar.

Garred leaves the room. When he returns, his hands are stuck in his pockets. He watches the man and the woman.

"Where's the chink?" he says finally.

"The Oriental—uh—gentleman?"

"That's the one."

"Well—"

Garred walks past Osgood Fetters, whose eyes are blinking behind his spectacles, and goes outside. Some moments later he returns with a duffle over one shoulder.

"Better do something about your luggage," he says.

"Our luggage?"
"It's piled on the road."
"What do you mean?"
"It's piled on the road."
"But that man—"
"The chink's gone."

8.

The cenote lies in the center of the building: the exact center of the building, directly beneath the dome which rises perhaps forty meters overhead. Although we are given to understand that this building is a reproduction, that it was built recently for the purpose, specifically, of this film, we are suspicious. It looks old. More importantly, it feels old. It has that deep darkness, that ancient weight, that only an old building can possess. Moreover, around one side of the cenote is what must be centuries of accumulated bat guano. Would a movie company be so interested in verisimilitude as to import bat guano? Living in the bat guano are fungi, specifically the *Bacillus subtilis* Cohn and *Bacillus mycoides* Flugge, of the order Eubacteriales. These fungi are phototactic, capable of fruiting when light is entirely absent, and can rapidly decompose proteinaceous materials. The cenote itself is actually a cave, as are all cenotes, in this case of the two-cycle solution type, which is indicated by its irregular, reticulate form and the presence—perhaps we shall discover these later—of high-vaulted chambers. There is a considerable pool of water perhaps ten meters, or about thirty-three feet, below the irregular surface. Doubtless because of the presence of this large body of water, the air temperature in the center of this building will vary only between 23.2 and 27.9 degrees Celsius, with the humidity maintained over 90%. Within this cenote and around its edge live troglophile, troglobite and occasionally trogloxene animals. Some authorities (Arndt, 1923; Mohr, 1928) name these creatures troglobitic, troglophilic, ombrophilic and euryphotic, while others (Gebhard, 1932; Kolsavary, 1934) prefer the terms eutroglobionts, hemitroglobionts, pseudotroglobionts, tychotroglobients, and additionally, troglocheimadas. In any case, many of these creatures, however they are classified, are blind, colorless, hydrophylic. There are rhabdocoeis and triclads, rhizopods and ciliates, several varieties of nematodes, simple polychaetes, oligochaetes, leeches, rotifers, pulmonate and prosobranch snails, sphaerid clams, many cave crustaceans such as cladocerans and copepods, including parasitic species, archaid anispidaceans, several aquatic and terrestrial isopods, many amphipods and palaemonid shrimps, arachnids such as aquatic and terrestrial mites, ticks, many spiders, pseudoscorpions, whip scorpions, scorpions, millipedes and centipedes, thysanurans and collembolans, psocids and earwigs, cockroaches, phasmids, beetles, dipterans, and cave crickets. In the water itself are fish such as the amblyopsid, the silurid, some cyprinids, brotulids, and symbranchid eels. The amphibians are chiefly salamanders, both aquatic and terrestrial, often with degenerate eyes. The troglophiles include lizards and snakes. Many of these creatures are blind, but are recompensed with unusually effective tactile and olfactory organs. Their bodies may be pale and pellucid, without pigment; small, stenothermic; and hydrophylic. Many of the fish, and some of the crustaceans, are luminescent. The silurids have long tactile and gustatory barbels on their heads. The bats are nocturnal and feed largely without using their organs of vision; some, in fact, have degenerate eyes. The cave crickets subsist entirely on the remains of insects in the bat feces. Many of the other creatures we have named feed also on the organic remains found in the guano, which is fecund. Other creatures simply eat each other. We shall deal more specifically with some of them, and the details of their lives, later.

The building, as we have said, resembles a fat cross. The three actors sleep in the red room. The red room comprises the eastern arm. It lies precisely on that cardinal direction. The northern room is the white-painted adobe room, filled with artifacts. At this hour it is empty of people, if not of other creatures. The surface of the cenote is occasionally disturbed by movements of schizopods, sphaeromids, cirolanids, amphipods, blind brotulid and amblyopsid fish. The sleep of our actors is disturbed also. None of them can be comfortable. For the woman and the priest, this is their first night, ever, beneath the shroud of a mosquito net. The room, of course, is filled with both anopheline and aedene mosquitoes; the former carry malaria, the latter yellow fever. The "beds" on which these actors sleep are no more than burlap stretched over wooden frames. There are no sheets. Blankets are not needed in this heat. There is no movement of air, although the windows in the room are all open. Even if the air did move, the mosquito nets would largely prevent the air from sliding over, and thus cooling, the skin of our sleeping actors. Garred Haus, the husband, lies in a pair of bikini underpants. Osgood Fetters, the priest, lies in boxer shorts and singlet. The woman Virginia White has troubled to change into pajamas. When she tosses from side to side—which she does often, half awake—her breasts, loose, unconstrained, flow beneath her pajama tops like waves moving the surface of the sea.

IO.

There is a drop of blood on her arm. The blood—a single drop—appears when the woman scratches a mosquito bite. She is still in her pajamas, which are decorated with small figures of an anthropomorphic rodent called "Mickey Mouse," a creation of the American entrepreneur Walt Disney. This creature has that wide, idiotic smile, that maniacally cheerful innocence, which Americans feel is their patrimony. On her feet are "bunny slippers." On her bed, still shrouded by netting, is the "teddy bear" with whom she slept the night. Is this possible? Are we exaggerating? Can we believe that this grown woman, who must be more than thirty years old, even if she looks younger, would travel with, or even possess, Mickey Mouse pajamas and bunny slippers and a teddy bear? This morning, despite scratching blood from one of many mosquito bites, despite being tousled, smudged, unwashed, this woman sits sleepy-eyed on the edge of her bed, feet and legs together, hands on knees, a bright smile on her face, like a child expecting applause or perhaps a trip to the zoo.

Last night she was not so cheerful. She and Osgood Fetters rushed out to the road. Halfway there, Fetters suddenly faltered, a grimace on his face. What is it? the woman said, pausing. Are you all right? It's nothing, he answered, just a muscle cramp. He did not know it, but a blood vessel had burst deep within the calf muscle of his right leg. In a few days the leg would be swollen and blackly bruised. Now, however, slowly, carefully, he hobbled to the road where their luggage, indeed, was piled.

He brought in one suitcase, then another. She carried two at a time, wobbling on her high heels. He made more journeys, in obvious pain. The woman's face was dusty and tight-lipped. They piled their luggage inside the door. Garred Haus was nowhere in sight. At last they found him in the "red room," which was apparently where they were all expected to sleep. Garred had already selected his bed there, the largest, and was reclining on it, smoking one of his Gauloises. The woman and the priest then carried their luggage into this room, one and two at a time, past the artifacts, past the cenote, past the bat guano. The woman's white clothes were filthy. She plunked herself down on her "bed." Her mouth pushed open and shut like the mouth of a fish taken from water.

"What," she said, "is going on here?"

Although the question was rather tossed out into the air, it was actually addressed to Garred, who ignored it.

"I have never been so despicably treated."

Garred blew smoke into the air.

"I am going to complain," she announced, "to the producer."

Osgood Fetters had put his leg up and was massaging the calf.

"We shall all complain," he said, as though he were capable of speaking for Garred. "This is intolerable. Youre quite right."

"No one should have to put up with this."

"No one."

"This isnt a movie; it's a torture chamber."

"Exactly."

"This isnt even a hotel."

"It's not even a decent dormitory."

"Am I supposed to sleep on one of these things?"

She banged at the burlap, from which rose a cloud of dust.

"Where's my shower? Where's my bathroom? I want my own bedroom. We need a cook—someone to do our clothes—decent accommodations—"

"Hear, hear."

"I wont put up with this. I simply wont."

"Youre quite right."

"I simply," she repeated, "wont put up with this."

She then sat there, looking around, as though expecting something to happen.

After a while she pushed out her lower lip and began to sniff. No one noticed. Garred, droopy-eyed, was blowing smoke into the air. Osgood, pant leg pulled up, was still massaging his calf.

She whimpered, softly; then again, more loudly.

Osgood leaped up.

"My dear!" he said.

He limped to her side and put an arm around her.

"Are you quite all right?"

"No," she said, suddenly gasping with sobs. "No, I'm not all right. I'm filthy, I'm all dirty, I cant do my hair, I feel ugly—"

"My dear!"

"Nothing is going right, nothing ever goes right, I dreamed of this, I dreamed all my life, and now look at me, a filthy mess!"

"My dear!"

"It's not right! It's just not right!"

"Here, here now!"

"It's not fair!"

"My dear, surely, tomorrow all this—"

"I dont *care* about tomorrow! It's not right *now*! Tomorrow will be just as horrible! I know it!"

"No, no, really—youll see—"

"I dont see! I dont want to see! I dont want to see any of this!"

"My dear! My dear!"

She buried her head on his shoulder.

Yet the evening, and the night, passed, as we have indicated. There was a five gallon bottle of water mounted on a swivel base, allowing its contents to be poured into a chipped enamel cup. On a shelf were three tins of tuna fish and two papayas. There was an outside toilet of sorts, a dank, smelly shed, more like a simple outhouse than a bathroom. The woman used it, almost in tears, peeling down her Ironweave Pantihose, letting out a discreet fart and then a dribble of shit. The toilet paper came from Garred, who alone seemed prepared for these eventualities. Garred had put a bucket of water just outside the door for washing. The bucket had a long rope attached, and the water came from the cenote itself. The bar of soap was Garred's, of course. The woman, used to American motels which supplied everything, carried no soap with her, although in her luggage she had two brands of shampoos, three different hair conditioners, a mouth wash, and sundry other items of personal hygiene, including what must have been a year's supply of tampons. Garred showed her and Osgood Fetters how the mosquito nets worked, which was simple enough, and they crawled under them as the sun—kinich-kach-moo—fell below the horizon and the mosquitoes rose from their fetid pools and shadowy lairs to take over the night.

But morning comes. The dawn then is as rosy as a woman's—as Virginia White's—cheeks, and all seems possible again, even if you are perched on the edge of a burlap-covered bed. Her blubbery lower lip now retracted, sleepy-eyed but pert, clothed in her infantile pajamas and bunny slippers, as charming as a well-behaved twelve-year-old, the American woman Virginia White is ready for anything.

Nothing happens. They dine on a papaya—the Swiss army knife comes from Garred's duffle—and take turns sipping at the enameled cup. At nine o'clock Garred announces he will walk to town. He collects a few dollars from each of the others ("Diet Coke, please") and immediately leaves. His absence creates an odd stillness in the room. The two remaining people, the "priest" Osgood Fetters, with his sore leg, and the "wife" Virginia White, in her Mickey Mouse pajamas, stare at each other across the room.

II.

In her luggage the woman has several white dresses, plus white skirts and blouses. Many of the blouses are embroidered. Some have what are called Peter Pan collars. There are also frail white brassieres, white panties, white slips and camisoles, white shoes, and several pair of white Ironweave Pantihose. There is clothing in other colors, too; we will describe some of them later. But for today she wears only the rodent pajamas and the bunny slippers. Osgood Fetters is doubtless aware of the looseness of her breasts beneath her torso. She certainly is. When she walks, when she shifts her torso, these breasts seem to move independently, swinging right and left, up and down, whichever way they please. But a woman could hardly be accused of seductiveness or overt sexuality in Mickey Mouse pajamas and bunny slippers, could she? Could anything be more innocent? She chats with a kind of childish happiness of her career, her upbringing in Iowa, her boyfriends back home, her dream of being a famous actress. Osgood, a bit donnish, a gentle man—he should really have a pipe in his mouth—encourages her expansiveness. His avuncular air, combined with her innocence, allows her—rather perversely, we are afraid—to swing her breasts more than necessary, and to frequently cross and uncross her legs, as though her cunt itched, and to coquettishly pat at her hair—to flirt, in fact, the way a little girl will flirt with a favored uncle. It is all quite innocent, and thus allowed, surely. The two of them stroll through the garden outside, Osgood limping, the woman plucking flowers, including the ic-bac nicte, or Little Girl Plumeria. Neither of them notice the locusts or scorpions, the xulab or the chac uaya-cab, or the hanging pupae. The sunlight is warm, the air reasonably dry. Beyond the road rise the giant trees of the forest. There are hills on three sides, all deeply forested. The air is quite still, awaiting developments. When they go back inside, the woman places the flowers around the room in bottles and tin cans. That seems more cheerful, she says, and Osgood agrees. He has been talking now of his career—rather, his failures—as a playwright; and with this charming girl, in this place, with the sun just so, his failures seem, even to him, amusing. He tells anecdotes of producers who chewed cigars, of method actors who chewed lines, of the amateur groups (housewives from Queens, gay men aging into their toupees) who did put on his plays, and the resulting discomfort of their audiences, who understood nothing. He chuckles over the despairing jobs he held on the fringes of the theatre world, of waiting tables, clerking at hotels, at last finding a more-or-less stable part-time job with a law firm, writing briefs and other missives. The two lawyers for whom he worked seemed relieved to have someone who could make their presentations sound suitably, correctly opaque, yet someone who could adorn their letters with an occasionally lucid sentence. Osgood's mastery of legalese was quick and easy—writing is writing, after all—and he amused himself within its constraints with subtle turns of phrases, with lines in iambic pentameter, with obscure echoes of Eugene Ionesco and Samuel Beckett. Things no one but him, he was sure, would be aware of.

Thus the morning passed pleasantly enough. For lunch Osgood opened a tin of tuna, using Garred's Swiss knife, only cutting himself once. The woman wished, wistfully, for tea, Osgood for gelata and a good expresso. The afternoon passed with more strain. Perhaps the woman's role as child was beginning to weigh on her. How cheerful can one be, when there is no trip to the zoo in the offing? no tea? no finger sandwiches? no boyfriends? no admiring glances from passing strangers? no full-length mirrors in which to admire oneself? no stores in which to shop? no bedrooms to adorn with teddy bears and other anthropomorphic creatures? no hot water for a bath? no tub for a bath? no television "talk-shows?" no music to set her feet atwinkling? no car to drive? no telephone with which to hold long, chirping, cheerful

147

conversations with girlfriends? And besides, Osgood was stumbling now over his anecdotes, which were becoming morose and boring. There was an embarrassed look about him, too, a bit of lustful confusion, guilty desire—her breasts had apparently gotten to him—which she did not find amusing. Uncles were supposed to know their roles, after all. But that was the trouble with men. They were infuriatingly incapable of taking her innocent display—she meant nothing by it— in the spirit in which it was offered. At least, with his injured leg, she could evade him if this became necessary. But his tumescence was discomfiting. She sat straightly on the edge of her bed, and buttoned one more button of her pajama top. Mickey Mouse would defend her.

But at last a battered car comes up the road, blowing steam and leaking water. Garred Haus gets out with two jute sacks. He carries them with deceptive ease—they are actually quite heavy—through the white room, past the cenote and the bat guano, into the red room. There he finds Osgood Fetters and Virginia White in the attitudes we have described. The woman becomes immediately animated. Osgood hunches his shoulders, as though trying to hide. Garred unloads from his sacks two sixpacks of Cokes—no Diet Cokes, no diet anything, no one in that country is on a diet—more tins of tuna, a can of kerosene, a pressure-type lantern, two bottles of rum, three bottles of Chinese brandy, mosquito coils, two long loaves of crusty bread, mangoes, papayas, a pineapple, a bunch of bananas, and two more tin cups, one of which he immediately fills with Coke and a healthy slug of rum. Young Virginia claps her hands, breasts swinging again. Somehow the top button of her pajamas has unbuttoned itself. Garred takes his cup to his bed and starts fishing out a cigarette from his crumpled pack. "They are behind schedule," he says. *All* movies were behind schedule. They were shooting a scene when he reached town: GIs marching through the street with crowds cheering and girls throwing flowers. Garred does not go into detail. The girls, however, *we* understand, were bar girls imported especially for this scene. They were suspended in gilt cages above the street. They threw flower *petals*—the waxy lobes of the plumeria—onto the marching GIs, but first they rubbed the petals on their pussies. "Hey, GI! You want fuckee-fuckee? You want suck pussy? You come to mama-san, baby! I suckee-fuckee good time boy!" Pulling plumeria petals redolent of their effulgent secretions from their bikini bottoms, tossing them, watching them float serenely onto the upturned faces and opened mouths of the young soldiers. The GIs cheered, or the extras playing GIs cheered, marching down the street in one direction, then turning and marching back up it . "More flowers!" someone yelled. "Get those girls more flowers!" The girls plucked at their own teats and rubbed their famous pussies against the bars of their gilded cages.

"I dont remember," Osgood says from across the room, after clearing his throat, "any GIs in the script."

"We only have part of the script."

"Yes, I know. But soldiers—there's nothing there about soldiers. I mean, there's no place in the story for soldiers—"

"Scripts change, Fetters."

"Yes, surely. But—"

"Soldiers are popular now in America, arent they?"

"Yes, but in Yucatan?"

"What difference does it make?"

"I know scripts—I write them. You cant just stick in some extraneous element—I mean, for no reason—"

"This is the movies, Fetters."

"Yes, surely. But—"

"Anything can happen."

"I dont understand. I just dont understand these soldiers."

"Wait," says the woman, who has been staring back and forth at the two, rather like a spectator following the ball at a tennis match. "What about us? Did you talk to anyone about us?"

"Someone's coming for us tomorrow."

What the man—he was identified to Garred as the Assistant Director—actually said was, "Just stay cool, buddy. Someone'll getcha tomorra, okay?" He was a tall man, a bit gone to seed, a hard man turning soft in a sweat-stained T-shirt and jungle fatigue pants. A duckbill cap was pushed back on his head. His accent was southern American, bayou country, Louisiana maybe, juicy like a swamp. He had eyes with hardly any color. He pushed Garred out of the way—put his hand flat on Garred's chest and just shoved a little, hardly any effort, moving aside a minor irritation—and stalked off to some obscure duty, perhaps to get flowers for the bar girls. There was a .45 pistol stuck in his back pocket. Garred wandered through the crowd. He talked to a lighting man holding big aluminum reflectors, a key grip in a floppy hat, an assistant cameraman who tried to bum cigarettes from him. When the street scene, the marching GIs, was finished, close-ups began: closeups of the suckee-fuckee girls, close-ups of GI faces, a snatch of dialog repeated from three different angles, an aluminum reflector here, another there, diffusion screen overhead ("Get rid of that shadow!"), interminable waits while everything was put together, while sound men swore and cameramen snapped. It was all melee. In the confusion Garred slipped from group to group, Gauloise smouldering, listening.

He tells little of this to Osgood Fetters and Virginia White. We ourselves will not repeat the conversations he had or the fragments he overheard. Some of the information contained in them will become apparent shortly. For some time he sat in a dark little store. It was owned by an elderly Chinese. Garred sipped beer and watched the afternoon wane. Finally he acquired all the items we have mentioned. The Chinaman himself—his shop, small as it was, contained canned Lychee nuts from Shanghai and rodent poison from America, Tiger Balm from Singapore and White Horse Whiskey from Canada—supplied most of it and sent out for the rest. He also summoned the car, the local "taxi," and provided the jute sacks and two boys to carry them. All was paid for with a fine sheath of local currency, which Garred had acquired, presciently, in the provincial capital .

Garred stuck his thumb towards the open door of the shop.

"What you think?" he asked.

"Ah," said the Chinese. He touched a finger to his eye. "I look. I see. I say nothing."

"Wise old bird, arent you?"

"Yes, yes, very wise old bird indeed!"

He chuckled. Garred got into the car.

12.

The woman wears a white dress. First, however, she bathes. She is adamant. She will not meet the director, perhaps the producer, perhaps the producer's *girlfriend*, without shampooing her hair and washing her body and putting on fresh clothing, that is, a clean white dress, a red leather belt, and red high-heeled shoes. Her bath is arranged in the following way. The bucket is brought back to the cenote, which is where Garred originally found it. He tosses it into the water thirty-three feet below, drags it full, and hauls it back up. She dips her hair into it—the hair is long, fullbodied, and rather tangled now—and, humming, spends several minutes lathering it. She wears a cotton robe and thong sandals. When the lather has risen to her specifications, Garred pours the bucket over her bent head. "Oooh!" she cries happily. Garred brings up more water. She rubs conditioner into the wet hair. After one minute Garred pours again. He pours a second time. Finally he brings up another bucket and leaves. She is ready now to bathe, a more private act.

Only we shall watch. The two men are in the white room, the door closed. The woman stands naked at the edge of the cenote, in a spot clear of bat guano. The door to the red room, the room which faces east, which faces into the rising sun, is open. Some light comes through this door. Because it comes from only one direction—the center of the building is otherwise quite dark—and because the light is faint, she is deeply shadowed. Her breasts are illuminated on one side, and dark on the other. The hollow of her belly, as she stands at an angle, is shadowed. Her swelling mound of Venus, however, glistens—the pubic hair is wet and each drop of water shines like a diamond. As she turns, pouring cups of water over herself, light illuminates her cleft rump, then one swelling breast, then another. As she soaps herself she continues to turn. Perhaps it is best if we see her from a distance, from near the top of the domed ceiling, for instance, where the bats are hanging. From that distance she is a marionette turning, turning, turning below. Her hands can be seen moving over her robust body. Each breast is given attention. Each thigh is soaped. The light from the door of the red room functions exactly as a spotlight would function. She turns in this spotlight. Her head falls back, exposing her throat. When both breasts are turned into the light she lifts them, one hand to each breast, as though offering them to an audience. Each breast is rinsed individually. All this time she is humming into this vast, dark room. All this time her wet hair hangs, sometimes down her back, sometimes across one shoulder, sometimes, as she turns, and turns, across one breast. All this time she is alone, except for the sleeping bats, except for the silurids in the water below, except for the crickets in the guano and the whip scorpions, false scorpions, and scorpions living beneath the lip of the cenote.

She dresses. She pulls on, awkwardly, white Ironweave Pantihose. She slips her small feet into the red shoes with high, high heels. A brassiere is strapped around her breasts. It is so delicate, a man's hand, stroking a breast through this brassiere, would tear the fabric. She puts on a white cotton dress, a shirtwaist, buttoned down the front and collared. Buttons are left undone so that the thin, delicate brassiere, and the flesh beneath it, may be glimpsed. In the white room she props a mirror on a display case—it contains a terracotta balam, or jaguar—and makes up her face: mascara and eyeliner, a touch of color on the cheekbones, red thickly on the lips, then covered with gloss so the lips are wet, lubricated, inviting. Into the mirror she smiles. She touches her collar. She shifts her breasts, slightly. She is perfect.

Slowly, delicately, perfectly, balanced exactly on her high heels, she returns to the red room to wait.

13.

She wears a white dress. It is the dress we have described. She is clean and shining. Gradually however she begins to wilt. The heat becomes stultifying. She sits and sweats. There is no wind. No one comes for them. Breathing itself becomes difficult. The flowers outside droop like open mouths. There is no escape from this heat, which today lies heavily on the red earth.

In the afternoon Garred walks through this heat back to the town. Within the town he finds two slinking dogs, some iguanas and geckos, and ravens pecking at unidentifiable carcasses. Yesterday's flower petals—already brown, already rotting—lie in the street. Many of the buildings are false fronts, apparently constructed just for the scene Garred witnessed the day before. The gilt cages lie behind them, some on their sides. A musky odor hangs there, rather like the perfume of a woman who has just left a room. Garred sniffs, lips peeled back, teeth together: it is the face of a feral animal. He bangs on doors. The Chinaman's shop is shuttered. The train station, the only concrete building in the town, is deserted. The tracks are hot and already rusting. He finds a metal rod there and uses it to pry open a window to the Chinaman's store. The shelves are bare, except for a pile of jute sacks. When the shadows lengthen, he starts back. He finds the other two in the red room. The woman wears the white dress. A red belt is around her waist. On her feet are red shoes with high, high heels. Her legs are crossed at the ankles. The priest is bony and thin. His leg, propped up before him, is now swollen. Bruising is visible. Garred explains what he has seen. There were things he did not tell them yesterday. People yesterday talked nervously of an attempt against the government. There were rumors of a coup. Something like that, he says, must have occurred. The movie company, in any case, had deserted them, perhaps unavoidably. The villagers themselves were gone, although they were possibly hiding in the hills. Perhaps the town lay on the route of an invading army. Perhaps the government had forcibly removed them. Who could say? Luckily they were provisioned for several days. They had fruit, water, canned fish. He himself was fond of Chinese brandy, a taste he had acquired some years before, in Bangkok. There were worse places to be marooned. In a few days the coup would either succeed or fail. The villagers would return; possibly even the movie company. The trains would run, perhaps the buses, perhaps they could hire a car and drive to the provincial capital. Garred lights two mosquito coils: it has grown dark. He fires up the pressure lantern. He peels himself a mango—the juice dribbles down his chin as he eats it—and pours a cup of brandy. In the meanwhile, he says, they could pass the time by practicing their lines. If the movie resumed they would be ready.

"What do you think, Fetters?"

"It seems we have little choice."

"And you, my dear?"

"I dont know what to say."

"We are agreed, then. Brandy, Fetters? Miss White? Or do you prefer rum and Coke?"

14.

She wears a white dress. She sprawls on her bed. Her face has that slackness that one sees in drunks or in people deeply, exhaustedly asleep. The room is quite dark; the lantern has gone out. Fortunately the mosquito coils are still glowing: only Osgood Fetters, in singlet and shorts, has crawled under his netting. Garred Haus, shirtless, the top button of his fly undone, snores softly .There is no moon, or if there is a moon, it is entirely obscured by clouds. The only illumination comes from the tracer bullets arcing overhead and the occasional flare which drifts onto the hills from the east. The weapons firing these bullets make rattling, sputtering, and popping sounds. These weapons are a mixture of M-16s, M-14s, AK-47s, CAR-15s, 9mm automatics, .45 automatics, Swedish-Ks, M-60s, ZPM-2s, and an occasional Stoner 63 A1 MK23. After a while mortars, Mark 18 grenade launchers, and RPGs open up—from both sides, both east and west—and then, waking Garred at last, the whine and thump of incoming 105s.

He stares out the window. He puts a cigarette in his mouth but doesnt light it. His sweaty face glows; his eyes droop. When he sees figures moving from the tree line, he goes to Osgood and shakes him awake. "Get under your bed," he orders. Bullets begin to splat against the walls of the building. One whines into the room. Garred rolls Virginia White off her bed onto the tile floor. He lies on top of her. When she tries to speak, he slaps her. By now footsteps are audible outside. Voices flutter past, rather like the wings of bats: dry rustling noises in the dark. A weapon—it is an AK-47, its sound is quite distinctive—goes pop-pop-pop just outside the window. Garred uses this moment to pull open the woman's bodice. A button pops. One brassiere cup, as delicate as we have indicated, rips quite away. Only the underwire remains intact, and this has the effect of pushing her breast up and out, into the mouth which Garred lowers. Once the plump nipple is in his mouth—in better light we would have glimpsed the roseate bud—he begins to bite and suck. It takes a moment for the woman to react. Then she tries to push his head away. The mouth, however, is locked onto her teat. She twists beneath him. A face, meanwhile, appears at a window, looks quickly right and left, somehow misses the figures squirming on the floor, and ducks away. A mortar shell lands just outside. People breathe heavily as they race past. The woman likewise is panting. Garred has left her breast. He is pulling and tugging and jerking at the Ironweave Pantihose, which is as unyielding as jute. The woman's legs are flying in the air. One shoe comes off, and spins across the room. The exposed breast—it is quite lovely in the sporadic light from the tracers—rolls and heaves while the other remains confined within its delicate lace cup. All the while bullets pock-pock-pock against the walls. Occasionally a tracer spins eerily into the room, sizzling like meat on a fire. Osgood Fetters peers out from under his bed. "Garred!" he whispers. "What are you doing?" Garred is still pulling at the Ironweave, while the woman twists and kicks beneath him. "Garred! Are you crazy?" Osgood crawls out from under his bed. A mortar shell explodes outside, sending shrapnel skittering through the room. Osgood ducks back. In any case, it is too late. The Ironweave has been peeled off of one leg, and hangs now about the ankle of the other. The red high-heeled shoe remains somehow on that foot, kicking into the air. The shroud of the pantihose flaps about like an injured animal. Garred rises triumphantly over her—what superhuman effort he has expended!—and plunges into her body. His organ unerringly finds her orifice, like a ferret slipping into its hole. She bucks and twists, but he has impaled her. He rises over her like a lizard. His eyes—they reflect the red light of the tracers—glow like the eyes of a lizard. He thumps, thumps, thumps away at her, while mortars and 105s thump, thump, thump at the hills outside. Osgood crawls over the tile. "Garred! Garred! Youre crazy!"

Garred swings an arm. His backhand catches Osgood in the face.

"Wait your turn, priest!"

People garbed in black race past, making sounds like the wings of bats. After a while they are gone. A few more tracers arc overhead. An M-60 opens up, briefly. Then everything is quiet. Only smells remain: cordite, burnt flesh, singed air, semen.

15.

The husband stands at the edge of the cenote. It may be that he has no fear of the darkness. He is naked. He seems wiry in this light, the light that comes through the door of the white room. His body is striated with muscle. Only his belly is soft. He pours a bucket of water over himself, then another, dragging it up from the cenote. He shakes himself—he seems almost to growl—and then pulls his pants on over his wet body.

Outside the air is thick from a recent rain. The earth swells, the way a sponge will swell when dipped into sea water. Steam rises from the earth. This rich effluvium is palpable. It is as pungent as the farts of old men, as acrid as the scut of the balam, as sour as old urine. The red plumerias, the scarlet plumerias, the white-petaled plumerias exude an odor as dense as oil. The air itself is as dense as oil. Through this turgid air banks an F-4 Phantom, its engines throttled back. It moves very slowly. It seems almost to pause as it banks away from the eastern hills. The pilot, goggled and masked, is visible through his plexiglass cockpit. As he passes overhead the shriek of his engines causes the woman to rise on her burlap bed. Her movements are sluggish. Across from her, head sunk into his hands, sits the man we call the priest. Visible through the windows are small boys scurrying across the open spaces and along the edges of the hills, putting brass shell casings into jute sacks. The F-4 floats slowly past once more, this time leaving behind an ochre burst of napalm. The woman at last comes upright. She pulls her bodice over the one breast which has lain exposed. Her left eye is blackened. Her lips are bruised. Along the wall nearby moves a swollen iguana—a ppuppulni-huh—which has found its way in from the garden. Through the open door leading to the cenote comes Garred, the husband. Following him are scorpions, false scorpions, whip scorpions, and other insects which will be named. He smacks them with his shoe and piles their carcasses together. Although he has just washed, he is already oily with sweat. So is the woman, who raises her head.

"Why are you angry with me."

"I'm not angry."

"You hit me."

"You never listen to me."

"Tell me what you want."

"If only you would put yourself in my hands."

He has lit his Gauloise. Smoke drifts upward, past his sweating face, past his colorless eyes, past the dank hair lying on his forehead. The tip of his cigarette glows with the same ochre color as the napalm spreading itself on the hills outside. In this turgid air only the smoke moves, rising upward from the corners of his mouth.

"What are you staring at?"

There is no response.

"What are you staring at?"

There is no response.

"What are you staring at?"

"Nothing," she says at last. "I am staring at nothing."

PART THREE

I.

Garred rushes off the set. There is no ready explanation for his behavior. A wardrobe woman tries to stop him—his toupee has come loose—but he brushes past her. "Coo," she says. "Aint 'e the one?" Meanwhile, an SP-2H Neptune drones overhead. It carries a Night Observation Scope, AN/PQ-92 Search Radar, FLIR and LLLTV Sensors, Side Looking Airborne Radar, Real Time IR Sensors, Moving Target Indicators, Digital Integrated Attack and Navigation Equipment, and a Black Crow Truck Ignition Sensor. It is armed with twin 20mm cannons in its tail, several miniguns, a 40mm grenade launcher, 500-pound general purpose bombs, and incendiary weapons. It is a lovely sight unloading its weaponry on its digitally displayed targets. There is a kind of serenity to the sight. The Neptune moves slowly. Its LLLTV sensors, its AN/PQ-92s, its Moving Target Indicators pick out, with delectable delicacy, the warm bodies hiding below, moving or not, the truck engines, ignited or not, and the children, alive or not. No one can escape the Night Observation Scope or the Side Looking Airborne Radar. No one can evade the Digital Integrated Attack and Navigation Equipment. Tracer bullets stream from the tail and the miniguns. At the touch of a button 500-pound bombs and incendiaries tumble out, unerringly finding their targets. *Red were the beards of the children of the sun, the bearded ones from the east, when they arrived here in our land. The strangers to the land are white men, red men. There is a beginning of carnal sin. Oh Itza! Make ready. There comes a white circle in the sky, the fair-skinned boy from heaven. Fire shall flame up at the tips of their hands.* Meanwhile, the woman and the man—the ones we call Virginia White

161

and Osgood Fetters—have strolled to the yellow, or southern, room of the cross-shaped building. He shows her a figure carved in wood. It is reclining. It is full sized, that is, as large as a living person. The face is blissfully suffering. Is that possible? The expression on the face reveals both suffering and bliss. There are terrible wounds on this figure. The woman wrinkles up her nose. "Ugh," she says, "that's disgusting." She refers to the roll of intestines visible in the abdominal wound. Black blood has flowed from this wound and crusted at its edges. The black blood has flowed from the wounds on the knees, on the feet, on the hands, on the head. These wounds are depicted in great detail. "It was carved by the Indians 200 years ago," says Osgood, referring to a pamphlet. "It's supposed to be the Christ, of course. But the Indians claim it is really a statue of Jacinto Canek." "Who?" "Jacinto Canek. A rebel, apparently. Caught and executed by the Spanish." Canek was captured following the Maya rebellion of 1761, which he led. His followers were hung, then disemboweled, and pieces of their bodies sent to outlying villages. Jacinto himself was tortured publicly in the square in Merida. Thousands watched. All were silent. Red hot pincers tore open his flesh, making wounds in his abdomen, his hands, his feet, his knees, his head. Perhaps his intestines rolled from the wound at his side. Black blood poured from him. Iron bars broke all his bones. All this time he did not cry out. On his face was an expression of bliss and suffering. Did he enter into death peacefully? No one could tell from his expression at what moment he expired. At last his body was dismembered and cast upon the city refuse dump, where it was guarded until the flesh decomposed. *There are rains of little profit, rains from a rabbit sky, rains from a parched sky, rains from a woodpecker sky, high rains, rains from a vulture sky, crested rains, deer rains. There is fighting; there is a year of locusts. The diminished remainder of the population is hanged. They are defeated in war. Sad shall be the havoc at the crossroads.* Meanwhile, Garred Haus drives his Mercedes convertible down Santa Monica Boulevard. It is dark. Each car racing up and down the street weighs two or three tons: two or three tons enclosing mere pounds of flesh, of meat, of blood, of hair, fingernails, teeth, bones, intestines. Garred, one of these creatures, pulls his tons of metal and glass and rich upholstery to the curb. A boy gets in. Garred lifts an eyebrow: "How much?" "What do you want?" "Suck me off." "Give me twenty dollars." "While I drive, okay?" Garred opens his pants. *The kinkajou claws the back of the jaguar amid the affliction of the katun, amid the affliction of the year; they are greedy for domination.* Meanwhile, a line of horsemen descend the defoliated eastern slope of the hills, threading their way between ochre blossoms of napalm. Meanwhile, Osgood Fetters and Virginia White—breast tucked carefully into the bodice of her dress—stroll beneath the statue of the Virgin Mary, which is given pride of place high on the wall above them. Her bisque face shines. Her cheeks are plump and ruddy with health. Rich robes adorn her body. She looks down on the broken Jacinto Canek, or on her broken son Jesus, she looks down on the few wooden pews which remain on the ruined floor, on the rubble of brick and stone, and says nothing. *Then shall come to pass the shaking of the plumeria flower. Then you shall understand. Then it shall thunder from a dry sky. Then shall be spoken that which is written on the wall.* Meanwhile, Garred Haus, zipped back together, gives the boy $20 and some Big Mac coupons. The boy shuffles away, into the depths of Santa Monica Boulevard, wiping his mouth. Garred drives to a Denny's Restaurant. There are several in the city. The restaurant never closes. A hostess always greets you cheerfully. As Garred enters, an older couple are leaving. "Say," the man says, "arent you Gerald House, the actor?" "No." "He sure looks like Gerald House, dont he, ma?" "He surely does." "You sure you arent that feller?" "I'm sure." "I think Gerald House is younger," says the woman, "and he's got more hair." "Maybe youre right, ma." Garred goes in and says to the hostess, who is short and fat and has nothing to be cheerful about, "Give me a table in the back." She waddles towards the rear. "There's a meeting back here," she says, "is that all right?" "Just bring me coffee, okay?" Beyond him a man is speaking to a number of waitresses in their very gingham, very American, uniforms, plus one man in cook's whites. He is an *active* man, this speaker. He bobs up and down. He punctuates his words by slapping his fist into his hand. He continually smiles. "When they *finish* eating," he is telling his audience, "dont just walk up and *ask* if they want anything more. How do *they* know what they want? Do *they* remember the menu? No, of course not. *Make* a suggestion. *Help* them out. This month we're pushing strawberry pie. So go up to them and say, How about a *nice* piece of *strawberry* pie. You'll be surprised how many will say, Yeah, sure. But they *wont* say, Yeah, sure, unless you *tell* them what they want—" "Shit," says Garred, loudly enough so the nearest waitress, who has short brown hair and blank brown eyes, can hear. He takes another sip of his coffee, leaves a dollar, and walks out to his car. *"Son, bring me a very beautiful woman with a very white countenance. I greatly desire her. I will cast down her skirt and her loose dress before me." "It is well, father."* Meanwhile, the others have gathered in the red room. When Garred returns they take their positions. The woman removes her white dress. She lies on the burlap bed. The iguana—the ppuppulni-huh—crawls toward her.

"I heard screams last night."

"Screams?"

"I'm certain of it."

"I heard nothing."

"I was awakened—they awakened me—"

"Awakened?"

"I dont know the time."

"You were possibly dreaming."

The priest lifts his head.

"No," he says. "I heard them, too."

"You?"

"Distinctly. Quite—quite distinctly—"

"Sound effects."

"What?" says the woman.

"Sound effects. If you heard anything at all."

They lie silent. After a while the woman begins to moan. The ppuppulni-huh has crawled up between her legs. Its head is at the cleft of her body. Oh, the woman says, oh, the woman moans, dont do that. Oh, no, please, dont do that. The lizard sucks. Oh, no, oh no, the woman moans, not that, oh please, not that. Her white body begins to buck.

164

2.

The day begins with everyone called to the set. Positions are allocated. The three actors are arranged on their burlap beds. It is early morning, or what is supposed to be early morning. One actor lifts a head: "Listen!" Another stirs: "I dont hear anything." The third: "It's a helicopter!" The three lines of dialogue are repeated. "Listen!" "I dont hear anything." "It's a helicopter!" The helicopter—a UH-1C—comes thump-thump-thumping over the hill, on cue. It looks like a flying black insect. Below it dangles a net filled with dark objects. The copter hovers a moment, and then releases one end of the net. Immediately the black objects fall. From this distance they look like bodies; perhaps they are merely papier-mâché heads and pants and shirts stuffed with kapok. "No, no ," an electronically amplified voice shouts, "you assholes, not in the trees!" The bodies have indeed fallen into the arms of a ceiba tree. Heads, legs, a few arms and torsos are caught in the branches. "Jesus Christ!" the voice roars. Even over the electronic amplification system the southern accent is distinguishable. "Jesus Christ! Cant you assholes do anything? Go on—get outa here! Get another load, and for Chrissake do it right!" Suitably chastened, head drooping, the insect-like helicopter thump-thump-thumps away over the hill. Petulantly it fires a couple of 2.5-inch rockets and a couple of bursts—at 6,000 rounds a minute—from its two XM-21 Miniguns. The trees below shake at the impact. Meanwhile, the horsemen, winding their way down the eastern hillside, pause to watch. A twin-engined UC-123 Provider passes overhead, a fine mist trailing behind it. The mist drifts through the ceiba trees, the red zapote, the tall balche trees, and onto the horsemen. They wipe the Dioxin from their faces, the 2,4,5-T from their hair. The ponies shake their heads. Then they continue. *The sea upon which I go burns. The face of the heavens is tilted.* Meanwhile, the woman Virginia White takes advantage of the break to stroll into the nearby mall. She wears her white dress. The bodice is askew—a white breast can be glimpsed rolling about. Around her waist is a red belt. On her feet are red shoes. Past her hurry people. Many of them appear bloated, like the bodies seen occasionally in the rice paddies. They have tiny, suspicious eyes. They are all very pale. They are going to Karen's Kloset ("Nothing over $10!") and Pay-Less Drugs and Sav-Mor Shoes. Virginia White stands in a line at Swiss Colony—which has nothing to do with the Swiss—near clear-plastic-wrapped boxes of homogenized cheese and wax-coated fruit. When her turn comes she asks a tall man for a cup of tea. "What kind?" "Just tea." "We've got Red Zinger, Purple Passion, Yellow Zinger, Spicy Tamarisk—" "No, no, just tea, regular tea." "Ma'am, we dont have regular tea. You want regular, we got regular coffee and decaf coffee—we got regular Coke and Diet Coke—" "Diet Coke." "Large, Extra Large, or Jumbo?" "Small." "Lady, our large is small." "Large, then. No ice. And warm it up." "Warm it up?" "Just put it in your micro-wave—just for a minute—" "Lady, we dont heat up Coke." "Just warm it—just a little." "Look, lady, I'll give it to you with no ice, if that's what you want. But we dont heat up Coke." "Just no ice, then." "Large, right?" "Small—yes, Large." He shakes his head and turns to his Coke machine. *There is knife-thrusting strife, purse-snatching strife, strife with the blowgun, strife by trampling people, stone-throwing strife. The fighting ends in the heart of the forest. There is sudden death with hunger; the vultures enter the houses because of pestilence.* Osgood Fetters, meanwhile, decides to bathe. He draws water up from the cenote. His naked body is lean, but fallen: that is, the muscles and the flesh seem slack. Within the water that he pours over himself, in the air around him, in the bat guano and the dirt and the limestone beneath his feet, are various organisms. There is the *Geoplana multipunctata*, with its hundreds of eyes, its sinuous ejaculatory duct , and its short female duct which enters the rear end of the atrium. There is the *Parabascoides yucatanensis* whose

166

oral sucker is approximately the same size as its acetabulum, and the related *Anenterotrema auritum*, whose sperm ducts arise from the anteromedian ends of its testes. In the water are leeches, such as the *Glossihonia magnidiscus*, whose caudal sucker is a very large, thin disk, and whose anus is a conspicuous opening on the narrow caudal peduncle. In the dirt crawls an *Eodrilus oxkutzcabensis*, its copulatory pouches in front of its prostatic duct. Among the arachnida near Osgood's feet are the *Tarantula fuscimana*, *Schizomus cavernicolens*, the scorpion *Centrurus yucatanus*, whose ventral plates are shining but rugose, whose cauda are long and slender, whose keels are granular or subserrate, and the *Cryptocellus pearsei*, with its whitish carapace. The false scorpions abound, and include the *Pachychitra maya*, completely lacking eyes, but whose palps are robust, and the *Lustrochernes minor*, which possess eye spots but no true eyes, and the pallid *Parazaona cavicola*. Present also, unknown to Osgood Fetters, who is briskly drying himself, are the araneida and the nematodes, the acarinids and the cave crickets, the heteropterida and the ubiquitous blattida. In the bat feces are coleopterida, both larval and adult. Crawling every-where—they crawl over Osgood's feet—are the myrmicinae and the dolichoderinae and the formicinae. Some of these creatures may appear later, and will then be described in greater detail. Osgood, however, has finished bathing. He dresses: boxer shorts, loose slacks, socks and sandals, and a white shirt, which is left untucked. He returns to the red room, where, meanwhile, the woman Virginia White has returned also. *Then it was that fire descended, then the rope descended, then rocks and trees descended. Then came the beating of things with wood and stone. Then Oxlahun-ti-ku was seized, his head was wounded, his face was buffeted, he was spit upon, he was thrown on his back.* Meanwhile, the three actors are arranged once more on their burlap beds. Virginia White's hair is fluffed. More oily sweat is applied to Garred's face. Osgood's leg, still swollen, is propped up before him. One actor says: "Listen!" A second responds: "I dont hear anything." "No," says the third, "it's a helicop-ter!" The UH-1C comes thump-thump-thumping over the hill, on cue. The net, filled again, sways beneath it. "A little further!" booms an electronically amplified voice. "Keep coming. Keep coming. Keep—

167

all right, *now!*" One side of the net is loosened. Somehow, however—perhaps a gust of wind upsets it—the edge of the net catches on some protrusion beneath the helicopter. "Shit!" booms the voice. The net, with its grisly burden, real or not, swings from side to side, rocking the copter. The copter quickly descends, spitting fire from its exhausts. The rolling, swaying bodies in the net hit the ground. The landing wheels of the helicopter bounce on top of them. "Assholes!" booms the voice in undisguised electronic fury. "I dont think I can watch this," says Osgood Fetters. He limps out, past the cenote, past the bat guano, past the *Pachychitra maya*, which, lacking eyes, fails to see him, and then through the western or black room, into the garden. He passes the black laurel, the black ceiba tree of abundance, and the rows of black speckled corn. Black wild pigeons are flushed from the black tipped camotes. Black bees hum. Scent from the black Ix-laul fills the air. The air itself is blackened with clouds. At the end of the garden stands a white man. It is a moment before Osgood sees him. The man is soft, plump. His clothing bags around him. He is dressed in the green camouflage uniform of a soldier, perhaps a marine. His face is pallid, pellucid, although not blind: blue eyes have turned to look at Osgood. He is pissing. The penile organ itself, which he holds between the forefinger and thumb of his right hand, is pale and pellucid, perhaps hydrophylic, though lacking tactile or gustatory barbels. One might call him trogloxene, or perhaps euryphotic. Wisps of blond hair have escaped his duck-billed cap. He is pissing into the open mouth of a dead man. This dead man lies at the blackened end of the garden. His body is swollen; the skin taut. A trail of intestines leads from his stomach across the blackened grass. The boy who is pissing—he does not seem old enough to be a man—shakes his pellucid organ. A few golden drops of urine fly about. He tucks the organ away, bending slightly at the waist. He looks again at Osgood. "They told me to do it," he says. His words fly away in the wind. He begins to walk, limping a bit, like Osgood. *The face of the lord of the katun is covered; his face is dead. There is mourning for water; there is mourning for bread. His mat and his throne shall face the west. Blood-vomit is the charge of the katun.* Meanwhile, the horsemen have stopped at the edge of the forest. Five men are visible. They have dismounted. The details of their clothing and their armament are not clear at this distance. Meanwhile, Osgood, his face pale, has returned to the red room.

"There's a man out there—he was pissing—"

"Pissing?"

"On a dead man."

"Pissing on a dead man?"

"Pissing into his mouth."

"There's a man out there, you say—"

"A soldier, a marine—"

"What?" says Virginia White. "What are you saying?"

"There's a man out there—"

"Are you quite sure?" says Garred.

"I saw it—"

"You saw a man—a soldier—pissing into a dead man's mouth?"

"I saw it."

Garred gets up. He walks out. There is an embarrassed silence. Virginia White avoids looking at Osgood. One of her hands plucks at the torn cup of her brassiere. Then Garred returns. "There's nothing out there," he says. Osgood starts to protest. "Nothing," Garred says firmly. "Nothing at all."

3 ·

The woman wears her white dress. Lights come on, illuminating her. Outside all is dark. Only the SP-2H Neptune cruises overhead. Occasionally—perhaps its Night Observation Scope or its Black Crow Truck Ignition Sensor has found a target—it lets loose a stream of tracer bullets or a load of incendiaries. When this happens everyone stops to watch. Conversation becomes general. People lean on each other to see out the windows. When the display is finished all resume their places. Garred's toupee is adjusted. Osgood's leg is placed just so. The white woman's bodice is arranged so more breast shows. A wardrobe woman sniffs: "No better than she needs to be, that one." The F-4 pilot next to her says: "I wouldnt mind a piece of that." The wardrobe woman nudges him with her elbow: "Coo, you men!" Angles are calculated. The actors begin to speak. "I'm going to complain." "We shall all complain." "This isnt a movie, it's a torture chamber." Occasionally they are interrupted. Lines are repeated with cameras at different positions. "I cant do my hair, I feel ugly." "No, no, everything will be all right, youll see." "I dont want to see." When the lights are turned off they make crackling noises as they cool. *The dog is its tidings; the vulture is its tidings. The opossum is its face to the rulers. Then came Hunpic-ti-ax as an affliction, the jaguar and Canul for an affliction. These were the eaters of their food, the destroyers of their crops, the boboch, the destroyer of food.* Meanwhile neither the artificial lights nor the flashing tracers have any effect upon the brotulid and synbranchid fish in the cenote. The brotulid, *Typhlias pearsei*, and the synbranchid, *Pluto infernalis*, are wholly devoid of eyes, even vestigial eyes. As the *Typhlias* swims in the black water its large, clasper-shaped penis emerges from the vulvate-like folds around it. The eel-shaped, *penile*-shaped *Pluto* emerges from a crevice: its head moves left and right as though searching for something it cannot, and never will, see. Meanwhile, the five horsemen have waited until dark to cross the open space. At last they tether their mounts to a ceiba tree. The lighting here is ochre and sporadic, supplied by the munitions of the Neptune, which continues to drone overhead. Because of the intermittent nature of the light these five men are indescribable until they enter the red room, where the gas lantern continues to hiss. This lantern casts a ruddy glow. The glow is so dim that special, ultra-sensitive film must be used to capture the following scene. Yet even so, shadows shall predominate. Shadows shall exaggerate each movement. The camera position will be low—the figures thus looming and sinister—and the lens a wide angle, allowing both a deep focus and a certain distortion, a certain *disorientation*, of space. In this way is the first man illuminated in the doorway. He has a braid of red hair down the left side of his head. The right side of his head is shaved. He is lightly bearded. He, and the men who follow, are garbed in camouflage uniforms and festooned with weaponry: pistols, hand grenades, bandoliers, K-bars, dangling rifles. We identify two M-16s, one M-60, and an M-79 grenade launcher, among others. When the woman Virginia White sees the first man her face blanches. She has by now read several pages of her script, and recognizes what must necessarily follow. "No," she says, however, "*no*," she protests, "*wait*, I'm not ready." The man steps forward one pace. "Fucking *round* eye," he says. The second man is in the doorway, weapon erect. He is quickly followed by the third man. These two are both black and wear their hair in mohawks. One has long black hairs sprouting from his chin. The fourth man is white. The fifth man is white. He is plump, with pellucid cheeks. "Fucking *round* eye." "Let's dick her." "Fucking *A*, man." Her bodice is ripped wide. The one loose breast rolls. "Fucking *tits*, man." Osgood makes a feeble interventionary gesture. An M-16 fires six rounds—pop-pop-pop, pop-pop-pop. Stucco blasts from the wall. Osgood sits abruptly. "Fucking *tits*, man." The woman is thrown onto the floor. Her head bounces on the tile. She is

171

stunned but conscious. "No, no—you cant—I'm not ready—" Her skirts fly up. "Fucking *cunt*, man." "Dick her." "Fucking *A*, man." She tries to squirm away. The black plastic stock of the Colt Armalite M-16 whacks the left side of her face. The sound is oddly hollow. The woman spits blood and what appears to be, in this dim light, white pieces of teeth. Her eyes are huge. "Fucking *still*, cunt." Her voice, when she speaks, will now be slurred. The words will be scarcely recognizable. We shall give careful attention to them. At all times a rifle barrel will be held close to her face, first an M-16, then the M-60, then the gaping muzzle of the M-79, which surely could not be used in such close quarters. The first man is already between her legs. His red ass rises and falls. Seconds later the next man is between her legs. His black ass rises and falls. "No, no, why are you doing this—" "Fucking *ass*, man." The third fucks her. While he fucks her, the fourth man grabs her by the ears. He lifts her face and turns it. He jams his pellucid but erect organ into her mouth. "Suck, bitch." Blood speckles the white shaft of this organ. "Fucking *suck*, bitch." The first man—he is identifiable, even in this dim, hissing light, by the red braid of his hair—is already back between her legs. The fifth man, however, is standing at her head. He has opened his pants and is fiddling with his dick. When the woman's head is thrown back down—it bounces again on the tile floor—this fifth man begins to piss on her. He holds his pale, perhaps hydrophylic organ between his thumb and forefinger. The woman sputters and gasps beneath this golden shower. The man between her legs is thumping her so hard she is being driven across the floor. All this is visible in the glow of the gas lantern, augmented occasionally by the ochre flare of incendiaries outside. All this, even where we have not specifically noted it, is deeply shadowed. It is not always clear what is happening, in spite of our careful review. The woman is driven—thump-thump-thump—across the tile floor, spitting blood, spitting semen, spitting urine, spitting teeth. Perhaps the darkness adds to the atmosphere of gloom and violence, or perhaps it is carefully planned to give an artistic dimension to the scene. Certainly the leaping shadows are dramatic. The low angle of the camera adds a special flair. Osgood's sorry face, his lugubrious face, is visible to one

172

side. Garred's poise is feral, that is, like a wild animal prepared to leap. It is beyond his window that we see the Neptune SP-2H as tracers spit from its nose. It cruises the black night, spitting fire, illuminating the shadows and making the ground dance beneath it, as though the ground were itself celebrating its own death. *Then began their reign; then began their rule. Then they began to be served; then those who were to be thrown into the cenote arrived; then they began to throw them into the well that their prophecy might be heard by their rulers.* Meanwhile, the Neptune SP-2H has left the hills. Cries can now be heard. Rifles and RPGs and Swedish Ks open up, sending their tracers from the eastern hills to the western hills, and from the western hills to the eastern ones. All this, however, has no effect upon those in the building, where the rape scene is coming to an end. Each man seems sated. One has pissed as much as his bladder held, the others ejaculated until their testes ached. Their movements are now slower, turgid. The woman lies bloody on the floor. One man—the first one, the one with the red braid of hair—picks up his M-16 and injects the barrel into her vagina. "Fucking *A*, man." "Bust *caps*, man." He pulls the trigger. Fortunately for this book, and this film, the weapon fails to fire. The trigger clicks again and again. He jerks it from her cunt, tearing the tender flesh. "Fucking *car*bine." He hurls it across the room, where it clatters against the wall. He takes the woman by her long hair and drags her across the floor. She leaves a trail of blood and semen from between her legs. The others herd Garred and Osgood. The building, of course, is shaped like a fat cross. The room they enter is in the center of the building. It is dark, except for the light from the lantern in the red room. Their shadows are thus thrown forward, to the edge of the cenote. The eight people gather at the edge of the cenote. They pause there for only a moment. "The fucking *water*, man." The woman is jerked by her hair half upright. Her hair looks particularly delicate in this dim light. Her dress is mostly off her body—held, in fact, only by her red belt. The one free breast rolls, and rolls. A boot shoves her. A little over a second later her body splashes into the water. Osgood and Garred follow, nudged forward by the barrels of, respectively, an M-60 and an M-16. The men then begin shooting into the cenote. The M-16 makes pop-pop-pop sounds. The

173

M-60 goes brrrrrp. A .45 automatic pistol makes the loudest noise of all. Smoke drifts in the air. Hot shell casings pile up around them. Finally one man—it is the one with the red braid—unhooks a grenade and tosses it into the cenote. The explosion it makes ends this scene. The sound reverberates away. After a moment there is an electronic squeal. Then:

"Fucking *round* eye."

"No, wait, I'm not ready."

"Fucking *tits*, man."

"Shee-*it*, man. Five times. And I'm a honkie, too."

"That's some Class-A organ, man."

"Let's dick her."

"No—you cant—I'm not ready—"

"With my old lady, I get it up once a week, man, I'm lucky."

"Fucking gun, man."

"Got that rapid fire *function*, man."

"No, no, why are you doing this—"

"Fucking *suck*, bitch."

"Get it on, honkie."

"Fucking *A*, man."

There is another high pitched electronic squeal. And then, finally, silence.

4·

The woman is laid out on her burlap bed. Everyone gathers around her. They inspect her wounds. Her labia are black with blood. Elsewhere she is bruised and torn. Her hair is a mat of reeds. Her cheeks are swollen. They are like the swollen bisque cheeks of the Madonna. Her eyes are brittle. They are like the brittle glass eyes of the Madonna. Garred sticks a cigarette in his mouth. He rolls the pack into the sleeve of his T-shirt. It was he, of course, who hauled the woman from the cenote. He climbed out. The rope was lowered to Osgood, who tied it under her arms. The black water luminesced around them. She dripped water, like tiny lights, as Garred pulled her up the wall of the cenote. She glowed, phosphorescent, sheeted with water. During the night, they had all glowed. They had drifted under a high vaulted ceiling of the two-cycle solution type cave. The current carried them. Garred pulled himself onto a shelf of limestone. He helped Osgood, and then, as she drifted near, the woman. Her dress had at last come free from her body. It continued past, like a white soul loosed from its flesh. The woman was garbed then only in the remains of her brassiere. On the shelf of limestone they waited, perhaps for hours, perhaps all night. They heard the bullets splat into the water of the cenote. They heard the explosion of the grenade. Dead fish—silurids, brotulids, the blind synbranchid *Pluto infernalis*—floated past. These fish were not phosphorescent. They were dead. The walls, however, dripping water, glowed, as though the walls were alive. *Their faces had been trampled on the ground, and they had been overthrown by the unrestrained upstarts of the day and of the katun, the son of evil and the offspring of the harlot, who were*

175

born when their day dawned in Katun 3 Ahau. Meanwhile, the Assistant Director enters with a syringe in his beefy hand. Meanwhile, the two F4s swoop low over the eastern hills, pummeling them. Meanwhile, Garred Haus wanders through the black garden. He has not stayed to watch the ministering to the white woman. He passes black flowers and black insects. He pauses at a row of five black heads. The heads are black with blood and their own decay. The heads are like turnips. They are lined up. Each has a cigarette in his mouth. The ears have been cut off. Doubtless someone, perhaps someone in the cavernous forest, the forest that has not been denuded by defoliants, is wearing the ears around his neck. Garred stares at the heads for only a moment. He grinds his own cigarette under his heel, leaving a charred mark in the dirt. He leaves. Meanwhile, the wardrobe woman has led the Neptune pilot to the wardrobe room. Hanging there are camouflage uniforms, white dresses, Ironweave Pantihose, boxer shorts, trousers, red belts, and delicate white brassieres, many with one cup torn loose. The wardrobe woman bares her ass. She does this by leaning forward and flipping her dress up onto her back. The Neptune pilot has sheathed his penis in black latex. He attacks her from behind. The woman grunts. The dresses sway. Uh-uh-uh-uh-uh, grunts the woman. The pilot gives a final lunge—a paroxysm of a lunge—and whoops. "Coo, you men," says the wardrobe woman as the black-sheathed penis withdraws. She pats her clothes into place. "Now dont you come out for a few minutes, hear? We dont want the others thinking anything, do we?" "Getcher ass in gear, then," says the pilot, grinning. The woman elbows him. "Coo!" *Then begins the lewdness of the wise men, the beckoning of the katun. The katun begins to limp; it is all over the world. Carnal sin is its garment, carnal sin is its face, carnal sin is its sandal, carnal sin is its head, carnal sin is its gait. They twist their necks, they twist their mouths, they wink the eye, they slaver at the mouth, at men, women, chiefs, justices, presiding officers, everybody both great and small. There is no great teaching. Heaven and earth are truly lost to them; they have lost all shame.* Meanwhile, Garred walks along the tracks. Old railroad cars stand there. The jungle is just beyond them. In places the jungle has reclaimed the railroad cars. Some of the railroad cars have words still visible on them: The Great

White Way. The Southern Route. Ferrocarilles de Sonora. Vive el Corean. Visible within one railroad car are three beefy men. They are playing cards and drinking tepid Cokes. They chew on cigars and Cheese Doritos. They glance at Garred as he passes. Below them, on the ground, men are working. They are slitting open the bellies of corpses. Using thickly gloved hands they pull the intestines into buckets. The buckets are carried away by boys. Into the abdominal cavities are placed packages wrapped in plastic. Another man—he is dressed in white—sews the abdomens back together. The bodies are then put into heavy rubber bags and lifted into another railroad car. The intestines are yellow, red, and black, and emerge in great looping coils. Because of the stench everyone wears gauze masks. Garred does not. He hurries past, past men holding Uzis and MAC-10s, past men holding clipboards, past diesel trucks filled with black rubber bags, past spitting children, past Congressmen with sweaty faces and rotund bellies, past a steam engine hissing on rusty tracks, past railroad cars filled with whores, past cages holding prisoners of both sexes and several races, past cook shacks where T-bones are frying, past piles of rags that women are picking through, past graves marked with sticks, crosses, and plumeria flowers, past piles of ears, some of them plastic, past briefing rooms, past pilots with "Air America" tattooed on their biceps, past marines sleeping in the shade of ceiba trees, past television reporters in safari shirts, past wrecked helicopters and APCs and Caribous and six-bys and T-54s sagging on their treads. Finally he pauses at the last row of railroad cars. "Hey, GI! You want fuckee-suckee?" Women whistle and lift their sarongs, their saris, their skirts, their legs, their asses, their breasts. Garred goes up to one. A small boy lies with his face in her lap. The woman has dark, thin lips. Her eyes shine like polished copper. "GI got dollar?" "I got dollar." "You want fuckee-fuckee?" "I want fuckee-fuckee." "You give me five dollar." Garred taps the boy's rump. "I want fuckee-fuckee boy." For a moment the woman says nothing. The boy does not stir. "You give me ten dollar." She holds out her hand. When Garred finishes, the little boy is crying. The woman watches Garred walk away. Then she turns to the boy and slaps him. *Then descended Bolon Mayel, the fragrant one;*

sweet was his mouth and the tip of his tongue. Sweet were his brains. Then descended the two mighty demon bats who sucked the honey of the flowers. Then there grew up for it the red unfolded calyx, the white unfolded calyx, the black unfolded calyx, the yellow unfolded calyx. Then there sprang up the five-leafed flower, the five drooping petals, the ix-chabil-tok, the little flower, ix macuil xuchit, the flower with the brightly colored tip, the laurel flower, and the limping flower. Meanwhile the red room is quiet. The lantern hisses. Shadows gather in the corners. The white woman's swollen face turns right and left. Osgood sits at her side. His shadow is cast onto the wall. Garred sits on his bed. His shadow is cast onto the wall. After a while the woman tries to speak. She tries to speak through her bruised and broken mouth. Osgood leans forward. "What? What? I dont think you should talk." "I saw something." "You saw something?" The pupils of her eyes are dilated. They wander right and left. Garred, unlit cigarette dangling from his lips, comes to the woman's bed.

"What did you see?"

"The cenote is a mirror."

She breathes heavily for a moment.

"I saw it," she says.

"You saw—the cenote—as a mirror?"

"It is a mirror."

"Anything else?"

"I saw people below."

"People?"

"When I tried to look at them they beat me."

"I see."

"They called me Ix Zacbeliz."

"What does that mean?"

"I dont know."

She breathes heavily again. Her eyes wander up and down, right and left. She is silent. She does not speak. Only her breath can be heard. At last the hissing lantern is quiet. The shadows move freely through the room. The Ix Zacbeliz—the white woman who travels on foot—lies on her burlap bed. Her flower is agape. Red mucencabs—the wild bees who drink honey from flowers—cluster around it. Her white and red

178

blossom is their cup. Then come the black mucencabs. Then come the yellow mucencabs. Then come the white mucencabs. They drink from her. Then comes Nohyumcab, the lord of the hive. Her blossom is his cup. Then come the black bats. They drink from her. Then comes Ah Puch, scepter in hand. His red eyes glow. Her blossom is his cup. Then comes Hapay Can, the sucking snake. He drinks from her. Her blossom is his cup. They cluster at her open flower, at her five petaled flower, at her five unfolded calyx. Then comes the ppuppulni-huh. He crawls up to her. His tongue flicks, once, twice. He lays his throat, his soft throat, on her wounded flower.

5.

The day begins as scheduled. Positions are taken as directed. A fleshy boy in jungle fatigues jiggles his dick. "There's a man out there." "Are you quite sure?" "I saw him." Men and women with coppery eyes press their faces at the windows. The white woman puts on her red high-heeled shoes. "I need a break." She walks to the nearby mall. Mean-while, stubby A-1 Skyraiders, capable of carrying 8,000 pounds of external ordnance, and Vought A-7 Corsair IIs, single seat jet attack planes, begin appearing overhead. They circle along with Caribou C-7s, a few Republic F-105 Thunderchiefs armed with 20mm Gatling guns, and one AC-47 Dragonship. Mingling with the airplanes are CH47s, some loaded with up to 65 troops, and Sikorsky H34 Choctaws. The SP-2H Neptune, with its FLIR and LLL TV Sensors blinking and flickering, is joined by an Aeronavale PB4Y Privateer. Soon others will appear. As they appear we shall describe them. All of them circle overhead, waiting their cue. *There shall come multitudes who gather stone and wood, the worthless rabble of the town. Fire shall flame up at the tips of their hands. Prepare yourselves to endure the burden of misery which is to come among your villages.* Meanwhile, in the mall everything is ready. The people are arranged. They stand at intervals in front of the shops. Every fourth person is obese. Some have tiny eyes. These eyes are sullen. The eyes do not move. The eyes glower: tiny, sullen, staring straight ahead. When the white woman passes in front of them, the eyes do not acknowledge her presence. The white woman wears her red shoes with very high heels. She wears her white bra with its one cup torn away. Her face is swollen, like the swollen bisque face of the

Madonna. Her eyes are brittle, like the brittle glass eyes of the Madonna. Her flower is crusted with black blood. Young girls hiss at her. These young girls stand in front of boutiques. Each boutique has a name like Hot Metal, or Deep Pink. The young girls stand in small groups. They hiss as the white woman passes. They hiss as the white woman walks by. The woman goes to Swiss Colony. She stands in line. When her turn comes she tells the tall man she wants tea. "Red Zinger, Purple Zinger, Orange Zinger—" "No, Diet Coke." "Large, Extra Large, Jumbo—" "Small—I mean, Large. And heat it up." "Lady, we dont heat Coke." "Just a little—" "Lady, we dont heat Coke." "No ice, then." There is a *Holocompsa zapoteca* climbing the wall. The woman plucks it from the wall. She bites off its head. She puts the rest of it in her mouth. "Lady, that's disgusting." "It's *your* cockroach." "I'm calling the security guards." The five security guards come. They jostle her. They tug at her arms, they pluck at her mat of hair. Their hands anonymously brush her buttocks, squeeze her breasts, stroke her belly. They put her down on the floor. They pry open her mouth and take out the remains of the *Holocompsa zapoteca*. One of the guards puts his hand between her legs. Fingers grope at her. Then they escort her to the door. "Dont come back," they warn. She steps out across the acres of hot asphalt. Cars race by. Overhead pass a squadron of B-57s and a lone F-100 Supersabre from the 429th Tactical Fighter Squadron. Douglas A-26 Invaders thunder past. Following more slowly are UH-1Cs, UH-1Ds, UH-1Hs, UH-1Ls, and a few UH-1Ms, their blades making thump-thump-thump sounds. Even slower is the Antonov AN-2, a fabric-covered, single-engined biplane with a wooden scimitar propeller. The pilot looks down and waves, or perhaps makes a threatening gesture. *Then it shall shake heaven and earth. In sorrow shall end the katun of the plumeria flower. No one shall fulfill his promises. The prop-roots of the trees shall be bent over. There shall be an earthquake all over the land.* Meanwhile, the woman continues walking. Night appears to have fallen. This, however, may be a trick. A filter may have been placed over the lens of the giant Panavision camera. If that is so, the moon which appears to be high in the sky is actually the sun, filtered. Nevertheless all is coordinated. The cars as they race past have their headlights on. The street lamps appear to glow. The woman walks, in her red high-heels, past boys and girls who stand patiently on the street corners, dimly lit. One of them is the boy Garred picked up not long ago. The boy appears very sweet. The camera examines him. Then he turns his face. A sly smile appears. A white fluid begins to dribble from the corners of his mouth. Quickly we move away. The woman continues past open doorways. Through these doorways may be glimpsed stairways, some rising, some descending. An occasional balam stands there, or a kinkajou, or a Quetzal bird with iridescent feathers. Sometimes men stand at the tops of stairs. Sometimes women stand at the bottoms of stairs, wearing masks. The white woman does not pause. Meanwhile, a T-28 hurtles past, followed by a U-17 and a Volpar and a pair of Pilatus Porters. Joining them are Douglas SDB Dauntless dive bombers, a single F6F Hellcat, and a SB2C Helldiver. Easily identifiable, lumbering low over the hills, is a PBY-5A Catalina and a Grumman JRF Goose. Meanwhile, the woman passes an alley. Standing there, half obscured by the darkness, is a boy in camouflage uniform. A rifle is slung by its strap over one shoulder. The boy's face is pale, pellucid, wet with sweat. He is pissing. His organ is held between his thumb and forefinger. It is not clear what he is pissing on, or into. The boy shakes his dick and tucks it away. He watches the woman in red high-heels pass. He says nothing, but he does move his lips, licking them. At last the woman returns to the cross-shaped building, where the crew have been practicing tai chi and tae kwon do. She arrives at the same time as the O-1, the O-2, the OV-10A Black Ponies, the A-4 Skyhawks, some carrying 2,000 pound bombs, the F-8 Crusaders, who are not on a crusade, the UC-123 Providers, who provide a fine trailing mist of Dioxin, the C-47s laden with their electronic gear, the RF-4s providing reconnaissance, the T-33 Shooting Stars—they shoot across the black sky—and finally, the F4U Corsairs. The woman takes her place. Lights hiss as they turn on. Makeup people circulate, touching up the sweaty faces. Garred's toupee is adjusted. Osgood's leg is placed just so. "Listen," says one of them, perhaps Osgood. "I dont hear anything," another replies. "No," says the third, "it's a helicopter." The helicopters swoop in. Each copter dangles a net. The first copter is an

HH-3E. Bodies plummet from its net to the ground. It is followed by
an H-21C. Its bodies plummet to the ground. Then comes an H-46 Sea
Knight. Its bodies plummet to the ground. Then comes the CH-3C,
and the Cobras, the CH-47s, the Sikorsky H-34s, and a line of UH-1s—
the UH-1C, the UH-1D, the UH-1H, the UH-1L, and finally the UH-
1M. Each releases its net of blackened bodies which plummet to the
ground. An electronic voice shouts: "Yes! *Now!*—Yes! *Now!*—Yes!
Now!" Heads roll over the ground. Torsos bounce right, torsos bounce
left. It is difficult for us to identify the ages, sexes, races, and nation-
alities of these torsos, these heads, these arms, these legs. All of them
bounce, roll, break apart. Finally the last helicopter thump-thump-
thumps into the distance. "Fucking *A!*" cries the electronic voice. *Their
hearts are submerged in sin. Their hearts are dead in their carnal sins. They sit
crookedly on their thrones; crookedly in carnal sin. They are the unrestrained
lewd ones of the day, the unrestrained lewd ones of the night, the rogues of the
world. They twist their necks, they wink their eyes, they slaver at the mouth, at
the rulers of the land, lord. Behold, when they come, there is no truth in the
words of the foreigners to the land.* Meanwhile, the blackened and denuded
hills are silent. The black sky is silent. The helicopters have fled, except
for one, an H-23 loaded with cameras. All wait. Sweat drips from faces.
The ppuppulni-huh crawls into the white woman's arms. The wardrobe
woman rearranges her skirt. Key grips, sound men, gaffers crouch at the
windows. Then the first jet makes its bombing run. It comes out of the
west. It comes low over the building. The sound is like thunder from a
dry sky. It unloads its napalm on the eastern hills. The jet shrieks away.
It is followed, however. It is followed by another F-4, and then the A-1s,
the A-7s, the C-7s, the F-105s. These are followed by gunships,
spraying six thousand rounds a minute. The eastern hills shake. The
black stumps of trees collapse. Cameras catch all of it. There are
cameras in the H-23. There are cameras on the open ground. There
are cameras mounted on platforms on the dome of the cross-shaped
building. There are mobile cameras and stationary cameras. Men
race through the gardens, carrying cameras. Other electronic
instruments capture sounds. Each roar, each shriek, each peal of
thunder is captured on electronic tape. They capture the sounds of the

Dauntless dive bombers and the Pilatus Porters and the T-28s, the Volpar and the Antonov and the Supersabre, the Shooting Stars and the Privateers, the Goose and the Catalina, the Marlin and the Orion, the Hellcats and the Helldivers. Electronic voices shriek in glee. "Keep *coming!* Keep *coming!* Fucking *A!*" Finally the B-52s—so high overhead they are scarsely visible—begin dropping their ordnance. They drop 500 pound bombs, and 750 pound bombs. They drop 1,000 pound bombs, and 2,000 pound bombs. They do this in conjunction with ordnance fired from PT-76 tanks, 80,000 pound tanks, Sheridan tanks and Patton tanks. APCs fire M-60s. 122mm rockets flash past. 60mm mortars fire, and 57mm guns, and Hawk surface-to-air missiles, and 155mm howitzers, and 104mm howitzers, and 175mm artillery, and five-inch shells from ships offshore. There are Walleyes and Willy Petes exploding, and napalm, and tear gas, and Bouncing Bettys, and CBUs. M-14s mounted with Starlight infra-red night sights begin to fire, along with M-16s and Kalashnikovs and Uzis and MAC-10s and Swedish Ks and Stoner 63s and CAR-15s. Ochre tracers flash across the arch of the sky. All this is caught on film and on tape. One camera focuses on the explosions caused by 1,000 pound bombs dropped from a B-52. These explosions move slowly along the eastern hills. They follow in a line, one after another. The explosions are like flowers that burst open. Their calyx unfold. Their petals unfold. The earth bursts into the air like flowers bursting open. Each step is visible. The 1,000 pound bombs continue across the open space. One falls into the eastern, or red garden, onto the red zapote and the red ceiba. One bomb falls onto the red room itself, another onto the dome which is set, as we have said, in the belly of the cross-shaped building. One bomb falls into the black room. A final bomb falls into the black garden, dispersing the five black heads, which look like turnips, the black-speckled corn, the black mucencabs, the black laurel, the pupae hanging from the black ceiba tree, the plumeria, the white, the red, the scarlet plumeria, and the balam, whose fur is thick with oil. When this happens the filter is removed from the last camera. It is daylight, as we have suspected. Small fires glow on the eastern hills. Smoke rises into the bright air, the air blazing with sunlight. The sky is empty. The earth is littered with craters, with metal, with bricks, with concrete. The cross-shaped building is mostly rubble. The dome has collapsed. The cenote is visible. The air is so bright that we have to blink our eyes. What a change, from night to day! We move away from the rubble, from the steaming earth, the blackened earth. After a moment I stop and turn around.

"What are you staring at?"

"Nothing."

"Nothing?"

"Nothing at all."

"Let's go, then."

She takes my arm. We leave.

PART FOUR

I.

The first draft of this novel I wrote during five months wandering through Mexico. I mention this because it may be important for an understanding of this book. I have been a wanderer all my life. My life has been episodic, scattered around the world. It is not a life one would choose. I am a stranger everywhere I go. Nevertheless I am alive, which is perhaps a victory of sorts. Three fortune tellers predicted I would not survive into middle age. One was a Chinese in Decker Street, in Singapore. Another—long ago—was a Parsi woman in Bombay. My future embarrassed and flustered her. The last was a self-proclaimed psychic in Yucaipa, California, surely an exotic place. Yet I see today that my beard is gray, and that my hair is becoming gray. It is not a young man that peers from my mirror. I am middle-aged, and I am alive. I ascribe my survival to my constant wandering. Death could never catch up to me. It is amusing, at least, to think this. It is as good an explanation for my life as any. I have been fleeing death. During the course of this novel I fled death in Lagos de Moreno and Merida, in Aguascalientes and Uruapan. I hid in Guanajuato, in the Casa Kloster. I moved quickly through Querétero and Morelia. I slipped into Xalapa. I write this now in Pátzcuaro. I am in the Hotel Valmen. The sun enters from my right, through a tall window. Birds sing in a courtyard to my left. Altogether it is a pleasant enough place. The town itself is quiet. Tourists come here for the Indian market and to see Janitzio, a town on an island in the nearby lake. It is amusing to watch the tourists and guess where they are from. The Americans are the easiest. Many of them dress as Indians. They go into the mercado and buy white pants

187

or cotton skirts. They put on sandals and straw hats. The women wrap shawls around their shoulders. We saw one of these Americans this morning. We were crossing the plaza chica. We were on our way to breakfast. The woman was middle-aged herself. She had a pale face with a silly smile on it. She seemed pleased with herself.

"Americans," I said, "are a costumed people."

"Costumed?"

"They have so little identity of their own they must constantly put on costumes, and pretend to be something they are not. But the disguise is always superficial, like their television."

"She seems happy."

"She seems silly."

"Perhaps Americans are only happy when they are silly."

"She reminds me," I said, "of Virginia White."

"Is that what happens to her? She becomes a middleaged 'Indian' in Pátzcuaro?"

"No. But that is an idea."

An episodic life produces an episodic novel, that is what I am trying to say. This novel appeared piece by piece. When I become too comfortable in any one place I moved on. The novel, like the life, is thus oddly discontinuous. It is discontinuous, episodic, segmented. This continues to be true even now, in Pátzcuaro, as I write these final pieces.

2.

We came to Pátzcuaro to see the film of *Maya*. It has never been released in the United States. Doubtless this is because the film is so terrible. Perhaps someday it will appear on late night television or videocassettes. In the meantime the countries of the third world will absorb virtually any film, no matter how badly done, that has a blonde American actress in it. Virginia White, therefore, may be considered responsible for this movie's appearance in Mexico. Photographs of her are prominently displayed on the posters outside the theatre. Her bare breasts, unfortunately, have been inked out. This is a common practice in Mexico. In relatively sophisticated places like Mexico City and Guadalajara, where these movies first appear, the posters remain unmarked. As films progress through the countryside, which is more conservative, exhibitors begin inking over breasts and buttocks. Sometimes they draw brassieres and slips and panties on the bare flesh. There is something titillating about all these women blacked out with ink. I have wondered at times if the exhibitors do this to make the films seem more salacious than they actually are. No one, however, blacks out scenes of violence. In the posters of the film playing with *Maya* can be seen stakes driven through foreheads, blood bursting from bodies riddled by machine guns, and so on. Violence is clearly more acceptable than nude women. A naked breast, we may assume, is more dangerous than an M-60. No one goes so far as to ban these films, however, no matter how titillating they may be. They are the mainstay of the Mexican cinemas. Men will line up for hours to see them, especially on Sundays. The theatres fill with restless men, shuffling their boots, spitting on the floor. They pay the equivalent of about fifty cents to see someone like Virginia White bare her breasts. This seems a bargain. I would pay fifty cents any time to see Virginia White's breasts moving on a picture screen. No one could complain about their size, shape, or the profound delicacy of their nipples. It is unfortunate that the woman never learned to act. Whenever she is on the screen, you can see that she is yearning to turn to the camera and smile. That is all she really wants to do. She seems a little embarrassed at having to bare her tits so often, but it is all for the sake of art, isnt it? Besides, she is proud of her tits. One can see, throughout the film, this conflict running through her. She wishes to show off her tits. She wishes to demurely hide them. She is proud of them. She is embarrassed by them. But even in the middle of her embarrassment, as her face flushes, she yearns to turn to the camera and smile.

The movie, of course, has been retitled for its Mexican release. It is now called *El Sacrificio Sexual de las Mayas.* The ambiguity of this title is interesting. We discussed it this morning, after breakfast. We were walking through the cemetery which starts just beyond the mercado. I like Mexican cemeteries with their encrypted bodies, their anarchic jumble. No two tombs are alike. Sarcophagi, some broken, are everywhere. Stelae are moss-covered. We stopped at a large englassed crypt. Within were perfect plastic flowers and a large, gaudy picture of the Virgin Mary.

"I think you're wrong about the Mexicans," she said to me.

"In what way?"

"I think they prefer the Virgin Mary to Virginia White."

"The men, you mean?"

"The women, too."

It is certainly true that the Virgin Mother—resplendent, glowing— is given prominence in Mexican churches. Jesus, on or off his cross, will be relegated to a side chapel. Often we saw women crawling across the floor, kissing the tile at each pause. Others walked on their knees, gazing raptly at the indifferent, serene face high above. But one seldom saw men adopt these attitudes of reverence. I pointed this out.

"No, they dont need to. They *marry* the Virgin."

"Ah. Their wives—"

"Precisely. Who then play the role as perfectly as they can. Have you seen how Mexican women adore their male children?"

"The spoiled brats."

"The Virgin Mother holding the infant Jesus—that's what the Mexican women copy. They adore their sons, and mostly ignore their daughters."

"Yes, I've noticed."

"I didnt know you were so fond of tits."

"What?"

"You were going on there about Virginia White's bosom, werent you?"

"Well, just for the sake of illustration—"

"A bit tiresome, this masculine obsession with tits."

"I assure you—"

"Yes. Youre a leg man, arent you? Or so you say."

It is never wise to continue conversations like this with a woman. I mentioned the Spanish title of the film. Had she noticed the ambiguity in the wording? She nodded.

"But I doubt if it was on purpose," she said. "I think they just wanted the words 'sex' and 'sacrifice' in the title somewhere."

"The Mayas did sacrifice women—presumably virgins."

"Presumably."

"Or does the title suggest," I said, "that the Mayas themselves were sacrificed, sexually? I mean one could argue—"

"And doubtless you will."

"One could argue—couldnt one—that the Spanish invasion of Yucatan was a kind of rape."

"Quite literally, when it came to the native women."

"But *symbolically*. The army of men—those lances, and spears, the muskets—the horses—"

"I do rather like the horses."

"And didnt the Kaiser—I mean, during World War I—didnt the Germans keep referring to their country in masculine terms, as in the Fatherland—and the Low Countries and France, which they invaded,

191

in feminine terms?"

"What are you trying to make of this?"

"And the American invasion of Vietnam—it was an invasion, wasnt it?—those tanks, the artillery—"

"Youre not only obsessed with tits, youre obsessed with symbolism, arent you?"

I shut up. We walked silently through the graves. After a moment she knelt at a small mound of dirt and a wooden cross. On the cross was the name Paco Garcia, handwritten in black paint. It was easily the smallest, least opulent grave in the area. A little farther along I could see a field of corn, and then rows of adobe houses. The sky was black towards the west, but here we could feel the sun on our shoulders.

"Poor little Paco," she said.

She stood up and looked at all the marble and stonework and glassed-in cages of the dead around us.

"I'll bet," she said, "I'll bet he was loved more—more than all these—"

She gestured, head thrown back. Her eyes were suddenly fierce.

"You may be right," I said.

"I am right."

She stalked off. I followed.

3 ·

Pátzcuaro is famous for its market. It is divided into sections. At one place Indians sit at long wooden tables with their fish. These are black bass and carp and live axolotls, which look like big tadpoles, and of course the prized pescado blanco. But there are fewer of these fish, in particular the white fish, every year. The lake from whence they come is gradually turning into a swamp. It is fed by runoff from the hills. But the hills have been largely deforested. Silt washes down each year into the lake, which was already shallow. Water lilies and hyacinths are choking the waterways. Sewage descends with the silt, washing down with blood from the slaughterhouse. This is not, of course, a problem for me. I am only a visitor. It is a problem for the Mexicans, in particular the Indians who live off the lake. These Indians are called Purépecha. They once had a civilization which rivaled that of the Aztecs. Their capital, named Tzintzuntzan, lies now in ruins. Tourists visit it. It is only a few miles from Pátzcuaro. Everything dies, of course. Old civilizations. Cities. Races and cultures. People and lakes. One cannot dwell on such things, or on the accumulation of misery, the weight of eons of suffering. Yet death is visible everywhere. It is even visible in the market. We walked through it after the cemetery. At first glance all was the bustle of life. People gathered there from the neighboring villages. The market was bursting with produce, with fruit and meat, with cheese and bread, the wealth of the earth. There had been a rain earlier, and the ground was wet. We walked over cantaloupe skins and crushed tomatoes, peppers ground into asphalt. Bananas, including the huge ostions and the tiny dominicos, lay everywhere, turning black.

193

Papayas, plucked from their trees, were already dead. Rot had settled in everywhere. Apples had wormholes and brown spots. Carrots were limp. The Indians, the remnants of the dying Purépecha, stared at us with coppery eyes. We stopped at a display of pig heads. Their snouts were soft to the touch, very pale and delicate, and very dead. But there was noise everywhere, the noise of life, amid the dying grapes and ciruelos, the hanging slabs of beef and pork, the salchichas, the flesh ground up into sausages, the chorizo that we ate daily between soft tortillas, sustaining ourselves. We passed great round slabs of cheese. We smiled at the Indian women presiding over their baskets of bread. We passed tables laden with dead food, supplied by the earth, the earth that was washing down into the lake below, killing it.

We stopped at La Princesa Restaurant to sip at tepid Cokes.

"All this," I said, gesturing at the scene before us, "this mixture of death and life—does it ever bother you? Do you ever get depressed, watching it? Or angry?"

"Never."

"Why not?"

"Why not? Why on earth should I?"

"It depresses me."

"You must remember I am a woman."

"I wont forget *that*."

She silenced me with a look.

"Dont be cute," she said. "It doesnt suit you."

"Well, go on, then."

"I am a woman. I am capable of creating life. And when I dont create life, every month I discharge blood from my body. I am—involved—in all this."

"This market—"

"You like symbols. This market is me. All this life, and this death—this ripeness, this decay—that is what I am. That is what a woman is."

"I'm not sure—"

"You are a man. You make a good beast of burden, carrying fruit to the market. And youre good at sowing, too, at planting, I'll admit that. But the fruit itself—all this produce—the market—the earth—all of that is female. That is why I sometimes despise you men."

"Despise us?"

"Because of what you do to the earth. You are cruel. If you had your way, you would destroy everything."

"I dont think I am cruel."

"Arent you? But in any case we are talking in generalities, arent we? About men—not a man. About women."

"Women are cruel too."

"Yes, we are cruel. I can be cruel. I was cruel the other night. I bit you."

I winced.

"Yes," I said. "The mark is still there."

"That was no love bite. I was angry."

"Why?"

"At your failure to acknowledge me."

"I dont understand."

"That's what I mean."

We sipped at our Cokes. They were cloying with sugar.

"Let's talk about something else," I said.

"All right. I notice you are limping again. Your ankle?"

"Yes. I stepped on a loose rock at the cemetery."

I had sprained the ankle a month earlier, in Aguascalientes, playing baseball with Gallo and his relatives. It was still weak and inflamed.

"It's nothing," I added.

"I noticed Osgood Fetters was limping all through the film."

"Like me, you mean?"

"He is your character."

"I think I look more like Garred. We're both blond—"

"Your belly is flatter."

"Yes, there is that."

"What happened to them? After the movie, I mean. They didnt die in that explosion, did they?"

"No, no. That was all special effects. No, Osgood went back to New York. He has a rent-controlled apartment there, you know."

"I thought he was adequate in the film."

"Yes. Competent. Nothing more, I'm afraid. Well, it was his first and last movie, anyway. He still acts once in a while on stage—community theatre, that kind of thing. And works for his lawyers."

"Is he writing?"

"No. Once in a while he talks about it. But no—just briefs, letters, case notes. He's getting old, you know. He looks bonier and bonier all the time. But he isnt as bitter as one might expect. He really thought he was good, you see. As a writer, I mean. And to never be acknowledged—well, that would make anyone bitter. But he seems to find a kind of—oh, odd pleasure—in his bitterness. He enjoys it. You know what I mean? His bitterness animates him, you see, and this animation—this pleasure—keeps the bitterness from being—from being—"

"Too bitter?"

"Exactly."

"So he is reasonably content?"

"Who knows? He's a solitary fellow. But at least he isnt consumed with anger."

"And Garred?"

"Ah, yes. Garred. That's another story. Look, shall we go on? I cant take any more of this Coke. How about a *feminine* taco in this *female* market?"

"You are a sweet man," she said.

Perhaps she meant it. She took my arm as we started across the market.

4.

Pátzcuaro is an old town, a 16th-century town. It lies in the hills of Michoacán. It is chilly at night. The morning sun, however, comes through the window, warming me as I sit at my typewriter. From the window I can see adobe walls marching up the hillside to the basilica, which I can glimpse just beyond some trees. The red tile roofs are all blackened with age. The streets below are paved with flat stones. At the corner, sitting near the entrance to Muebles San Jose ("Lo que su hogar necesita nosotros lo tenemos!"), is an old man with a wooden cart, selling ciruelos and peanuts. A policeman stands at the intersection periodically blowing his whistle, though at what is not clear. Earlier today school children marched down to the plaza chica, or the Plaza Gertruda Bocanegra, as it is properly called, after a local heroine of the Revolution. The children marched quite in step. They blew bugles and beat at drums. Speeches were made in the plaza. Then a marathon began, the runners leaving from Parroquia El Santuario, trotting along behind police cars with sirens wailing. Later in the day there will be a parade. It will pass beneath the hotel, skirt the plaza, and end at the Parroquia. All this is in celebration of Columbus' discovery of the Americas, the discovery which made the invasions of Cortez and Pizzaro and Francisco de Montoya possible. What was interesting to me, however, was the sense of community displayed. The school children in their uniforms, the men and women lining the streets—all of them belonged here. All of them, that is, except the Indians, who came into town from their villages and stayed close to the market, and the people like me, too tall, too red, too foreign to blend in. I was as

197

much a stranger here as I was in the streets of southern California. Or Kudat, in Borneo. Or Darwin, or Mombasa, or Tangier. I suppose that was why I liked Garred. He too was an outsider, and knew it.

"But so was Osgood."

"Yes. But Osgood never accepted it. He wanted to belong. It was part of his despair, part of his bitterness, that he could never fit in."

"And Garred didnt mind?"

"Garred made it part of his life. He became a *dangerous* man."

"Dangerous?"

"Like an old elephant outside the herd. Short tempered, rather vicious. Unpredictable. And rather proud of his alienation."

"I will never forgive what he did to that boy."

"And to Virginia?"

"Given the context, I am more irritated with her. I despise the games such women play."

"Yes, you would."

We were in the Restaurant Los Escudos, on the plaza grande, having coffee. The tables were covered with cloth. The waiter wore a white jacket. We couldnt often afford to eat there, but we could drink their coffee. Outside, the marathoners passed for the second time, behind the wailing police car. Now there was a group of four in the lead, the rest straggling behind. School children, released from their duties but still in uniform, cheered them on. Bringing up the rear, far behind, were two fat men, flesh bouncing, faces bursting, soggy already with sweat. The school children jeered.

Pátzcuaro is unusual in having two plazas. The plaza chica I think of as the Indian plaza. The market begins there. The hotels around it are poor, run down. The plaza is busy, noisy, dirty, full of the swarthy Purépecha. The second, larger one is named after Don Vasco de Quiroga, a Spanish bishop sent from Spain in response to complaints by the Indians of maltreatment. This plaza is quiet. Around it one finds the expensive hotels and restaurants, like Los Escudos. Children play in the grass, and pretty women stroll about, arm in arm, in the evenings. It is a peaceful place, and we often go there in the afternoon to sit and read. If it begins to rain—we are at the end of the summer rainy season—we hurry into Los Escudos for coffee. On this day clouds piled up to the west, but the rain still held off.

Because of the two plazas, Pátzcuaro seems divided in half, as is much of Mexico: the poor and the rich. The villagers and the townspeople. The Indians and the mestizos. But in the towns like Pátzcuaro and the provincial cities like Aguascalientes, the culture somehow holds together. Only in Mexico City, and perhaps now Guadalajara—with their urban poor, the crime, the palpable misery, the poisonous air—does the center fail to hold. In this respect Mexico City is like an American city, or one of the old English manufacturing centers like Manchester. One sees there the despair of modern, Western life, the spiritual failure of a civilization. Osgood would rail against it. Garred would move through it, through the underworld, in this case more like a panther than an elephant, sleek, vicious, burning, his ochre eyes triumphant.

"Is that where he is now? In New York, or Hamburg?"

"No, no. Although he did go back to Europe, where he made a couple more films."

"And is he European? German?"

"He never liked to say. He liked being—secretive. But he spoke several languages, including German, quite fluently."

"You speak of him in the past tense."

"You noticed."

"So he died?"

"He died."

"Let me guess. He contracted AIDS."

"Youre too quick for me."

"You are so obvious."

"Well, why not? It is such a modern disease—and such an American one."

"Yet it began—"

"I know, I know. In Africa, where it has been even more devastating. But I think of it as an American disease—or as a modern, Western, Christian disease. Americans are so righteous about it, so judgmental—"

"Yes, yes, we know your thoughts on the subject. But Garred—how

199

did he take it? Did he suffer?"

"Do you want him to have suffered?"

The tip of her tongue appeared between her teeth as she thought.

"Yes," she finally said. "Why not? He would suffer anyway, and probably find pleasure in it."

"Youre right. As the symptoms appeared—the lesions, the emaciation—-he seemed to gloat. As though the pain, the corruption, proved something. And of course he spread the disease around, too. If anything, he became more promiscuous than before. If he could have, he would probably have put the virus in the water supply."

"Let everyone get it."

"I think he believed—how shall I say it—everyone already had it. He was just making it visible. AIDS was already there, everywhere, in the polluted air, in the devastated earth, in the streets, the schools, the churches—well, everywhere. He became a symbol of the corruption he saw all around him."

The marathoners passed again, this time with one man in the lead, two others half a block behind, and then the pack, running determinedly together. There was no sign of the two fat men. The leader's face was shining, and not just with sweat. He was triumphant, and knew it. I watched him circle the Plaza Vasco de Quiroga. As he passed the far corner he lifted a clenched fist. Above him were black clouds, and the first hints of rain.

"Well," she said at last, "I shall leave Garred in his grave. But I shant forgive him."

"No," I said. "I dont suppose that would be possible."

We sipped at our coffee. After a while I saw one of the fat marathoners. He was walking, almost stumbling, his face purple. He went to a bench and sat down. He sagged there, defeated. There was a red bandana around his forehead. It was clearly foolish for him to have attempted such a run. An official, perhaps concerned, drifted towards him. Then it began to rain, and the wind blew darkly through the trees.

5.

Much of this novel was written in Mexican cafes. I remember with fondness the Cafe del Olmo in Morelia, with its sombre lighting, and the Cafe La Flor in Xalapa, where they roasted their own coffee beans. There were sidewalk cafes, too, in Merida and Uruapan and Guanajuato, and other towns. Many of these have unfortunately become expensive and are thus frequented mostly by tourists, who seem a bit dazed by Mexican street life, and local businessmen who resentfully ignore the tourists. Nevertheless I found some cafes that were pleasant, mostly the older ones, not yet spruced up to attract big spending foreigners. I liked the arched portales looking out over the streets, and the old men playing guitars for a few pesos. I liked watching the dark-eyed girls strut by on their high heels, the men gesturing constantly with their hands, the small boys drifting from table to table, selling chiclets, the traffic cops bargaining with motorists who were illegally parked. But my favorite cafe was not open to the street at all. It was the Cafe Excelsior in Aguascalientes. The front part was a bookstore. People gathered at the tables in back, talking and gesticulating, sometimes with passion. It was possible in the Excelsior to play chess, to argue politics, to compare Jorge Luis Borges to Octavio Paz, to contrast Velasquez to Goya. Odd things could happen there. A lady once sat at my table and gave me a rose. She stared for a long time into my eyes. "My mother killed her five children," she finally said. "I'm sorry to hear that," I responded politely, and returned to my book and coffee. When I left an hour later she was still there, still staring. Rosa Maria, at the counter, shrugged her shoulders. Once I saw a chess player get angry and knock over the board, not because he wasnt winning—he was—but because his opponent was taking too much time in losing. With Susan, who had married into a wealthy Mexican family, I discussed photography and the failings of modern psychology; and with Dan, a missionary, I argued the lineage of Arianism and the Christian ideals of Nikos Kazantzakis. Elida and I discussed Mexican politics and American culture, and José and I the difficulty of a life devoted to art. Yolanda and Norma, like two flowers, blossomed at my table, admired by all. All this was possible in the Excelsior, and other Mexican cafes. And none of it, alas, would be possible—

"—in American cafes."

"That's right."

"What do they talk about in America?"

"What kind of car to buy, what was on TV last night—the prices of things, like cigarettes—which athletic shoe is the one to get this season—"

"And this is where you want to take me?"

"Well, just for a while. You should see it."

"I hardly ever wear athletic shoes."

"I noticed."

She turned her foot so we could both see her instep, which was arched in her red, high-heeled shoe. We had gone back to the hotel and changed—myself into faded jeans and a gray jacket over a white shirt, she into a tight black skirt and her heels. When the rain let up we strolled to the Fuente de Sodas Tim's, near El Santuario. We were sipping again at coffees, for her a Capuchino, for me a Cafe Americano, black and rich. On the street outside, people had already gathered. Tables were set out. At the iron gates of the church stood a white-robed priest surrounded by his faithful. All of us awaited the parade, which would end here. It was darkening outside, and yellow lights had begun to glow in the shops. The street was emptied of cars. There were only people murmuring, and the dark clouds tumbling overhead.

While we waited I told her more about Virginia White. Originally I had seen her crawling out from the ruins of the cross-shaped building. The earth was glazed under the brilliant sun. Flies buzzed around bodies, half in and half out of the rubble. In the red garden a broken helicopter smouldered. There was no sign of Garred, no sign of Osgood. Virginia herself was bloodied, bruised. All she wore was her brassiere, its one cup still intact, thanks, of course, to the supply in the wardrobe woman's closet. It was rather interesting, watching one breast bound, one breast unbound; one contained, one wobbling. But her face was awful: left side swollen, black, still bleeding, the eye closed, teeth missing. Her long blonde hair fell everywhere, like dirty straw tossed in the wind. She crawled down from the rubble in a series of close-ups and medium shots, and then stood in the open space, near a crater, while the camera backed away and rose into the sky, thus emphasizing her isolation. Finally she moved off, a tiny, solitary figure, down the dirt road towards the town. Within the town were only more bodies—soldiers sprawling from windows, lying amongst shell casings in doorways—but at the train station was a great mob of people, coppery-eyed natives, women crying, children wailing, men hurrying to and fro. At last a train came. Everyone pushed to get on board, including Virginia White: white flesh pressed amid all that copper. It was a struggle for her. She cried in pain. But at last she got in, just as the train started to move and people fell back to the tracks. She was shunted up against the door at one end, squeezed there, scarcely able to breathe. For a while the camera just stared at her, moved in close to her panicky face.

Then she turned and looked through the window. There was another carriage behind the one she was in. Three men were there. They wore gray slacks and white shirts. They looked like oil company executives. All were Europeans with short, well-brushed hair. They were studying sheaves of paper, which they passed back and forth. Virginia banged on her window. She pressed her face against the glass. She kicked at the door. At last one of the men looked up. There was no expression discernible on his face. He walked down the corridor, past the leather seats, to the door of his carriage. His face was thus no more than thirty-six inches from hers. It remained expressionless. It was partially obscured by sunlight glancing off the glass. Then he reached up and pulled down a shade. Virginia White slid slowly to the floor.

6.

It was not quite dark outside. The crowd had grown, but they were quiet. We could hear fireworks exploding in the distance.

"But you chose a different ending?"

"There didnt seem to be a choice. An ending eventually writes itself. One simply has to step back out of its way, and let it proceed— sometimes in directions one doesnt expect. I could not force Virginia White out of the rubble, into that train."

"She balked."

"What she did was just get up, walk off the set, and return to Iowa."

"Dressed, I hope, in more than that torn bra."

"Yes, yes. Her face bandaged, too."

"Did the production company pay her bills? It sounds like she needed extensive care—a doctor, a dentist—"

"And plastic surgery. But no. The company immediately declared bankruptcy, and the principals vanished from sight. Only Garred got anything—he had insisted on half his pay up front. The rest were lucky they survived."

She flew to Iowa. The jet hissed through the sky for hours. She changed planes once, perhaps twice. She was shuttled down one chute, up another. Anonymous hands plucked at her clothes, her breasts, her buttocks. In Iowa she immediately married a cocky, bow-legged man, considerably older than her, who worked in sales. The plastic surgery and dental work they could afford could not entirely restore her face; and scar tissue had built up within her vagina and cervix, making intercourse difficult and pregnancy impossible. At first she tried to resume her previous life. She tried to behave as though everything were normal. But nothing was normal any more. She began to eat. She went on food binges. Sometimes she threw up afterwards, on purpose, but the vomiting made her sick. So she just ate and drank. She grew as bloated as the bodies in the rice paddies. One day she cut off her long blonde hair. After that she would not go out. Her husband had to do all the shopping. He didnt seem to mind at first. He brought home bottles of Jack Daniels and Hiram Walker coffee flavored brandy and all the cakes and pies and ice cream she wanted. He continued to brag at work about his moviestar wife. He would take out photographs and show them to everyone. When people wanted to meet her, he would compare her to Greta Garbo: she just wanted to be left alone. He didnt tell anyone she was fat. Virginia sat all day in front of the television, watching soap operas, old movies, and Phil Donahue. She ate and drank. After a while her husband started to beat her. But it was never very serious. He just slapped her around a little. The bruises hardly showed. He grew a paunch himself and started losing his hair. The day he made vice-president in charge of sales, he came home drunk, found his wife snoring on the floor, and beat her more intensely than he ever had before. The next day, however, he apologized. Sometimes he watched television with her. Her eyes had sunk into her cheeks, and were scarcely visible. She overflowed the chair. Her bed had to be reinforced. She didnt leave the house again until she died a few years later. Doors had to be removed so her corpse could exit. Her husband put a photograph of her on the casket, so everyone could see how beautiful his wife had been. The casket itself was closed. He respected, he said, his wife's wish for privacy. But he continued to take photographs from his wallet to show people, especially when he drank. Some were publicity stills, and quite professionally sexy. He did this even after he remarried. His second wife was thin, pale, lackluster, and spent much of her time sleeping. He had no photographs of her.

7.

She was silent. We went out onto the street. After a while she began to talk. While she talked, the night descended. More people pressed around us. Three tourists passed, two girls and a pale boy, speaking German. They were dressed in the ragged remnants of their civilization.

"You are hard on women," she said. "I dont think you can claim innocence in this affair. To some degree you must admit Virginia White is your creation. No, no. Dont interrupt. I know as much about art as you do. I do not deny the independence of your creations, or the people who portray them. But you put her in harm's way. You set everything in motion. If you had selected someone stronger than Virginia White you would have had an entirely different ending—an entirely different story. You knew quite well—from the beginning— that her survival was in doubt. You degraded her. She did not deserve such torment. Bloated, indeed—like a dead body in a rice paddy. I'm surprised you didnt have her intestines spill out. How did you describe it? 'Great looping coils.' This work has become perverse. I wonder if every woman you are associated with is so brutalized. You are deceptive. You talk about masks. Do you ever reveal your true form? If I remove this mask from you, is there another one below it? Do you imagine you are one of those god-impersonators, manipulating everyone around you? What are your plans for me? Is there something you have in mind that you would like to explain to me? Do you have a script for me to read? If you think I am going to slavishly follow your directions you are quite mistaken. I am not a foolish innocent like

Virginia White and the rest of your American friends. You will not catch me unaware. You are a cruel man. Cruel, and perverse."

The rocket man came up the street. He held the rockets between thumb and forefinger and lit them with the glowing tip of a cigarette. The rockets shot up into the air, making sizzling noises, and then exploded. A boy trailed behind, handing him the rockets. The cigarette glowed ochre.

"Look," I said. "Here's the parade."

It was led by a police car and boys carrying a large portrait of the Virgin Mother. Then came taxis—there must have been fifty of them, perhaps every taxi in town—all maroon and white and festooned with ribbons and balloons and crepe. On the hoods rode little girls in frilly white frocks. We were silent, watching them. The crowd pressed us close together. I took her arm, and felt her hip against mine. After the taxis came beribboned buses, belching fumes. The crowd was quite silent: women dressed in their best clothes, men in straw hats and gleaming shoes, children made up like dolls. We could hear music approaching, and at last, following the buses, came groups of men playing accordions and saxophones and bass fiddles and guitars and drums. Interspersed were more portraits of the Virgin, held aloft, her serene, indifferent face high above the crowd. The taxis, buses, and trucks turned left at the corner. But the people all went forward, through the iron gates, into the church courtyard. After the last band the spectators spilled onto the street. People were packed curb to curb, marching to the Parroquia. We let them press past us with difficulty. Anonymous shoulders, breasts, hips pushed against us. We worked our way back to the sidewalk and to a table covered with Coke bottles and bowls and a large pot of pozole steaming over a brazier. We wedged ourselves against the wall. An old man gave us bowls. The pozole was hot and rich. I watched her spoon it into her mouth. I watched her lips part, and her tongue emerge.

A yellow light glowed above her, casting shadows down her face. She turned her eyes to me.

"I said you are cruel," she said.

"I wont argue with you."

"And perverse."

"I acknowledge what you say."

Her lips were painted so they were almost black. She put down her bowl.

"Pay him," she ordered.

I gave the man two thousand pesos.

"Rico," I said.

"Sí, muy rico."

He grinned up at me. His teeth were brown. The woman pulled my arm.

"I want something sweet," she said.

We pushed through the crowd. I put my hands on her hips. My fingers felt around to her belly, where her belly narrowed into her crotch. She stopped at a stall where a woman made pancakes. The old woman smeared cajeta on a pancake and handed it up. I paid, and we moved on. "My fingers are sticky," she said after a moment. She stopped and turned so she faced me. I could see the cajeta, syrupy, on her fingers. She began to lick at her fingers. I watched her for a moment and then took her wrist. I put her fingers into my mouth. Her face was expressionless, but after a moment her lips parted. At the corner the crowd eased. A rain began to fall. I watched the droplets gather in her hair. As we crossed the plaza the yellow lights on their poles made her hair luminesce. When she shook her head, the lights in her hair scattered away. Our faces became damp. Drops of water rolled down my shirt, and down her blouse. At the far corner of the plaza men and women shivered around a stall selling seafood. Their faces turned in our direction. A gas fire hissed. Our feet made little splashes in the water glowing on the street. All the lights—the street lights, the lights in the buildings—reflected up from the puddles beneath us. We were illuminated from above and below. As we hurried forward the lights kept shifting. Sleek sheets of water rippled as we stepped into them. Her hair was wet. Her eyelashes were wet. I saw water at her throat. We went faster.

In our room she stopped and turned. She seemed very tall and dark. I could smell her wet clothes. I pushed her onto the bed. Her black skirt bunched up at her waist. Her white thighs lifted over my shoulders. "No," she said after a moment. "Oh, no," she moaned. "No, not that." Her white body began to buck. Her red shoes kicked in the air. I raised myself over her. Our eyes met. In her eyes I saw horror, and pain, and desperation, and greed. I hovered there, above her, while she stared up at me. Rain spat against a window. Her blouse was torn open. One breast lay exposed. She stared up at me. I hovered there, on my outstretched arms, raised above her.

"My lizard," she said. *"My lizard."*

I plunged into her, into oblivion.

The Queen
of
Las Vegas

PART 1
BLUE MOVIE

I.

We begin with the woman sitting on her throne. She crosses one leg over the other, as ordered. A single light is to the side—her right, our left. She makes no movement except the crossing of the leg, which she repeats several times. The nylon surfaces of her stockings hiss faintly as they slide one against the other. The camera hisses too. Film races through it at 24 frames per second. These hissing noises—her stockings, this film—are the only sounds audible in the room. The camera is a Mitchell NC. It is constructed in two parts, allowing the hinged body to swing away from the lens. With the body out of the way, direct focusing is possible on a ground glass screen positioned behind the lens. If the camera body were racked-over at this moment—instead of hissing with its racing film—the ground glass screen would reveal the inverted image of the woman sitting on her throne. She is darkened, shadowed by the single lamp situated to our left. That is, the light has the effect of hiding rather than revealing her. The light creates the shadows which obscure her. It is this paradoxical situation that we wish to stress. She is obscured, not revealed, by the light which illuminates her.

The woman sits. She crosses one leg over the other. The camera, and her stockings, hiss. At last the man clears his throat.

"Do you know what this film is about?"

"No—not exactly—"

"You know it is pornographic?"

"Well, they said X—"

"Not just X—triple X. Pornographic."

"Will I have to—you know—"

"Yes."

She sucks in her breath. He says:

"Have you done it before? In front of a camera?"

"Yes—I mean, once—"

"Not simulated—"

"No—no, it wasn't simulated."

"There's nothing simulated in this film."

"I understand."

"What's wrong with your face?"

"My face?"

"That side—your left side—"

"I try to comb my hair over it—"

"I can see that. What happened?"

"Boiling water—when I was a child—"

"Someone spilled boiling water on your face?"

"I dont want to talk about it."

"All right. What did you say your name was?"

"Dominique."

"All right, Dominique. That will do for today."

Good-bye, she says. She leaves. She walks along the edge of the mercado. This is after she passes the bridge, the slaughterhouse, the opera house, etc. At the mercado the Indian women—they are shaped like turnips—rearrange the plastic tarps which protect them and their merchandise. Their language is indecipherable. Dominique continues her stately walk to the portales. These portales form a kind of porch or arcade in front of the buildings which surround the plaza. There are pharmacias, restaurantes, the registo civil, and a ferraterria. All are made of adobe. One large building has a sign: Hotel del Lago. Some years ago, however, its roof collapsed during an exceptional monsoon. Through its unglazed windows is visible the fallen interior of tile and stone and adobe overgrown with bushes and vines. Some flowered stalks—their blossoms are red, yellow, purple—stretch out through the windows, into the portales. Dominique, her stride as graceful as that of any young hoofed animal, passes these blossoms heedlessly. As she walks men lean towards her right ear and whisper. The men are small and dark. Sometimes they have to stretch, like the flowered stalks, to reach her ear. The women—the turnip-shaped Indian women sitting wrapped in their rebozos before their piles of tortillas and ciruellos—stare at her without expression. Each brown face wreathed in wrinkles is expressionless. These faces, that is, are expressionless until Dominique moves past. Then the women look at each other. Their eyes and their lips become mobile. They communicate something to each other, something secret. We cannot decipher these communications. Dominique, in any case, seems unaware of the stir of movement that follows her. Her black patent shoes with their very high heels click on the stone paving. If she is aware of the Indian women, or the men breathing words into her ear, she gives no indication of it. At last she goes into a cafe. She sits at a table. She orders a cup of coffee. She brushes back, with her left hand, the hair falling over the side of her face. No one in the cafe makes any comment. We do, however. It is our belief that her beauty would be incomplete without this disfiguration thus revealed. Could her right eye be as beautiful without the left? That eye, blank, milky, lifeless, protrudes slightly, as though ready to fall from its scarred socket. The stiff parchment skin around it is finely wrinkled. The ear is nearly gone—only a lump of cartilage remains. Her mouth, on her left, does not seem to end but continues as a scar nearly to her throat. Could her mouth be as lovely without this scar? We believe not. Her beauty, her disfigurement, is entire, of a piece. She sits in the cafe, her beauty complete, sipping at her coffee. Soon a man joins her. A cigarette dangles from his lower lip, which seems wet and excessively red. He talks to her. She does not look at him. Occasionally she nods, or makes some agreeable noise. Finally he stands. He makes a last comment. She nods again, looking down at her hands. Then he leaves. After a while she pushes aside the cup of coffee. She stares vaguely around her. She puts money on the table. Then she leaves.

2.

She enters from our left. The door parts; light spills into the darkened room. She takes her place, as ordered, on the throne. She crosses one leg—her right—over the other, her left—

The room has been kept darkened, perhaps for days. As the door parts, light springs with a feral eagerness across the room. This intrusion of light has an aspect of violence to it. The light leaps across the room with a tangible force. There is something of the raptor in this leap. Light and shadow are being manipulated in this scene to achieve some effect, some goal, before the filming even begins. The woman, however, seems a willing participant. It is she who slides back the latch. Though well-oiled, it clicks loudly, the metal tongue drawn against its internal spring by a knob rotated counter-clockwise, then released. The door itself appears heavy. The side facing us is ornately carved. We see a gargoyle's face amid resplendent leaves. Lizards coil at each corner. The door moves easily, in spite of its weight, which is supported by three brass hinges, releasing, as it opens, the light which springs unbounded across the room with something very like an audible noise, so sudden is its intrusion. At the same time, thrown obliquely across the floor and entirely within this shaft of light, is the shadow of the woman. The shadow, and the woman, pause for a moment, until the quartz light on its tripod is turned on. This appears to be a signal, for the woman now steps into the room and shuts the door—whose latch once again snaps audibly as the tongue slides back, then rebounds—shuts the door, we say, behind her, vanquishing at that moment both the light and her shadow thrown obliquely within it.

The camera hisses. A man speaks.

"How is your hotel?"

"My hotel?"

"Your room—your room in the hotel."

"It's all right."

"And your trip?"

"My trip—"

"Your journey down here. Was it comfortable? Easy? Pleasant?"

"It was all right."

"All right? Not—difficult?"

"No."

"Yet you were late. A week, is that right?"

"Was it a week?"

"You delayed your flight a week. Seven days, exactly."

"There were things—-it took longer than I expected—"

"As it happens it doesn't matter. There have been delays here. The set isnt ready. The script is—incomplete. Have you seen the faces in the mercado? In the portales?"

"Well—faces?"

"I mean the faces for sale. The wood carvings especially. Youve seen them?"

"I noticed something—"

"Do you know what they are for?"

"No."

"What is your interest in film?"

"In film?"

"Dont stop crossing your legs. You can talk and move your legs at the same time, cant you? A little higher—bring the leg a little higher as it crosses. And when you lower the leg, slide it—slide one calf against the other. You have splendid legs, Dominique. It is Dominique, isn't it? Young, coltish. No, keep the legs parallel—one pressed against the other. Hold them there for a moment. You must give us a chance to admire them, mustnt you? Then uncross—as before—slowly—"

"Like this?"

"That is fine. You are an actress, Dominique? A real actress?"

"I did another—you know—film—"

"No, no. What I mean, Dominique, is acting a passion with you? Is it your life?"

"I dont think—"

"Do you know who I am?"

"Youre the director."

"Yes, the director. The director, Dominique. That's who I am."

After a while the film stops hissing. Good-bye, she says. She walks past the slaughterhouse—the abasto municipal—where a steer shrieks as his throat is being cut. Her walk is graceful, slow. She wears very high heeled shoes. Her legs are sleek in fine stockings. Indian women squat on the sidewalk before baskets woven of tule. Mastiffs with swinging teats and drooling jaws sniff at her footsteps. Is she aware of any of this? She passes the opera house without a glance. In the opera house a movie is showing. Posters reveal a blonde woman thrown onto her back before brutal men. Her legs, in very high heels and fine stockings, are sprawled apart. One can see white thighs above the stocking tops. A breast has come loose from a torn brassiere. Para adultos, a hand-lettered sign advises. The film is called La Reina de las Vegas. There is no English translation. The brutal men hold their rifles upright, watching the woman sprawled before them. Dominique continues past the opera house, past the mercado with its faces, faces both carved and living, wood and flesh, on through the portales, at last to her hotel. A man awaits her in her room. It is not clear how he got in. They talk for some minutes. The woman seems uncomfortable. She does not look the man in his eyes. He laughs, finally, and gives her a small cellophane packet. She gives him money. He leaves. The door clicks shut. She goes into the bathroom. Her hands are trembling.

3.

He waits in the darkened room, perhaps for hours. The room is rectangular. It measures ten meters by twenty. He sits with his back to one long wall. A camera—the famous Mitchell NC—is in front of him. A door is behind him. The door leads to other rooms in what seems to be a very large building. At last the woman enters from our left. She takes her place. Her stockings hiss as their surfaces pass one over the other. The man, who has been waiting for her in the darkened room, lifts his head.

"You are late."

"Am I?"

"I've waited for hours."

"I didnt realize—"

"Nevertheless I've used the time well. I've been thinking, you see. Sometimes a man must think—in darkness, in solitude. Images come to a man then. Images that have roots, Dominique, roots that stretch backwards into time and outward into space—images that speak, that signify something. Do you know what I am saying?"

"I'm not sure."

"Everyone is waiting, Dominique. Complaining. Have you heard them? Are they whining into your ear?"

"I've not met—"

"Youve not met them yet? My crew of rats? Ghastly people, Dominique. Sometimes I am embarrassed to be in their presence—to be associated with them. Can you imagine wringing a performance from them? Any of them?"

"Is this—what I am doing now—part of the film?"

"Is it? Is the camera running, Dominique? Can you hear it? I am too tired to listen, my dear. I think I'll sit here for a while longer. The solitude soothes me. Noiseless—peaceful. Dont you agree, Dominique?"

The camera stops hissing. Good-bye, she says. She pulls down her skirt, which has ridden up her thighs. Her stockings wrinkle a little at the knee. Her walk is stately, as graceful as that of any young hoofed animal. She passes the bridge, the abasto municipal, the opera house where a line of men has formed. The men watch her, surreptitiously. Indian women turn to each other as she passes. Their eyes, their mouths become suddenly mobile. What secrets do they pass to each other? Men whisper into her right ear. The warm breath is not unpleasant, surely. Yet she does not turn, does not acknowledge their presence. She goes to her room. After a moment there is a discreet knock. A small, dark man enters. He is almost breathless, as though he has run up a flight of stairs. His breath hisses between his teeth. He seems close to panic. "Come in, then," the woman says. The man's eyes roll. "Digame?" he squeaks. She unfastens his belt buckle. His uncircumcised penis, like a dark tuber, lies lax against his thigh. "Youre so hairless," she says, as though surprised. She takes his organ in her mouth. Then she pulls him to the bed. She still wears her stockings, but her groin is bare, as hairless as his. When he stands back up—only seconds have passed—she holds out her hand. "Fifty thousand," she says. He stares at her in terror. He jerks his pants back on. He seems ready to run. "He told you fifty thousand, didnt he? You have it with you?" "Mande?" he squeaks. "Digame?" But he pulls from a pocket a soiled fifty thousand peso note. He looks around, wildly. "Here," she says, holding out her hand. The man drops the note and flees. Without looking at it—the bill lies dark and lax on the floor—she goes to the bathroom. Her one good eye is as hooded, as secretive, as blank as the other.

4.

She enters from the left, as ordered. Light springs with a feral eagerness across the room, which has been kept darkened for days. She turns to the side one foot clad in a very high-heeled shoe. Its shadow, cast forward by the sun low to the horizon, exaggerates the preternatural length and slenderness of this heel. There is no response, however, from within the room. At last she continues inside. The door swings shut behind her. For a moment she is invisible in the room suddenly black. Then she pulls at the heavy drapes which all this time have hung across the windowed doors behind her throne. An amber light spreads across the room, as thick and slow as molasses. She stares outside, at the lake, the docks, the incomplete construction with its clutter of wood and adobe. It is now possible—while she is thus engaged—to examine in more detail the room which hitherto has been kept darkened. Tapestries hang on the walls, their origins lost in the dim heights where the walls join the ceiling. Elsewhere hang wooden masks—faces crawling with lizards, two faces sharing three eyes, beards which descend into coiling ser-pents—and the famous mer-men of the lake district, each four or five feet in length: fish tails, scaly and finned, linked to the torsos of swimming men with protruding, feverish eyes and moveable arms. These mer-men, called sirenos, are carved from wood by a village's most adept craftsman, then painted by a bruja, or witch, using dyes from flowers, bark, and insects only. The fishtail and the man-torso are separated so that a woman can suspend the carving from her waist—thus the tail behind, the torso before—and, reaching forward, manipulate the arms to mimic swimming. Only women are allowed to wear these mer-men. Worn ritually during a waxing moon, they guarantee a woman's fertility. Men are not allowed to watch this unless they are covered by zapote leaves and their faces smeared with ochre clay. More items in this room will be described later. Dominique remains at the glassed doors—their ornate frames date from the 17th century—until she hears a noise behind her.

She turns slowly, leading with her head, then her shoulders, her hips following as she swivels on the toes of her high-heeled shoes. The gesture is rather affected, but undeniably graceful. Standing at the doorway—the doorway behind the camera, where the man usually sits—is a low, lumpish figure, scarcely visible in this amber light. After a silent moment—perhaps a cloud moves from before the sun—the light intensifies, and shifts from true amber to something rather more yellow. The lumpish shape thus becomes more defined. Perhaps aware of this—aware she is no longer hidden—the figure moves forward, exhibiting an odd, bouncing motion of her head, which is slung forward. Her shoulders are round. Her lower jaw extends beyond her upper lips. She looks rather like a hyena. The skin of her face is downy and mottled.

"My dear," this woman says. "You are early."

"But I thought I was late again."

"Not at all. I am quite certain of the time."

"Yesterday I was late—"

"So we heard. Endlessly, it seemed. Dominique, is it not?"

"Yes—"

"And tell me, my dear. Are you a domina*tor*—or a domina*tee*?"

"What?"

The woman brays suddenly with laughter.

5.

She walks in blackness to the window, whose heavy drapes she swings aside. A light, as thick and heavy as molasses, spreads through the room. We see sirenos, faces crawling with lizards, tapestries hanging from a ceiling too high to discern. A woman—she looks like a hyena—enters. The two of them talk. The woman brays suddenly with laughter. Her spittle flashes like a spray of tiny jewels in this amber light. It seems she wears jewelry everywhere. There are rings on each yellow finger, sometimes more than one, earrings dangling from earrings, rings in the flanges of her nose. We can identify jasper and sapphire, chalcedony and emerald, sardonyx, sardus, and chrysolite, fine beryl and topaz. Chrysoprase, jacinth, and amethyst are woven into her orange hair. Her fingers have long nails, lacquered green. Rubies, or perhaps garnets, are glued there. Her open toed pumps are festooned with tiny diamonds. Many of these jewels are coarsely faceted. There are gold chains and silver filigree dangling from each lobe, from each orifice. In the amber glow there is a nimbus of light surrounding her. Dominique retreats a step: the woman's breath, emerging hissing from between yellow stubs of teeth, is foul. They go through another door—this on the wall to our right, opposite the entrance—with the woman's hand grasping Dominique's elbow. In the next room hang racks of dresses, skirts, blouses, wraps, slips, half slips, camisoles, corsets, garter belts, and brassieres, some with their cups torn. Many are fine, delicate, edged with Belgium lace. In drawers are stockings, stoles, gloves, hats, some of them veiled, plus ribbons and costume jewelry. Shoes in their original boxes—we recognize Spanish and Italian brand names—are stacked on shelves. An iron chandelier dangles from the ceiling, which has trompe l'oeil scallops painted on it. There is yellow electrical light everywhere. Dominique is ordered to disrobe. This she does with an affected diffidence. She wears a twilight colored dress with buttons up its front. She steps out of it, and hangs the dress over a chair. The woman stares at her, grinning. No one could avoid pleasure in the sight of such a fine, slender animal, still clad in her high-heeled shoes, her legs sheathed in stockings, breasts contained in an underwired bit of lace, the bare mons nearly revealed through a thin wisp of silk. Her diffidence, under the woman's stare, begins to desert her. A flush spreads down her neck. She shifts her weight from one stiletto heel to the other. At that moment a door opens. A man steps into the room. A cigarette dangles from his lips, which are thin, wet, and surprisingly red.

"Dont turn your back to her, my dear. I warn you—our Sheba is prone to attack."

"Our Sheba?"

"Hasnt she introduced herself? You must be Dominique, our lurid starlet. Dominique, meet Sheba. And I am your co-star. Garred, my dear."

His cigarette wobbles as he speaks. His face has the rubbery look of a drunk. His cheeks are highly colored. He reaches over and hooks one finger under the elastic stretching from Dominique's garter belt to her stocking.

"A nice bit of crumpet, wouldnt you say, Sheba? Are we going to vie for her affections, you and I?"

She barks.

"Garred!" she says. "What a nice surprise. But wouldn't you say she is too old for you? And the wrong sex as well?"

"Arent we all, Sheba?"

"Have you a bottle with you?"

"Have you glasses?"

"The finest crystal, of course, dear Garred."

"Then shall we party? Dominique? Have you developed yet a taste for our Mexican brandy? A fine, burning liquid, Dominique, well suited to our cool evenings—"

"I dont feel so well—"

"Not so well? She hasnt started fondling you, has she? Sheba, that's enough to turn anyone's stomach."

"Better turn her stomach than her arse."

"Is that your preferred aperture these days?"

"Have you become discriminatory?"

"Any port in a storm—that's our song, isn't it?"

"It's your melody, I believe."

"Melody, malady—are you paying attention, Dominique?"

"No, really—I dont feel well—"

"She's not well, Sheba."

"She does seem pale, Garred."

"Can we do this—another time? Tomorrow?"

"Can we, Sheba?"

"Are you in a hurry, Garred? Certainly our director isnt."

"We are learning, Sheba and I, the fine art of intemperate dalliance, the inconclusive meanderings of day after day, of mañana, Dominique, we have all become infected with mañana—"

Garred peels his cigarette butt from his wet lips, looks at it a moment, then drops it onto the tiled floor. Good-bye, Dominique says. She walks over the bridge, past the slaughterhouse where hoarse cries reverberate, past the opera house, whose lights are now blazing, through the portales, to her hotel. Three men, small and dark, wait outside her room. There is a fine layer of moisture on Dominique's pale face, rather like the dew one finds in the morning on a white flower newly opened. There is an agitation about her that is only partially concealed. Her face, normally so fine, seems swollen. Her neck has thickened. Is this possible? Perhaps it is a trick of the light, the dim light in this hotel corridor. The three men waiting for her are dressed in what is clearly their best clothes: suit jackets bare at the elbows but recently brushed, white shirts only somewhat dingy with age, and shoes polished to a mirror shine. Just a minute, she says to them as she fumbles for her key. The men twitter and sing at each other. They move restlessly together. No, no, she says as one tries to follow her into the room, just a minute—un minuto—momento—just one minute. Their black hair has been greased back from foreheads, their faces scrubbed. Their skin is so smooth, so fresh, their cheeks so plump, it is impossible to guess their ages. Dominique shuts the door. Her hands are trembling. She hurries into her bathroom.

6.

She enters from the left, as ordered. Light springs with a feral eagerness across the room. Yet the woman seems a willing participant in this charade. It is she who slides back the latch, rotating a knob counterclockwise. As the door parts—it swings easily on its three brass hinges—the light leaps forward like a hunting animal eagerly released. It leaps across a quartz lamp on a tripod, across the chair we call the throne, and nearly to the distant wall, twenty meters away. The woman herself, as well as her shadow, lies entirely within this rectangle of light. She turns one foot to the side—the shadow of her stiletto heel is preternaturally lengthened, etc.—and moves forward with the grace of a young hoofed animal only when the quartz light is itself turned on, a kind of signal, perhaps, a cue already agreed upon. The door meanwhile shuts behind her, the latch springing closed with an audible click. For a moment she is in darkness. Then she sits on the throne, which is shaped—have we said this before?—as a giant lizard. Its hind legs form the "arms" of the chair. The head looms, lowers above, jaw partly open, eyes exophthalmic, hooded. This chair has been constructed—at some expense, we understand—by a craftsman imported specifically for this task, using papier-mâché mash laid layer upon layer over an existing wooden frame. This papier-mâché has been left roughly textured and gray, giving the illusion of stone, perhaps granite or oxidized limestone. Sitting in this chair exaggerates the palpable humanness—the warm fleshfulness—of the woman. This humanness beneath the overtly reptilian face, this fleshfulness enclosed entirely within reptilian legs, makes her appear not so much regal, we are afraid, as vulnerable. This is so even when she moves, lifting one leg—her right—over the other, her left, with a grace that is truly exquisite. No one, surely, faced with such a vision, could avoid a stir of pleasure—

The camera hisses. The woman is shadowed, not revealed, by the lighting. At last the director speaks. It is a man's voice which answers his.

"What do you think, Fetters?"

"If I knew what you were after here—"

"I'm after beauty, Fetters. Grace."

"Yes—yes, of course, I can see that. But as a technical matter—"

"Is there something technical here?"

"I mean as a matter of plot—to justify, you see, this scene—"

"Didnt you notice the way the light sprang across the room? Wasnt it like a leopard? A cat? Something wild, Fetters, something leaping free, something even ominous, threatening? And to have this figure back-lit—"

"Yes, of course—"

"She is luminous, dont you agree?"

"Surely. But plotwise—"

"What do you think, Dominique?"

"What?"

"No, dont stop moving your legs. Tell us, Dominique, what do you think, plotwise?"

"I'm not sure—"

"Really, John," says the man called Fetters. "I dont think—"

"You dont think she should have a voice? She's playing the role, after all—inhabiting it, so to speak—"

"I suppose if one's conception—"

"Tell us, Dominique—tell us what you are feeling—at this moment—"

"My feelings?"

"Your feelings."

"I dont know that I have—"

"Ah, Dominique. Feelings—if only we knew our own feelings—"

The hissing stops. A light moves slowly across the room, turning everything yellow. The air seems turgid, thickened. The two men greet Dominique. One, the younger, is blond, wearing khaki pants and shirt. The other, Osgood Fetters, is grayed, stooping. They stand close to Dominique, whose face is averted. Finally they shake hands, each with the other. It is a clumsy ritual. Good-bye, Dominique says. She leaves. After a moment the blond man in khaki follows. He remains a discreet distance behind her as she passes over the bridge, passes the abasto municipal—a sudden gush of blood washes down a concrete trough into the stream below—and the opera house where the man stops, briefly, to rearrange the tilt of the poster advertising his film. The woman strolls, with a liquid ease that is almost painful to watch, through the mercado, past piles of tortillas presided over by Indian women who squat like turnips, past chayotes, spined and not, past limp bundles of lechuga, glossy ciruelos, papayas sliced open to reveal their pink flesh, past pigs' feet stuffed into jars, past raw pig faces—their brains like coiled intestines—stacked in rows, past plucked chickens hanging from hooks and stalls where chorizo steams in liquid fat. All this time she is wearing her high, stiletto heels. Her legs are lean, sheathed in fine nylon. Her dress is the color of twilight. Blonde hair falls across the left side of her face, hiding—only partially—the limp eye, the parchment skin, the gnarl of cartilage left of the ear, the scar that extends her mouth into her throat. The man in khaki watches all of this. He watches men lean towards her and whisper words into her right ear. He watches the Indian women suddenly look at each other, their mouths and eyes becoming mobile. He follows her to the entrance of her hotel. A man awaits her. The man is unshaven. He has the surly face of a drunk. He takes her arm, a bit roughly. The woman does not look at him. After a while she gives him something, perhaps a sheath of bills. Others watch, also. Small Indian men in their best clothes—their eyes seem liquid—turn to each other and twitter and sing in their own language. The woman goes into the hotel. The unshaven man remains a moment at the entrance, hands thrust into his pockets. When he leaves, the Indian men—there are twelve of them—file silently into the hotel. Our man, dressed in khaki, watches all of this. A light rain begins to fall.

7.

It is morning. A thin sun has risen in the east. Dominique thrashes on her bed. Elsewhere smoke from chimneys settles on tile roofs. A church bell tolls. Owls hide in trees, lizards in bushes. Wagons pulled by men wheel into the mercado. Carcasses are unloaded, fruit and vegetables. In her bed Dominique's face looks sour. Has the disfigured part grown larger? This does not seem likely. Yet the right side of her face this morning is not pretty. Has she thickened, become swollen during her sleep? What dreams has she experienced? When at last she rises, she rises like an old woman. Naked she goes to the bathroom. Even her legs look swollen, shapeless. Her hair has been scattered like straw, like chaff. In the bathroom she boils a bead of brown heroin in water, using a cigarette lighter held beneath a spoon. Occasionally she shakes, a tremor that extends down her whole body. She holds the spoon with difficulty. When the water suddenly boils, spreading the brown heroin evenly through it, liquefying it, she puts a shred from a cotton ball into the spoon. Into this cotton she inserts the silver needle of her hypodermic. The brown liquid draws up into the plastic barrel. All this time buses and taxis pass outside. High revving engines howl. Somewhere, monotonously, a man bangs with a hammer at a piece of metal. Is the sunlight always this thin? this gray? this cheerless? A woman laughs beneath Dominique's window. Yet it is a sour laugh, a laugh without mirth, even vicious. In the bathroom Dominique is leaving blood everywhere. She cannot find a vein. Has the needle dulled at last? Are her hands shaking too severely? The needle slides into one ankle, then the other. Blood flows down her feet, onto the floor. The needle slides beneath the skin, but fails to penetrate the vein whose surface is hardened, scarred. She tries one arm, then the other. She spins her arm round and round, driving the blood into the metacarpal tunnel of her wrist. Blood flies from her wounds to the ceiling, to spot the walls in front and behind, to scatter like precious jewels onto the tiled floor. She wraps a scarf around her forearm. The needle seeks, slides, skips. She is sweating now, and breathing harshly. Her breath rales in her throat. Yet her determination is absolute. Her intentness is complete. At last the needle penetrates. Blood rises into the hypodermic, mixing with the brown heroin-water in the plastic barrel. She makes a soft noise of pleasure. Her head nods forward. Her shoulders relax. She presses the plunger.

Sleek, serene, she emerges from her hotel. Almost immediately the man called Fetters—gray, thin, slightly bent—takes her arm. He has been sent, he says, to lead her to the set being constructed at the lake's edge. Dominique's arm, in his grasp, is limp. Fetters smiles and nods as he explains his mission.

"I need some coffee," Dominique says.

"The coffee here is terrible."

"Just something to drink—"

"Have you tried the tea? At least the tea is tolerable."

"The tea?"

"Herb teas—chamomile, manzana. The water's usually tepid but the tea—"

"No," she says, "I need coffee."

The coffee comes, thick and strong. She gulps it, holding the cup with two hands. Her lipstick leaves a red bruise on the cup's rim.

"I must apologize," Fetters says, "for our director."

"Apologize?"

"I know you were expecting something more professional. I must say Ive never seen him so dilatory."

"I dont think—"

"Ive worked with him before, you know. Of course youve heard what happened to him. Perhaps that's an excuse—"

"Something happened to him?"

"Well, yes. He was taken off his last film. Surely youve heard the gossip—"

"No."

"Well. Well, I suppose that's neither here nor there. The point is we've all had misconceptions. I know Sheba is alarmed. It's mostly her money, you see—"

"Sheba?"

"Yes. Sheba Makeda. A rich Ethiopian woman. Youve met her, surely."

"Oh, yes."

"She invested in some of his other films—his early ones, I believe. The two that made money. Well, you know what Hollywood's like—"

"Yes," she says. "I'm ready now."

Fetters digs quickly into a pocket for change. Here, he says, waving his free hand at her, let me. Dominique does not stir as Fetters pulls from three different pockets coins and loose bills and inspects each one. Yes, yes, he says, here we are, this damned money—cant get used to it. He leaves copper and silver on the green tablecloth. Dominique rises with her usual willowy grace. They walk past the mercado, past the opera house, past the abattoir, over the bridge. Beneath the bridge blackish water flows over and around piles of trash. Paper, plastic and cloth hang on the weeds and spiny bushes above the water level. A black carcass—is it a dog's?—is wedged against a branch. Water eddies along its spine, nudging it. At this bridge the air smells of decaying flesh and decomposing sewage. Fetters wrinkles his nose. "I must say," he says, "you seem to have inspired him." "Him?" "Yes, our director. Since you arrived he's actually become animated—more like his old self. For the first time I'm hopeful—really hopeful—that something—er—finally will get done, you see." Fetters suddenly makes a little skip and hop. "Well," he says, "that is, I suppose this isnt exactly your finest—er—role—" But she ignores him. Fetters takes her arm again. "Here," he says, "to our left." They descend into Las Vegas.

8.

She makes a soft noise of pleasure. She withdraws the needle. Is it morning? A thin sun has risen in the east. Has morning always been this sour? this cheerless? this gray? A woman laughs beneath the window. There is nothing pleasant in this laugh, which reverberates as harshly as the cry of a crow. Dominique enters the shower. She pulls plastic curtains around her. We hear the water turn on. Steam rises. All this time buses snap and snarl outside, climbing the cobbled streets. A policeman blows a whistle. In front of the hotel paces Osgood Fetters. He has been up since dawn. Occasionally he glances at the façade of the hotel, and then checks his watch. Small Indian men watch him. Their eyes are liquid. Within the hotel Dominique steps at last from the bathroom. Wet hair falls around her face. She is fresh and clean. She looks like a child. She has a child's face, scrubbed and shining. She sits at a table. She leans into a mirror. Creams and powders are applied. Later we will name some of these potions, and describe their colors, their textures, their aromas, and the effect each has on her face. At last the face we remember emerges. Hair is dried. The left side of her face—the gruesomely beautiful side of her face—is half hidden by the hair. A black garter belt is attached around the small waist. Legs are sheathed in fine stockings. Each breast is placed in the lace cup of a brassiere. She puts on a dress that is the color of twilight. Sleek, serene, she emerges from the hotel. She meets Fetters. She insists on coffee. Her red lips bruise the rim of the cup. "I must apologize," Fetters says, "for our director. Surely you've heard the gossip. Only his first two films made money. Well, you know Hollywood—" They pass down the street. He takes her arm. They descend into Las Vegas. The director is there. Workmen are gathered around him, unloading a truck. These are small, dark Indians. John, the director, has plans unfolded before him. He points right or left as items come off the truck. When he sees Fetters and Dominique he sticks a pencil behind his ear and folds the plans. Other Indian men, holding hammers and saws, stop their work to stare at Dominique.

The director makes a sudden gesture as they approach.

"All realities are creations, are they not, Dominique?"

"Realities?"

"It is my conceit, of course, that as an artist I can create worlds."

"Come, come," says Fetters. "Surely—"

"I am not speaking metaphorically, my dear Dominique."

"You arent?"

"Fetters would have us believe that reality is a given. Something received, equally, by all of us. Isnt that so, Fetters?"

"Clearly it is not possible to argue—"

"Yet it is all lies. Lies, you see. And my lie—which you see being enacted around us—is just as real as anyone else's lie. Even God's."

"Reducto ad absurdum," says Fetters. "Your argument achieves success only within its own definitions."

"My definitions are the ones that matter, since they are the ones which form my own life."

"What are those?" Dominique asks, pointing.

"Slot machines, my dear. Well, Fetters would say not real slot machines. They are made of wood and papier-mâché, of course. By Indians in our local villages, and painted using dyes from insects and flowers. Yet they are real, are they not? Solid? They are genuinely something, arent they? If I call them slot machines—and it is my right to label them, isnt it?—how can anyone argue with me?"

"Do they work?"

"Work?"

"If you pull—"

"Ah, they work, Dominique. In the context of my film—they work."

Men with liquid eyes carry the slot machines past our group of three people. Each machine is slightly different from the next. That is, they are each approximately the same size and shape. Each has a lever emerging from its right side. Each is painted, mostly in muted shades, reds and yellows, some greens. The differences require a second or third look. Some have lizards crawling up them. Others have faces—some wounded, some smiling, some obviously dead—staring out from the carved wood and papier-mâché sides. Each slot machine, shouldered by a small Indian man, is carried across the open space where stand our three figures, past a stone fountain, and into a building to our left. This building is the casino. It is called—by light bulbs in different colors spelling out the name—The Quetzal Quesino. Come, the director says, to Dominique but perhaps including Fetters. He takes the woman's arm, which lies limply in his grasp. May I show you the reality in which you will perform? They start across the open space, Fetters trailing in their wake.

9.

The director is forty years old. His name is John. He stands six feet
tall in his leather shoes. Every day he wears a khaki shirt. Often a bandana
is tied around his neck; sometimes, perhaps as a talisman, around his
wrist. He is clean shaven and blond haired. When he is excited he looks
mischievous, the way a child will look doing something forbidden. At
other times his face sags. His eyes twist one way, then another. At these
times he moves, if he moves at all, without direction. We have seen him
sit for hours in darkened rooms. He will toy with his cameras. He racks
his Mitchell NC open. He slides the tips of his fingers over its metal
surfaces. He stares at the inverted image in the ground glass screen. The
camera hisses when he turns it on. Is it focused on anything? on nothing?
on infinity? It cannot be clear to him—nor to us—the direction he wishes
to go. Yet he is capable at times of moving in complete darkness with a
certain ease. At such times there is real grace to his movements. Within
the Quetzal Quesino his eyes shine. He appears even happy as he stares
around at what he has created. He moves easily between the banks of slot
machines—muted reds, yellows, greens—which are still somewhat askew.
He shows Dominique and Fetters the blackjack pit and the craps pit.
Both are mere tableless depressions. Only the poker pit has a few chairs.
The baccarat room is unoccupied. The roulette table has not yet been
placed, only its position marked. The keno corner, however, is complete,
with its glass box full of ping pong balls numbered from one to eighty and
its own bartender, a small, dark man industriously wiping with a white
towel the highball glasses which he then sets in a row behind him. He
nods at the threesome, as a good bartender would. The director, however, leads Dominique and Fetters to the lobby, which at this point is no
more than a bare desk and a rank of cubbyholes. Mounted on the wall
above these cubbyholes is the statue of la Virgin de la Salud. Dominique,
her mouth agape, stares up at this resplendent figure.

"Yes," says the director. "She is quite a sight, isnt she?"

"Who is she?"

"The Indians refused to work without her. She's made of something called pasta de cana—whatever that is. Corn meal, I believe. Perhaps they baked her in an oven."

"She's eerie."

"Isnt she? Quite properly blessed, too. They took her to the basilica. The priest did something with incense—waved it over her, I suppose."

"The Indians," says Fetters—he sounds as if he is apologizing—"are really quite superstitious here. One tries—"

"Perhaps they are merely more perceptive than we, Fetters."

"Who made her gown?" says Dominique.

"Nuns, I understand. Perhaps Indians—perhaps meztizos—"

"I cant tell," Dominique says breathlessly, "if she is alive or dead."

The Virgin looks down and says nothing. Her hooded eyes are focused elsewhere, distantly, perhaps millennia away. Her face is very white. Her lips are rouged. Her corona is gold and red. Her resplendor is arranged in two concentric circles behind her head. Her manto sagrado is blue. It is embroidered with gold. Her vestido is white embroidered with gold. The manto trails behind her. The embroidery, we understand, is done by hand by Carmalitos Descalzos—both Indian and meztizo—who never leave their convent attached to the basilica. Their lives are as circumscribed by their faith as are the lives of all of us. The Virgin's hands are pressed together. They hold a gold sceptro. There are pearls around her wrists and arranged in masses around her neck. Each finger has a ring. A media luna dangles from each ear. A large media luna is at her invisible feet. The gowns—the vestido and manto sagrado—spread widely, right and left. She looks down on the three people below and says nothing. The director nods. He leads them to stairs which rise, gently curving to the right. He opens a door. Its latch, though well coiled, clicks loudly. He gestures. "Your apartment, madam," he says. They enter—

10.

They enter from the left, as expected. Light springs with a feral eagerness across the room. The woman stands a moment silhouetted, the thrown shadow of her heel exaggerating its preternatural length. The shoes are black patent. The dress is the color of twilight. The legs are sheathed. The room they stand within is rectangular, perhaps ten meters wide by twenty long. At once an amber glow begins to spread through the room. Tapestries hang from the ceiling. Masks carved from the copalillo tree and painted using dyes obtained from insects and plants adorn the walls. A sireno hangs in the corner, waiting to be used. Chairs are ornate, weighty. One is formed in the shape of a giant lizard, its legs providing the chair's arms, etc. The lizard eyes are exophthalmic, hooded. The amber light luminesces around our three figures, the director dressed in khaki, the grayed Osgood Fetters, the fulgent woman who spins slowly on her stiletto heels—her gaze is hooded, although only one eye, the left, is exophthalmic—as she appraises the room which surrounds her, appraises its masks, its tapestries, its paintings murky with age in their gilt frames: the enthorned Christ, his blood black on his forehead, St Augustine embattled with demons, odalesques lucent as pearls, miraculous women rising from a black sea. The light does not reach to the fuliginous ceiling, which, we understand, is painted with trompe l'oeil scallops. A wind hisses at the windowed doors—their frames date from the 17th century—overlooking a parapet and the hyperentrophic lake below. This hissing, for some seconds, is the only sound audible in the room. Then the woman, whose pale hand—holding a sheath of paper— has lifted in some obscure gesture, speaks:

"What is the film about?"

"Havent you been told?"

"Only that it was rated X."

"Not just X—triple X. Pornographic."

"Will I have to—you know—"

"Nothing in this film is simulated."

She sucks in her breath. He says:

"We'll be filming from above, through a special mirror. Imagine a small, dark man lying spread-eagled on top of you, rather like a lizard, your white throat exposed to his teeth—"

"A lizard?"

"Dont you think men look like lizards? Seen from above, I mean? Have you noticed the lizards here? They bake on the walls, in the sun. They rise and fall on their legs, like a man doing push-ups. When I approach they scurry into bushes, into crevices. Some have opalescent collars. Their necks seem to glow, all purple and green. I'm sure it's because theyre in heat, if theyre female. Or displaying—eh?—if theyre male."

"In another film I did it. I mean, once—"

"In front of the camera?"

"It wasnt simulated."

"One draws inspiration from nature, Dominique. Yesterday an Indian woman tried to sell me a catfish from the lake. It had two heads. Very valuable, she said. Perhaps it was. I didnt buy it."

"A catfish?"

"I hear other stories. Calves born deformed—pigs with an extra set of legs. The animals graze alongside the lake, and the lake, you see, is the town's sewer—the town's cess-pool. You can see how black it is. Freakish things emerge from it. And the lake is also the town's water supply. A nicely closed system, wouldnt you say? You drink your own excrement. No, dont look so alarmed, my dear. You have bottled water to drink. We dont want you catching typhoid, do we?"

"I dont think I feel—"

"On warm days there is a miasma, a haze lifting off the water."

"I dont feel well."

"You seem pale, Dominique. Why dont you sit down? Cross your legs, one over the other. Yes, slowly. And when you lower the leg, slide it. I want to hear your stockings—hissing—"

"Like this?"

"Do you dream, Dominique? At night, I mean. Nocturnal dreams."

"I dont know—"

"Tell me your dreams, Dominique. You inhabit them, you see—just as you will inhabit this film. You will live here, within it. Trust me, Dominique. My film will rise around you like the miasma rising off the lake—"

Film hisses through the Mitchell NC camera. The camera retreats. After a moment Fetters becomes visible sitting to our left. He looks avuncular, perhaps priestly. He nods his head and applauds by tapping the fingers of one hand into the palm of the other. Good-bye, Dominique says, putting down the script. She rises with her usual liquid grace. She pulls at her skirt, which has ridden up her thighs. Pressed against the window behind her is visible a yellow face. The skin is mottled, hairy. The eyes seem ochre, like the eyes of an animal glimpsed at night in the glare of headlights. Dominique descends the curving staircase. Her hands float at her sides. She is exquisitely balanced. In the lobby la Virgin de la Salud watches as Dominique walks with the grace of a young hoofed animal out the open doors of the Quetzal Quesino. She passes the abasto municipal, where a steer bellows as it resists its death. She passes the opera house, where a man in a khaki shirt adjusts the poster of his movie. In the mercado, squatting like turnips in front of the slitted carcasses of papayas, Indian women hiss at each other in a language impossible to decipher. Men whisper into Dominique's right ear. They whisper entreaties, invitations, proposals. No one could avoid pleasure at the sight of such a splendid animal, her legs sheathed in nylon, her feet shod in stiletto heels of preternatural length, her dress the same color as the twilight which descends each evening over the black lake. She continues through the portales, past the ruins of the Hotel del Lago—coarse blossoms reach out from the rubbled interior—and at last to the doorway of her own hotel. Yet her face is already damp. Are tremors visible in her hands? At the doorway waits an unshaven man with the rubbery face of the habitual drunk. He takes Dominique's arm in a grasp which seems excessively tight. She averts her head but makes no move to evade him. Instead she digs into a purse for a sheath of bills. He grins, and slips her a cellophane packet containing something moist, brown, waxy. Indian men in their best clothes watch this transaction. More wait upstairs, in the corridor outside Dominique's room. They mill about, a crowd of them. Their eyes are liquid. They move aside to make a passage for Dominique. They twitter and hum. Their voices vibrate. "No, no," Dominique says, struggling to fit her key into the door. There must be thirty of the men, with more coming up the stairs. "No," she says, "you don't understand, I cant." The door at last swings open on its three brass hinges. A shaft of light leaps into the darkness with the eagerness of a hunting animal suddenly released. "I'm not ready," Dominique cries. The men twitter and moan. Restlessly, restlessly, they mill around her. "No, no, I cant—you have to wait—I'm not ready—" Drapes are pulled back as the door swings shut with an audible click. At once amber light spreads as heavy and slow as molasses through the rectangular room. A hissing noise is audible, perhaps a wind whistling through the cracks in the windowed doors, perhaps the combined intakes of breath of the thirty men, fifty men, hissing in the corridor outside her room. "Not yet," she says, one last time. "No—I'm not ready—" She hurries into the bathroom.

PART II
HEROIN DREAMS

I.

She lives (she dreams) in Las Vegas. She lives in an apartment. She can look down at a casino, whose lights keep blinking, and beyond the casino to a lake. The lake is black. Her lips curl cynically. She understands there are no lakes in Las Vegas. Las Vegas is a dry desert town. Its casinos look like temples, but there are no lakes, no rivers, no streams. Nevertheless this lake has black water in it. Speedboats race back and forth, pulling water-skiers. The water-skiers—they are all drunk on Budweiser—shout at each other and raise their fists. The water bubbles and froths behind them, creating criss-crossing lines. She, however, is trying to fix Dilaudid. The Dilaudid is crumbled into a spoon with distilled water. She seems to be holding a match beneath it. Is there a flame? The air itself is so hot and dry that no flame is visible. Yet the matchstick is slowly turning black. Why is she heating Dilaudid? The Dilaudid will not melt. It is synthetic morphine, made in a factory. It is orange, the same color as orange-flavored Kool Aid. The syringe is a U-100 disposable syringe. It has an orange cap. She recognizes it. Is the orange cap on the syringe significant? Is the orange supposed to be bright and happy, like the bright and happy Dilaudid? Why isnt she bright and happy, fixing Kool Aid Dilaudid in an orange-capped syringe? The grains of synthetic morphine bounce around in the spoon as the water boils. Yet they will not dissolve. They are as hard as glass. With alarm she notices that she is beginning to breath heavily. A beam of light falls on her. She can feel it. Is she bright? is she pretty? is she sweet? Hiss-hiss-hiss, she breathes as the light falls on her, a light as fierce as a leaping animal. She does not want to wake up. She does not want—

"But you wake up?"

"I always wake up."

"What do you do then?"

"You know—get my stuff out—"

"Heroin?"

"Yes."

"Not Dilaudid?"

"Well—in Vegas heroin was sometimes hard to find."

"So then youd use—"

"Anything. Dilaudid. Coke. Valium. I'd shoot Quaaludes."

"The coke too?"

"Sure."

"Why not snort it?"

"I guess I like the needle."

"I see," he says. "The needle," he repeats. He taps his pen on his knee. Soon he leaves. Outside the sun is thin. He pulls his coat tighter around him. At the opera house he stares critically at a poster advertising a film. The poster hangs in a wooden frame from a single nail driven into the adobe wall. He adjusts the poster's tilt. La Reina de las Vegas, the poster says. There is no English translation. Men holding weapons stare at a fallen woman. We recognize Kalashnikovs and Uzis, brutal steel machines held upright. Are the men guarding her? threatening her? The poster is deliberately ambiguous. Our man, however, seems pleased. He shifts slightly the brace holding the Arriflex IIC camera. Looking through the eyepiece he advances up the street and through the mercado. By now the mercado is nearly deserted. A wind swirls dust and scraps of paper around his feet and the feet of the few Indian women who squat, shaped like turnips, at their piles of tortillas and ciruelos. No one says anything to him. He continues into the fallen courtyard of the Hotel del Lago where a woman lies, legs sprawled apart, half hidden by coarse yellow and red blossoms. Her bare flesh is as pale as death, as pale as the death she portrays. Her face apparently has been flayed, or perhaps burned with acid. The ear is a gnarl of cartilage. The one eye exposed to us—blonde hair has blown like chaff around the face—is blank, milky, protuding slightly from its scarred socket. The mouth appears slit as far as her throat. The only sounds audible as the man stands there are the hoarse cries of a distant bird and the sibilant hissing, hissing of film racing through the Arriflex camera at 24 frames per second.

2.

She lives (she dreams) in Las Vegas. This is a dry city in the American desert. Nevertheless visible from her window is a black lake. Water-skiers—they are all drunk on Budweiser—criss-cross the lake behind speedboats, shouting curses at each other. Meanwhile she is melting heroin. Meanwhile someone is pounding on her door. Perhaps it is her lover, drunk again. She does not dare let him in. Cant he even wait until her heroin boils? He is always pounding on her door. Last night he tried to cut her head off. He knelt on top of her and put the blade of a kitchen knife at her throat. He was going to cut her head off because he believed another man—a man he didn't send—was fucking her. He was right. Men were always fucking her. Sometimes they paid her, sometimes they didnt. Sometimes there were more than one. They had penises like dead lizards—like the white bellies of dead lizards. They expected her to take these dead lizards into her mouth, into her anus, into her vagina. They were not satisfied until they had penetrated every orifice. The scales of the dead lizards hurt her. The lizard-men wrestled her beneath the shadows that they threw onto the walls. Sometimes they brought animals to her. Did they want her to bless them? No, she said, not the donkey. Its member unfurled, long and dark. Give me a lion, she said. Are there no lions? There were never any lions. Her lover bangs at her door. "I want to leave," she says. "I feel so trapped," she says—

"Are you trapped?"

"I dont know. I guess."

"You guess? Are there walls around you? Cant you turn right—turn left?"

"It doesnt seem to matter—"

"You dont care where you go? What happens to you?"

"I guess once I cared."

"Once? When?"

"I dont remember."

"Do you like your lover?"

"No."

"Why dont you leave him?"

"He keeps coming back."

"Is he your pimp?"

"Well—he sends—you know—his friends—"

"His friends?"

"We go to bars—he'll pick out—"

"He'll pick out men for you to sleep with?"

"He likes to watch."

"I see," he says. "He likes to watch," he repeats. He puts his pen back in his pocket. He looks at his scribbled notes. Finally he leaves.

The sunlight is thin. A wind swirls in the street. Dust and scraps of paper flutter about. He is forty years old. He is the director of a pornographic movie. He carries, attached to a body brace, an Arriflex IIC camera. This modern camera, manufactured by Arnold and Richter, is considered ideal for location shooting where mobility is important. It may be carried by a single person, especially when wearing a body brace. Unlike the Mitchell NC it utilizes through-the-lens viewing and focusing. Its shutter blades are silvered and set at a 45 degree angle between the lens and the film plane. The blades reflect the scene back through an optical system, including a prism, which magnifies and rightens the image. The image may thus be constantly monitored while filming. This is what allows our director to move up the street with his eye pressed against the viewfinder. He can see precisely where he is going and exactly what he is filming. Occasionally he stops and checks with an incident light meter the strength of the sunlight falling around him. He makes adjustments to the lens opening as necessary. The film hisses as he photographs a gush of blood, including a few soft organs, perhaps bladders, shreds of lung tissue, descending the concrete trough from the abasto municipal. The blood and viscera fall into the stream below, whose waters are red and black. He then continues through the mercado, which is nearly deserted at this hour. A single Indian woman, her head thrown back, is wailing at some real or imagined misfortune. The director photographs dead pigs' feet stuffed into pails. He passes a dangling row of plucked chickens. Butchers in gum boots slice at marbled haunches. He moves slowly, almost stealthily, into the fallen courtyard of the Hotel del Lago. Lying amid the coarse blossoms, half concealed by the rubble of brick and adobe and stone, is a woman. She is naked. She is very white. Clearly she has not been dead long. There are no signs of bloat. Her fine, slender body has not swelled. One can imagine touching her. Each breast is peaked with a small nipple. Her groin is bare, the mons invitingly lifted. Blonde hair is scattered like chaff. Nearby is a woman's shoe with a very high heel. The director moves it slightly, so its shadow is cast exaggerating its preternatural length. The camera hisses for some time, nosing about, right and left, as though searching for clues. This hissing is the only sound audible except for the distant cry of a bird, the muted rumble of buses beyond the portales, and the wail of the Indian woman somewhere in the mercado, her throat exposed as her head is thrown back, her figure scarcely visible now in the thin, waning sunlight falling coolly on our scene.

3.

She lives (she dreams) in an apartment in Las Vegas, a dry city in the American desert. She is lying on a bed. A man is fucking her. Seen from above—has she floated to the ceiling, leaving her body behind?—the man looks like a lizard. He has a long back. His arms and legs are arranged on each side of her body. His teeth are at her throat. He is pumping up and down. His shoes and socks—they are black—are still on his feet, but otherwise he is naked. His body is as thin and white as hers. After a while he rolls off of her. She sees her bare mons. Her slit looks like a wound—a vertical knife wound below the mons. Flaps of skin, still red and moist, fall open on either side of this wound. Close your legs! she hisses at the woman below her. If she closed her legs the wound might not be visible. But the woman does not move. The man has tattoos on his shoulder of lizards crawling through violent shrubbery. When he moves off the bed another man lies on her. She recognizes his back—it is Garred, who is playing her lover. He has been watching all this time. He cannot get into her, however. His penis is soft, like a dead animal. She watches from the ceiling as he puts this dead animal into her mouth. It is the same face—her face—that she sees in the mirror, but subtly altered. It is her face, but it is the face of a stranger. This stranger sucks and pulls at Garred's organ. Then he is on top of her again. Perhaps this time he is inside her. The other man is boiling heroin in a spoon. He is still naked, except for his black shoes and socks. His penis dangles, dripping fluids. Oh, she says, fluttering near the ceiling, let me have some. Oh please, she says, I want it. She watches as her broken face—the broken face on the bed beneath her—turns towards the dark man, who is now sticking a needle into his forearm. I want it, she cries. Oh please, I want it! It is at this moment that she realizes Garred, in his role as her lover, is fucking her in her ass. He has slipped his organ, now extended into a semblance of rigidity, into her asshole. Oh no! she cries. You know I hate that! She watches her face on the bed beneath her while one man fixes into his forearm and the other, laughing at her, fixes into her ass—

"Are you telling me there is a sexual aspect to fixing?"

"What?"

"Are you a Freudian, my dear? A needle—a penis—"

"I don't know what you mean."

"Dont you? How many times do you fix? In a day?"

"It depends. If I have—you know—the stuff—"

"We will imagine you have the stuff."

"Five, six—seven times—"

"That often?"

"If I have it."

"And men?"

"What?"

"How many men—in a day?"

"I dont know what you mean."

"Dont you? How many men would you take? In a day? Five? Six? Seven?"

"No—no, never that many—"

"I see," he says. "Never that many," he repeats. Restlessly he moves about. He examines a wooden mask—a terrified face crawling with lizards. He touches a sireno suspended by a rope from the ceiling. At last he shoulders his camera. He snaps it into the body brace. Good-bye, he says curtly. He leaves.

The sunlight is thin. He passes the abasto municipal, where a steer bellows as its throat is being cut. He seems oddly undirected. He goes up one street, then another. Finally he enters the mercado. Few people are about. Only the dregs of the daily market remain—wormy apples, burnt bolillas. Gap-toothed crones ignore him. Why is he so disoriented? He is a man who has directed five films. Only his first two made money. Well, you know what Hollywood is like. He was taken off his last film. Rumors flew about the event like bees around a hive. He is here making a pornographic film. A director has to direct, after all. A pornographic film, he understands, we understand, requires relatively little in the way of financing. A woman—Sheba Makeda, who claims a kind of queenship in her native country—has provided most of the money. Why not bring a real director to a pornographic film? Who knows what miracles might be manifested? A director of talent, a man of rigor, disciplined and hungry—perhaps even pornography could be turned into a work of art, or at least a work of some merit, some seriousness. "You must follow the formula," Sheba warns him at their meeting. "Yes, of course," he says. "You must have fucking," Sheba says—she has no fear of coarse language—"within the first few minutes. And come shots. At least one helpless woman—one brutal man—" "Of course," says the director, already dreaming. He hires, unseen, a girl from Las Vegas who has made only one film. "I want a Las Vegas girl," he tells Sheba, "someone who has lived in that American city, someone who knows it well. Oh, yes, and someone who has been a prostitute." "A prostitute?" "Of course," he says. "Prostitutes make the best actresses, don't they? Theyre already trained in the falsification of passion." He builds—it takes, naturally, longer than expected, and costs far too much for the verisimilitude he requires—a set in Mexico. The casino he wants is a specific place, a place on the edge of imagination, real yet unreal. "Yes, yes," he says, glowing, "slot machines made by village artisans—thick adobe walls—a black lake that has become a modern sewer—" "Remember," Sheba says, "fucking in the first few minutes—or I pull every penny and sue your ass off." "Fucking," he says. "Of course we will have fucking—" In the courtyard of the Hotel del Lago he finds the body of his star. Clearly she has not been dead long. Her body is still unbloated, unswollen, uncorrupt. A woman's high heeled shoe is nearby. He moves it, so the shadow of its heel—cast by the thin, falling sun—is preternaturally long. A broken hypodermic is half buried in dirt. Scraps of cellophane swirl in the wind. There is dried blood on the woman's wrists, her ankles, the insides of her arms. Her face has been flayed, perhaps burnt with acid or boiling water. Her mouth extends in a crimson gash almost to her throat. A roll of intestines is visible at her side, where a knife, or perhaps the point of a spear, has slipped under her ribs. Yet her bare mons is lifted invitingly. Each breast is tipped in pink. One can imagine, as the camera pans hissing over the body half hidden in coarse flowers, among bricks, adobe, fallen tile, one can imagine a man settling onto this corpse, his passion aroused by this exquisite, fallen grace, this splendid animal brought to earth before her time, whose tragic story demands, surely, the attention of an artist, a real director, someone sensitive, a man of discipline, hungry—yes, fucking, real fucking, morbid fucking if you like—but splendid, Sheba, splendid fucking, artistic fucking—the camera hissing like a hungry snake prowling through the coarse blossoms surrounding her.

4·

She lives (she dreams) in a dry American city. It is called Las Vegas.
Nothing grows there. Everything is piped or trucked across the flat
desert—everything, asphalt and concrete, masonite and Naugahyde,
boxes of saccharined cereal, vials of morphine, gallon jugs of cheap
vodka, tubes of Preparation H, multi-colored vitamin samples for multi-
colored doctors' offices, douche bags as flat and wrinkled as her mother's
tits, spatulate devices of stainless steel, beautiful in their purity, Phillips
Milk of Magnesia, L-tryptophan and Pepto Bismol and Maalox and Fleet
bagenemas with soap packets and Mylanta-II, all arranged in neat rows
on store shelves and in medicine cabinets, all trucked, entrained, piped
into town along with water carefully dosed with chlorine, meat full of
artificial hormones, vegetables waxed and tinted with USDA Red #3 and
Yellow #4, busloads of tourists glowing with artificial innocence, gaping
in synthetic amazement at the blinking lights, at the six-foot tall showgirls
in spangled tights, the great chrome Cadillacs, themselves hauled into
town on giant flatcars—and her, of course, another import. In the dream
the tourists gape at her as she descends the stairs into the casino. She is
searching for her lover, her connection, her cellophane packet of moist
brown heroin, the dark juice of the poppy, the beloved flower of peace.
The tourists this season are all small and dark, the men in their best suits,
carefully brushed, the women walking like hoofed animals in unaccustomed high heels. Why do they stare at her? They stop pulling levers,
stop throwing plastic dice, shuffling cards, snorting coke, stop ingesting
highballs. They all stop and stare up at her as she descends the gently
curving staircase. Isnt she exquisitely balanced? Don't her hands float
gracefully at her sides? Her shoes, with their very high heels, tap sharply
on the imitation marble steps. They make a noise like the clawed toes of
a cat. Then she realizes she is naked. Her legs are long and lean and bare.
Each breast is tipped in raw pink. Her mons is visible to everyone.
Bartenders in starched collars stare up at the slit exposed between her

legs. But she has heard the click of the door behind her. The door is shut. She cannot go back. She can only descend, clawed feet tapping, step by step—

"Did you enjoy it?"

"What?"

"In the dream, I mean. Or were you only embarrassed, walking down those stairs?"

"I dont think anyone could—"

"No? Wasnt it exciting? Even—arousing?"

"I was worried—my connection would never—you know—he wouldnt come to me—"

"Nevertheless—imagine it—wearing nothing but your high heels, descending those stairs. A vision, Dominique, a pale vision—"

"You want me to say it was—"

"I want you to say it was—stimulating."

"Stimulating?"

"Descending—naked—in those shoes—"

"To be naked—descending—in those shoes—"

"Everyone staring at you."

"Everyone staring at me—naked—descending in those shoes—"

"Yes," he says. "Naked," he repeats, "in those shoes." After a while the hissing of the Mitchell NC camera stops. He shoulders the Arriflex. Outside the sun is thin. He pulls his coat tighter around him. He passes the bridge, the abasto municipal, etc. At the fallen courtyard of the Hotel del Lago he watches—he films—shadows cast curiously elongated by the falling sun against the adobe wall.

5.

"Last night," she says.

"Yes?"

"When I came down those stairs—you know—in my dream—"

"Yes?"

"There was more."

"Tell me."

"I was embarrassed—I was ashamed—because—"

"Because?"

"There was—you know—come—all over me."

"Come? Semen, you mean? Ejaculate?"

"Yes."

"All over you?"

"On my belly—my titties—running—you know—down my legs—"

"I see. In the dream men had been fucking you."

"Yes."

"Fucking you—and then withdrawing? Coming on you?"

"Some just stood there—around me—"

"And what? Stood there—and jacked off onto you?"

"Yes."

"What were they like? The men?"

"They were just men."

"Old? Young? American men?"

"Yes."

"Old and young—tall and short—fat and thin—"

"Yes."

"And you just lay there?"

"Well—"

"Why are you so passive?"

"Passive?"

"Didnt you feel like getting up? Walking away?"

"There were men—all around me—"

"There are always men around you."

"Where would I go?"

"Where do you want to go?"

"Sometimes—"

"Yes?"

"I've had other dreams. I mean, dreams about other men."

"Other men?"

"These are different. They look different."

"In what way?"

"Theyre small—small, dark men. And—"

"And?"

"Theyre not circumcised."

"Not circumcised?"

"Most men—American men, the men I've known—theyve been—you know—cut. But these men—"

"These men—"

"They have—it looks like a hood of skin. It pulls back—"

"I see. Do they fuck you too?"

"Yes."

"They come on you?"

"Yes—no."

"Yes? No?"

"I mean—they come—but they dont withdraw. I feel them—they come into me."

"All of them?"

"I can feel them coming."

"How many are there? In your dreams?"

"Once there were fifty."

"Fifty!"

"Fifty of them."

"You took fifty of them? One after another?"

"Yes."

"All small—dark—uncircumcised—"

"Yes. And they all came—into me—"

"And it felt—"

"Different."

"Different?"

"Yes. It felt—different."

"I see," he says. "It felt different," he repeats. He puts his pen away. He rubs at his face. "I'm trying," he says, "to incorporate all this into the film. It's no good, you see, trying to impose a particular order on your material. The order—the story—has to grow out of its material. Do you know what I mean, Dominique? You are the material. You, and Garred, the casino, Sheba, all the others. Who am I? I am just the director. All I do is follow what is there. I sneak around with my camera—a thief—stealing images. Stealing images! A stupid job, Dominique, for a grown man. Stupid—because I get lost—we all get lost—in this miasma of imagery—" His voice fades away. His camera hisses. He scans the mercado, where an Indian woman howls in real or imagined pain. He slips through stalls filled with carved faces—both wood and flesh—where dogs draw back their lips over white incisors. A wind swirls scraps of cellophane around his feet. In the fallen courtyard of the Hotel del Lago he rearranges props. He moves the woman's shoe so its shadow is cast preternaturally long. The needle of the hypodermic is broken, the plastic barrel crushed. "What are you trying to tell me?" he shouts. Sheba comes stalking through the coarse blossoms. Her head is low to the ground. There is a feral odor to her, the odor of an unwashed animal. "Arent you pleased, my dear?" she says. "Our first snuff film!" She cackles gleefully. His camera pans hissing over the naked body lying in the rubble, the fallen adobe, the bricks, the tile of the Hotel del Lago.

6.

She descends (she dreams) a staircase. The staircase curves gently to her left. It leads into a casino. She is in Las Vegas, a dry city in the American desert. Everything is imported, including the tourists. This season the tourists are small and dark. The women hobble, unaccustomed to their high heels. They wear black skirts and white blouses. The men are in threadbare suits, carefully brushed. She is looking for her connection, her hateful lover, her moist brown heroin in its cellophane wrapping. She is naked. She wears only shoes with very high heels. There is come—the juice of masculine fulminations—on her breasts, on her belly, her shaven mons, running down her thighs. Nevertheless she is exquisitely balanced. Her hands float at her sides. Could anyone be unmoved by the sight of such a splendid young animal? Her breasts, glistening with ejaculate, tremble slightly at each step. In the poker pit white men wearing Stetsons—their jowls laced with broken veins—sit with cards fanned in front of them. One of the men calls her honey, and tries to slide a finger up her ass. The dark tourists part, allowing her to pass. They are pulling at slot machines painted in muted shades of red and green. They twitter and whisper as she passes. In the craps pit the auctioneer sing-songs monotonously. Keno runners—they are all young women, scarcely more dressed than she—race past. "Kee-no! kee-no! kee-no!" they cry like birds with a single refrain. Cocktail waitresses—one has a tit dangling loosely from her bodice—pass with trays of cocktails and cigarettes in lurid packs and ashtrays overflowing with butts. They look at Dominique with disdain. Some hiss at her, sticking out their tongues. Dominique tries to stop one. "Give me a drink," she says, "just a drink—any drink—" "Piss off, sister," the woman says turning yellow eyes towards her. The pit boss at the blackjack tables motions for her to keep moving. "Dont sit your ass down here," he warns. Across the room a singer croons in the lounge, toupee slightly askew. Three middle-aged women with beehive hairdos listen. They lean whispering towards each other—hairdos tip alarmingly—then straighten up to sip at their highball glasses. They see Dominique as she passes. "What's that on her tits?" one asks. "That aint mother's milk, honey," another answers. Dominique—as graceful as any young hoofed animal—moves on, hands floating at her sides, searching—

"You walk beautifully, Dominique."

"I remind myself to move slowly."

"Are you content with your wardrobe? Your apartment?"

"There seems enough of everything."

"Garred was drunk yesterday, wasnt he?"

"I tried not to notice."

"How will I wring a performance from them, Dominique? My crew of rats? Sometimes I am embarrassed to be in their presence."

"Is this—you know, these interviews—part of the film?"

"Is the camera running? Do you hear it?"

"I know you are filming—"

"I am always filming, Dominique. Each scene rises around us like the miasma rising from the lake. I am the director, but that means nothing. I have never felt so helpless. I keep throwing away Osgood's scripts. None of them make sense. His dialog sounds like old ladies at tea. I'm afraid I've rather annoyed him. I only know it is you—you, Dominique— at the center of everything—"

"Sometimes you frighten me."

"Yes," he says. "Sometimes you frighten me," he repeats. He shuts his eyes. Outside the sunlight is thin. A cold wind swirls around his feet. Indian women—they are shaped like turnips—watch him pass. The camera hisses just as the wind hisses, passing through the tarpaulins and shuttered stalls of the mercado, nearly deserted at this hour, the same sound as the women hissing between their teeth, speaking sometimes to each other in sibilant tones, a basilisk hissing, secretive, feral. It is the same sound that Sheba makes, parting the coarse blossoms on their tall stalks. "Yesss," she says, drawing out the word. "Arent you pleased, my dear? Our first snuff film!" Garred follows her, stepping with the loose-limbed clumsiness of the drunk over the rubbled interior of the Hotel del

Lago. A cigarette dangles from his lower lip, which is wet and unnaturally red. He nudges with the toe of his shoe the woman's high-heeled slipper. He turns to look at the director—to look, that is, directly into the camera, whose viewfinder is pressed against the director's eye—turning to look, raising himself as he does so to his full height, his face suddenly splitting into a loose-lipped, lubricious grin.

7 ·

Let us go then (she dreams) into the Quetzal Quesino. Osgood
Fetters is at her side, holding the script he has that morning prepared.
She is quite naked except for her high-heeled shoes, which click on the
imitation marble like the claws of a cat or perhaps the hoofed feet of a
goat—and the come, of course, the excretory fulminations of many men
spread liberally over her breasts, her stomach, her flanks. Waitresses
pass, bearing trays filled with cigarette butts and lipstick-stained glasses.
One has a tit dangling from her bodice. "Give me a drink," Dominique
says, "just a drink—any drink—" Fetters—in the dream he seems even
more haggard than in his real life—shuffles papers. He hooks the arm of
a waitress, who turns yellow eyes balefully at Dominique. "Piss off,
sister," the waitress says. Fetters nods and lets her go. The director must
be somewhere, because a camera is hissing, she can hear it. She cannot
see him, but everywhere she looks she sees mirrors and in these mirrors
is a blonde woman, naked, with shining breasts. The woman appears
confused, although perhaps this is a trick of the lighting. The man at her
side, diminutive, larval—he could be a gnarled priest—takes her arm and
turns her this way, that way. "Dont sit your ass down here," a man warns.
"Yes, yes," says Fetters, "that's good, that's it!" "Kee-no, kee-no, kee-
no," cries a young woman, pigeonbreasted in a tightly laced corset.
Dominique realizes she is trembling. She needs her fix. It has been hours
since a needle slid into a vein, since red blood, brown heroin mixed in a
plastic barrel. Oh, her white skin, bruised by the needle! "I need my fix,"
she tells Fetters, who has perched spectacles on his nose. "Yes, yes," he
says, searching through his papers which scatter behind him. "This
way—I'm sure it's here somewhere." In the poker pit sit burly men
wearing Stetsons. Garred is there too, although he is standing. He holds
cellophane-wrapped heroin—moist, lubricious—and a syringe. His belly
is bare, falling from a t-shirt over his loosely belted pants. Is that a penis
dangling from his fly? The men in Stetsons—their jowls are laced with

broken veins—push aside tables making room for her on the floor. A woman in a beehive hairdo peers over the pit. "That aint mother's milk, honey," she says. Her eyes glitter like sequins. Dominique, descending onto her knees, sees reflected in a mirror a vision. "Oh, what is it?" she cries as she settles onto her back, into the position of her trade. It is la Virgin de la Salud, resplendently garbed, pinned to the wall and surrounded by coarse blossoms. But the vision is replaced by Garred's face—and her heroin, her needle. "I want it," she says, she cries. "Oh please, I want it now!" The burly men in Stetsons unbuckle their pants—

"Are you sleeping well, Dominique?"

"Last night I heard screams."

"Screams?"

"Someone crying out—"

"I heard nothing."

"They awakened me—then they were gone."

"You were perhaps dreaming."

"Can dreams be so real?"

"Is anything as real as dreams?"

"Sometimes it seems I toss and turn—all night. And I hear things—like the screams. Hoarse screams. What do they mean? I cant tell if they are real or not. Could there be screams so late at night?"

"A woman's screams?"

"Yes."

"I heard nothing, Dominique."

"Yet they seemed so real."

"Yes," he says. He shuts his eyes. "Everything," he repeats, "seems so real." He taps with his pen at his knee. After a while the hissing stops. He leaves. He passes the abasto municipal. A stream below is black with cess and red with blood. In the opera house there are no operas, only films, modern films, triple X films. In the mercado he trains his Arriflex camera on an Indian woman. Her head is thrown back. Scattered about are crushed jicomates and ciruelos. A butcher in gum boots pauses at a marbled haunch. The haunch is so freshly killed it still twitches. The butcher looks through the camera into the eye of the director. What can he see? After a moment he runs a knife down the hanging flesh, which peels open like a ripe fig. The director slips away. He enters the fallen courtyard of the Hotel del Lago. Sheba comes through the waving stalks. Her lower jaw is slung forward. She looks like a bejeweled hyena. There are rings on all her fingers and emeralds in her orange hair. In the failing sunlight there is a nimbus of light around her. Garred follows, wetly drunk. All stare at the pale body festooned with blood lying amid coarse blossoms and fallen stone and brick. Garred turns smiling to the camera. His face is loose—it wobbles alarmingly. "Are we trifling now with necrophilia, my friend? Did our Osgood write *this* in his script?" His pants, loosely belted, hang beneath a protruding belly. His fly is undone. Is that his penis dangling there? A white sausage with a single eye? A drop of fluid—milky, viscous, perhaps poisonous—hangs from the eye like a thick teardrop. He moves disjointedly towards the body scarcely visible now in the thin sunlight falling into the courtyard.

8.

Let us go then (she dreams) into the Quetzal Quesino. Everything is arranged, as ordered. There are rows of slot machines. They are made of wood and papier-mâché. Indians stand there, pulling mechanically at levers. The Indians are dressed as tourists. The men wear their best suits. The women are awkward in their high heels. Their skirts are very tight. The younger women preen. Black hair falls in cascades to their waists. Some of the older women squat on the floor. They sit shaped like turnips in front of piles of chayotes and tortillas. Through them all moves the director in his khaki shirt. He clears a path for Dominique, who walks with the youthful grace of a hoofed animal. Her hands float at her sides. She can see herself in mirrors. Oh, her white skin is bruised! There are sores, scabs, track marks on her wrists, at the inner crook of each arm, even at her ankles. Elsewhere she glistens with ejaculate. Each breast is tipped in pink. Her mons is bare, freshly shaven. Are those her legs? They seem longer than she remembers. She turns a foot to one side, then the other. Her instep arches nearly free of her high-heeled shoe. "Is this what you want?" she says. "Am I doing it right?" The camera hisses. It is the Mitchell NC again. It is mounted on a ColorTrans hydraulic dolly which rolls smoothly on its eight pneumatic tires. Osgood Fetters, holding a sheath of paper, retreats with the dolly. He is mouthing words at her. Are they words from his script? Her own mouth is painted scarlet. Sheba's mouth—it opens as the face leans towards her—is not painted at all. It is yellow. A sparse moustache is on her upper lip. Her cheeks are hairy. Yet there is a nimbus of light around this creature, perhaps light refracted from the amethysts in her orange hair, from the emeralds dangling from each ear, from the rings which adorn each finger. Dominique blinks at the image reflected back at her. She too is dripping with jewelry, with jasper and sapphire, chalcedony and emeralds, fine beryl and topaz—just like Sheba, whose face is hissing—just like la Virgin de la Salud, who says nothing. The Virgin has come off the wall. She is borne aloft by eight Indian men who move smoothly through the casino. Coarse blossoms surround her. Thick petals, as waxy as heroin, fall in her trail. These petals are aromatic, splendidly scented. Their odor is as thick as oil. Then a woman in a beehive hairdo comes up to Dominique. Eyes glitter like sequins. "Piss off, sister!" A waitress with a dangling tit nods approvingly. Only Osgood frowns, searching through his script. Then Dominique is in the poker pit. Burly men in Stetsons unbuckle their pants. She assumes the position of her trade. Penises slide from pants like white snakes which each have a single eye. The Indians click and hum, watching. They stir restlessly. Even the director seems disquieted. His face is wreathed in frowns. He is as wrinkled as the old Indian women. Each white man beats her with his penis. "You're not fucking me," she tells them. "I know what youre doing!" They beat her with their cocks. They withdraw in order to shoot their come onto her. The ejaculate burns, like acid. Some falls on her face. The semen stings. She can feel skin slide away from flesh, flesh slide away from bone. One ear has burned off—only a gnarl of cartilage remains. The director is trying to talk into this ear. "No, no," he says, "this isnt what I had in mind—"

"It isnt?"

"No—no—not at all—"

"Can I have my heroin now?"

"Your arms are bleeding—"

"I want it," she says. "I want it now!"

"Here," says a burly man wearing nothing but a Stetson. "Here you are, honey. Here's a real piece of meat."

He jiggles it. Drops of liquid fly about.

"No, no," the director says, "that's not it—not it at all—"

"I want my heroin!"

"Your wrists are bleeding—"

"I've been good—havent I been good?"

"What happened to your face—"

"Oh, give it to me!"

"Your face—"

"Give it to me now!"

The sunlight is thin. The camera hisses on his shoulder. Through the viewfinder he sees a woman throwing back her head. Her throat is exposed. Shadows have grown dense in the corners. There is a murky glow in the deeper corridors. In the courtyard of the Hotel del Lago an amber light has begun to spread. It moves as slowly as molasses through the coarse blossoms, over the rubble of stone and brick. Garred follows Sheba through the gloom. His penis dangles from his open fly. "Are we trifling here with necrophilia?" he says with the careful enunciation of the habitual drunk. "Did our Osgood write *this* in his script?" Osgood— he is behind the director, trying to peer over the Arriflex camera— shuffles through his papers. "What?" he says. "What scene is this?" The woman lies pale and bloody, half hidden among the tall stalks. Beyond her, at the open windows of the Hotel del Lago, dark faces have gathered. Their eyes are liquid. The men are all in their best suits, carefully brushed. The women stand awkward in their unaccustomed high heels. They twitter and hum—they whistle and hiss—just like the camera as it follows Garred stepping loose-limbed, disjointed, awkward, over the rubble towards the body illuminated by the thick, heavy light flowing now over the ground.

9.

She is lying (she dreams) on her back. It is the position of her trade. Men are fucking her. But men are always fucking her. Sometimes they pay her, sometimes they dont. They have penises like dead lizards. They put these dead penises into her mouth, into her anus, into her vagina. They are not satisfied until they have penetrated every orifice. "I know what you are doing," she tells them. Not, of course, that they listen. "You are beating me. You say you are fucking me but youre not. Youre beating me. That's all youre doing." The women are just as bad. Since they dont have penises they cant pretend to fuck her. Instead they have to just beat her—hiss at her, spit at her, condemn her. They fill her with their shit, just like they fill the lake with their shit. Their streams of hate run into her carrying black cess and red blood. "I'm just your cess-pool," she says to the man grunting over her, the Stetson still on his head. Semen steams and hisses on her face. Her face is burning away—she can feel it. Do they care? "Have you no respect?" she says, arching her back. Her bare mons lifts invitingly. Could anyone resist the sight of such a splendid young animal? She sees herself in a distant mirror. Her wrists and her arms are bleeding from repeated injections. Garred is boiling more heroin. His features are loose on his face: his eyes and nose and mouth wobble alarmingly. She watches him hover over one ankle, then the other, jabbing the needle into her. She is lying in a pool of her own blood. The blood is as sticky as the semen the men leave on her belly. After a while she floats to the ceiling. She watches the scene below her. Her body lies, as ordered, in the poker pit in the center of the casino. The men crawl on, the men crawl off. Garred approaches, Garred leaves. The camera is a black beast hissing in the middle of it all. All these movements, however, seen from her vantage near the ceiling, are so slight they hardly seem significant. The real movement, the real significance, is at the periphery of the room, where eight Indian men weave their way between banks of slot machines—they are painted with dyes made from insects and flowers—and between craps tables and lounges filled with women in beehive hairdos buzzing at each other and keno runners and waitresses with dangling tits. The eight men carry la Virgin de la Salud. The Virgin tosses to each side coarse blossoms of such pungency that their aroma drifts to the ceiling. The Indian women chant and dance behind her. No one in the center of the room—not Garred, not Sheba, not Osgood—notices this procession, no one, that is, except the director in his khaki shirt who looks up from his camera, his face suddenly startled—

"What are they doing?"

"I dont know."

"Where did they come from?"

"I didnt see."

"What's wrong with your face?"

"Isnt it what you wanted?"

"No—that's not it—that's not it at all—"

"I can feel the rush—"

"Rush? What rush?"

"From my arms—my wrists—my legs—"

"What rush? What are you saying?"

"My lover," she says. "He's taking me."

"What do you mean? What are you trying to say? There's blood all over you. Your face is slipping away. I can hardly see you. Why is the light growing dim? I ordered strong lighting—harsh lighting—"

"Oh, cant you see the light?" she says. "Everything is glowing—I'm glowing—my lover is glowing—"

"You need to speak up—speak up, I say—"

"Oh," she says, "if only you could hear me—"

The camera hisses. After a while he puts down the script. White paper flutters to his feet. He leaves. He passes the abasto municipal. He adjusts the poster hanging in front of the opera house. In the mercado a woman laughs. She throws backs her head, exposing her throat. He watches her through the viewfinder of the Arriflex IIC camera. In the courtyard of the Hotel del Lago he films Garred who sniffs at the body lying half hidden in the rubble of brick and stone. Coarse blossoms surround her. Their aroma is pungent, thick. The air itself has thickened. An amber glow spreads. Sheba, low to the ground, is hissing between her teeth. Osgood searches desperately through the pages of his script. "What scene is this?" he cries. "What scene is this?" A wind swirls around them. Pages of script lie fluttering—like birds with broken wings—at the feet of the director, who is nearly engulfed by the black, hissing camera mounted on his shoulder.

10.

The dream ends. Dominique awakens. She is thick, heavy. She goes into the bathroom where she boils heroin. Her veins are scarred, hardened. Outside a man bangs monotonously at a piece of metal. Is the sunlight always this thin? this gray? this cheerless? A woman laughs beneath Dominique's window. It is a sour laugh without mirth. In the bathroom there is blood everywhere. At last the needle finds a vein. Her hands tremble so much she can hardly push the plunger. She showers. She dries her hair. She applies potions and powders and unguents to her face. She straps a garter-belt around her waist. She sheathes her fine legs in nylon stockings. Sleek, serene, she emerges from the hotel. Men whisper into her right ear. She passes the mercado. At the opera house she looks at the poster advertising the film. She adjusts the angle at which it hangs. Then she enters. She descends the aisle to our left, as ordered. We see her transfixed in a beam of light. Her shadow falls before her, cast preternaturally long. She takes her seat. A face turns towards her.

"Yes?" the director says. "Are you ready?"

"I'm ready."

The movie begins.

PART III
THE SILENCE
OF THE AUDIENCE

I.

Clang! goes the light. Suddenly visible is a woman. She is at the top of stairs. A hand flies up to protect her eyes. She is nearly naked. Her body is bisected by a black garter belt. She begins an uncertain descent. There is a scattering of applause from below. Then the screen goes blank. Sounds, however, continue. Heels tap, rather like the clawed feet of cats, on imitation marble surfaces. A camera hisses. Applause drifts on for some seconds. In the darkness below bodies seem to shift. There is a general sense of movement. Throats clear. *Clang*! Visible at the top of stairs is a woman. She takes a few uncertain steps. She looks to her left— our right. "Is this it? Is this what you want?" *Clang*! She pauses at the top of stairs. She twists away from the light. Her body is bisected. There is no color anywhere. The film, that is, is entirely black and white. There are no reds, no greens, no purples visible on the screen. Grain is pronounced. In black and white the woman twists away from the flaring lamps which illuminate her. Can a black and white film find favor with an audience? Perhaps not. Perhaps the film will be shown, if it is shown at all, in musty theatres in distant cities, subtitled in Urdu, or in tiny campus theatres where students can argue over the obscure references to Baudelaire and Eliot.

In the darkness below, Sheba glowers. She is on her haunches. She cannot be pleased. It is her money invested in this film, after all—her dollars, her pounds, her rubles, her zlotys, all valuable to her. She turns for consolation to the boy next to her. He is one of an endless supply. They are poor Mexican boys with sharp eyes and hair rank with oil. Perhaps for consolation Sheba imagines chewing with her yellow stubs at his dark member. Can we say any more what Sheba likes? It is rumored that once she was a man. It is said she lived in Paris years ago—as a raspy, jowly, very male expatriate with powerful shoulders. She lived with her—with his—Negro lover, whose biceps were encircled with gold bands. She decorated him with horsehair tufts and ochre daubs. My savage lover, she called him. One day the Negro vanished. Perhaps she had chewed too vigorously. Even then her teeth were yellow. Her pelt was yellow. Her eyes were flecked with yellow. Soon Sheba, still a man, began appearing in the cafes wearing dresses, toes stuffed into lady's pumps. His lips grew bulbous with lipstick. Nails became long, lacquered green. Finally breasts fell heavily down her chest. She invited hands to feel these fleshy sacks hanging in her bodice. She left smears of red on cups. "I lived a thousand years as a man," she boasted. Now she would live a thousand years as a woman. We cannot vouch for this story. Yet Sheba is a nighttime creature. There is always a nimbus of light around her. Her open-toed shoes are festooned with diamonds. The gems are crudely faceted. A leopard skin coat is askew on one shoulder. She looks past her boy in the direction of the director. *Clang!* Immediately a beam of light leaps across the screen. A woman sits before a mirror. Her chair is like a throne. After a moment she crosses one stockinged leg over the other. Their nylon surfaces hiss. Except for the stockings, the garter belt bisecting her waist, and her shoes with very high, very narrow heels, she is naked. In the mirror the director is visible as a reflection watching her. He asks:

"Do you want a drink?"

"Is there coffee?"

"Instant."

"That's all right."

"It's terrible coffee. The tea—"

"Yes?"

"Chamomile—manzana—"

"No," she says. "Coffee—just coffee."

We can see her face in the mirror. It is bereft of expression. For a long moment she is quite motionless. Then an amber light spreads throughout the room. As though this were a signal, movement resumes. She touches lipstick to mouth. Each eye is extravagantly made up. A mass of pearls is strapped around her throat. Breasts are placed into the cups of a brassiere. When she stands she tugs at her stockings, pointing as she does so the triangular toes of her shoes. One hand brushes the hooded clitoris suspended above her open lips. The gesture seems careless, but not without meaning. The director watches. We watch. At last a twilight dress falls into place, then the manto sagrado. "Shall we go?" They descend arm in arm stairs which curve to their left. Her heels tap on the imitation marble steps. They make a noise like the clawed toes of a cat. *Clang*! A light illuminates them. There is a scattering of applause from below.

Clang! A woman is pinned to the wall, as ordered. She is deeply shadowed. She looks towards the camera. For a moment she seems on the verge of speaking. Yet what could she say? She is immobilized by the light which has thrust itself against her. In any case the screen immediately goes blank. There is no opportunity for her to say anything. In the darkness below bodies shift. Men cough into hands. A woman laughs in a back row. It is a tittering sound more nervous than amused. *Clang!* She is pinned to the wall. The light is to our left, her right. She is deeply shadowed by this light. The light, that is, obscures what it reveals. If this is not clear nothing will be clear. She struggles in this light to speak. Her black lips move on her face. The screen goes blank. People stir below.

Garred Haus sips from a flask of mescal. The lids of his eyes droop. He lifts with care one leg over the other. The foot hangs. It does not move. He seems to have little interest in the film displayed before him. Of course he has been an actor all his life. He wears lifts in his shoes. There is a toupee on his head. The skin of his face has been tightened twice by surgeons. We have watched as every day he goes through a series of mechanical exercises. In spite of this his belly is flaccid. It protrudes over his pants. Over the years he has seen his shoulders settle. He has seen his thin breasts drop. He has seen his buttocks fall. All this has been visible in mirrors. In his apartment there are mirrors on every wall. He is his own best audience. Lighting is controlled by individual dimmer switches. In his mirrors he rehearses the gestures of life. All is simulated. Even his drinking is simulated. He sips until an equilibrium is reached and maintained. He is never as drunk as he seems. Since his penis will no longer come erect his sexual role has become passive. All this and more is widely known. It is widely known, for instance, that he receives male lovers and pays prostitutes, both male and female, to perform in his place. Such performers are not difficult to find in Western cities. His preference—we understand—is to watch each performance reflected in his mirrors. By the use of mirrors each performance is doubled, tripled, quadrupled. In his nest of mirrors he is surrounded by images. Without his images he can see himself only distantly reflected in others' eyes— in the eyes of Dominique, for instance, or Sheba, or the director, and of course the camera. Is that enough? In the darkness his eyelids droop lower as he watches the screen. He waits for himself to appear. *Clang!* goes a tungston-halogen lamp. Shadows leap right. The director turns to the woman. She is seated on her throne. She crosses one nylon clad leg over the other. She puts down a cup smeared with red. She asks:

"Are you content with your film?"

"I am never content."

"Perhaps you ask for too much."

"The artist can never ask for too much."

"At least the audience seemed quiet."

"Perhaps they didnt understand what they saw."

"Yes," she says. "Perhaps they didnt."

They watch each other in the mirror. Finally an amber light spreads through the room. As if this were a signal the two people busy themselves. She touches lipstick to mouth. The man works at his shirt buttons. The woman completes the creation of her face. All this time her eyes are hooded. The left side of her face has slipped. It has burned away. The ear on that side is a gnarl of cartilage. The eye on that side is a milky protrusion. The mouth extends as a scar towards the throat. Yet this side of her face is more beautiful than the undisturbed right. It possesses the numinous beauty of the disfigured. Nor does she neglect, with her potions and unguants, this left side. Each eye, even the exophthalmic one, is extravagantly painted. Each ear, even the truncated one, is adorned with a media luna. Pearls wrap around her throat. A garter belt is already around her waist. Her legs are sheathed. Her feet are encased in pointed-toed pumps with very high, very slender heels. She stands. She inspects herself. We, of course, approve the vision she reveals. We shall not mince our words. There are responsibilities here which we have no intention of evading. But in any case the woman is a willing participant. This seems clear. She admires herself. She strokes, as ordered, her vulva, which is quite hairless. The director watches. These mirrored inspections reveal nothing. Finally a twilight dress settles onto her shoulders, then the manto sagrado. "Shall we go?" They descend stairs. *Clang*! Lights come on. Applause is scattered below. Small men are in their best suits, carefully brushed. Dark women stand like hoofed animals in unaccustomed high heels. Burly men remove Stetsons. All stop pulling levers, stop throwing plastic dice, shuffling cards, snorting coke, stop ingesting highballs. All action ceases. When the applause dies away there is only the sound of Dominique's heels clicking, clicking, on the imitation marble steps.

3.

A woman speaks in an unending monotonal complaint. Finally someone nudges her. "Well!" she says, fluffing herself like a bird in its nest. Our attention returns to the screen. *Clang!* A woman is hurled across a room. She is dressed as we have described. In the auditorium below bodies shift. An eye is caught in reflected light looking back over a shoulder. *Clang!* The woman is hurled across the room. A legless beggar—his stumps are covered with leather—propels himself down the aisle. He pauses to entreat, right and left. People brush him away. A few coins appear. His progress down the aisle is pleasantly arrhythmic. His truncated body bobs with each swing. He is illuminated by light bouncing back from the rectangular screen before him. *Clang!* The woman, hurled across a room, goes to one knee. She looks up, perhaps fearfully. At any rate her eyes are wide. Her mouth opens. "Is this it? Is this what you want?" Blood begins to seep from a wound on one wrist. The blood is black, like her lips. None of this affects the beggar entreating right and left as he continues his descent. Once we catch a glimpse of his face, fiercely grinning. We nod in acknowledgment.

In the darkness Osgood Fetters removes his glasses. He wipes at his eyes. Quite loudly—perhaps he intends it as a statement—he clears his throat. He plucks at the crease in one pant leg. He frowns as he burnishes with his cotton shirt his spectacles. He is having trouble—we have heard this admitted—retaining respect for the director, whom he has known, professionally, for some years. "What you are doing is exploitative," he has argued. Osgood fumbles with his hair, with his sheath of paper, with the flaps and buttons of his clothes. "Well," he says, rocking back and forth on his heels, "you cant expect—that is, this violence, directed against, well, against women—I dont wish to psychologize, John, I know how you despise—er—such things—but surely—" He blinks his eyes owlishly. His pen falters. He cant seem to write what is required of him. His hands tremble in the darkness as he settles his spectacles back on his nose. He considers himself—perhaps he is—a fine and gentle man. His relationships with women are avuncular. He basks, gently glowing, in their admiration. Even his two ex-wives continue to respect him. One went on to marry a drunk who occasionally struck her. He was a doctor, however, and drove a Mercedes, which was some solace. The other went to live alone in a canyon near Santa Monica where she drank herself to sleep every night. "If only more men were like you!" she declared one night on the telephone. Like many American women she communicated best using this instrument. In America telephone wires hum with indiscreet revelations, confessions, confidences. Women sigh. Their voices become soft and seductive. They cradle their plastic instruments—available in designer colors—before their faces. Lips open. Tongues with great delicacy appear. There is such longing as American men and women sit miles apart, sometimes thousands of miles apart, declaring intimacies in solitary splendor! Osgood grimaces, meanwhile, as a beggar's hand touches his trousers. He blinks and fidgets. He looks away from the screen where light springs with such feral eagerness from our left to our right that it drives before it a woman nearly naked, certainly unprotected, her body merely bisected, her legs scarcely sheathed in their fine nylon, blood seeping from wounds on arms and wrists and ankles. Osgood coughs into his hands. *Clang!* The woman in the mirror glances at the director. She puts down her coffee cup which is smeared with red. She crosses one leg—her left—over the other, her right. The man asks:

"Did your role please you, Dominique?"

"There was something exciting—I admit it—in such total abasement."

"You seemed absorbed by your character."

"My surrender was absolute."

"You became transparent."

"That was your plan, wasn't it?"

"Of course."

"You watched it happen."

"With pleasure."

"You are a voyeur."

"Does that please you?"

"Yes," she says. "Why not? Yes, it does please me."

She stares into her mirror. A lipstick is before her mouth. Her face, and his, are bereft of expression. At last an amber light spreads, as slow and thick as molasses. Movement resumes. She touches lipstick to mouth. With one jeweled hand she strokes the hooded clitoris below her bare vulva. She stretches one leg—she pulls at the stocking top—and then the other, pointing, in each instance, the toes of her shoes, which are triangular like the heads of vipers. At last a twilight dress descends onto her, and a manto sagrado. "Shall we go?" *Clang!* Lights illuminate them at the top of the stairs. Applause drifts up from below. They descend arm in arm. A burly man slaps the director on a shoulder. "Liked your show, buddy." Women dressed in satin purse their lips. A man in a tuxedo—he represents a well-known studio—makes an indecipherable gesture. An Indian woman shaped like a turnip in a tight skirt squats on the floor. She winces as she removes her shoes. She sets out a pile of tortillas. A woman with chayotes joins her. Their voices fly back and forth like rain flurries. They fall abruptly silent as Dominique passes. They look at each other. Expressions alter. After a moment they resume the hissing and clicking of their language. Their voices, however, are now more guarded. Beyond this we can say nothing.

4.

A woman drones in monotonal complaint. This continues for some time. Finally someone nudges her. "Well!" she says in ruffled outrage. Elsewhere bodies shift. A man pointedly clears his throat. A legless beggar—his stumps are covered with leather—propels himself back up the aisle. There is nothing supplicating in his expression, however, which is occasionally visible in the light reflecting back from the illuminated screen. *Clang*! A woman crumples. Blood seeps. Each limb is askew. A high heeled pump is loose on one foot. A woman in the audience hisses. Outside the sky has a surly aspect. The apparent surface of the sky—that is, its clouds—has lowered. The mountain tops are no longer visible. In the valley the air has become leaden. In the plaza boys toot and drum in ragged rows. Occasionally their band leader, a man in white spats, glances at the heavens. It is at this time each year that the rains begin. Until they begin the air has a tangible weight. The tourists, standing in small groups, notice this. They wipe at their brows. The director, of course, must also be aware of the weight of the air and the imminence of the rains. It may be he has included this prospect in the schemata of his film. A film emerges, he has often said, from the images around one. It is his conceit that he does not create his films. He simply finds them, and makes them visible. All this has been alluded to previously. It is his own assigned role, of course, to play the artist, the rebel against commerce, the pure visionary in a currupt world. After his departure from the studios of Hollywood and the producers whose only talent lay in making deals—for money, for women, for cocaine—he found himself awakening in the mountains of Mexico. There was a town around him. Everything he wanted was there, he finally decided. He recognized the importance of the slate colored lake. A Purépecha woodcarver showed him the gnarled hands of his trade. In the mercado a woman with no teeth suddenly smiled at him. She patted the tortillas arranged in piles before her. He nodded in agreement. In this way, we understand, he returned to his original vision, his original sense of being. In the story within his film he tricks a wealthy Ethiopian woman into putting up money for a pornographic movie. "You must obey the conventions of the genre," she warns. "Of course," he says. Lies and deceits flow smoothly. In his story he creates at his mountain site an elaborage trap for the images that rise like the miasma from the lake. In the center of the trap he places a blonde woman. In spite of her profession she is innocent as only Americans be be innocent. "You are my lamb," he tell her, "my sacrificial lamb." "you are goint to sacrifice me?" "Only in a matter of speaking, my dear." The director—we recognize his profile in the audience—turns to the woman next to him. *Clang!* The woman is visible seated on her throne. She crosses one leg over the other, as ordered. A single light is to one side—her right, our left. We listen to her stockings hiss. She says:

"Your images are deceptive."

"Truth lies, Dominique—if it lies anywhere—in deception."

"So you say."

"Nature herself is devious."

"So you claim. As for myself—"

"Yes?"

"It may be my deviousness exceeds yours."

After a while lipstick touches her mouth. Finally they rise. They go to the top of the stairs. *Clang!* Lights come on. Applause breaks out. They descend arm in arm. Burly men slap him on the shoulder. "Liked your show, buddy." "This one went all out, guy." "Gotta hand it to you, pal." At a table three women in beehive hairdos lean towards each other. "Who is she? Is she the star? Do you know her name?" They each wear harlequin glasses studded with rhinestones. The hairdos tip alarmingly, then come upright. A bargirl whose breasts bulge over the top of her corset stands there. "Drinks, girls?" At another table men speak in booming voices about points and bear markets and junk bonds. Their women simper. They wear satin dresses. Their ankles overflow their shoes. Following the director and his star, people stream from the casino into the courtyard where Sheba, Garred, and Osgood await them. A group of rather scruffy mariachis—the silver ornaments on their pants are tarnished—thrum and toot near the fountain. A plump Mexican woman in a very tight dress—her skin is flawless, as tawny as her bleached hair—begins to sing. She sings a lament. Her voice is hoarse. A man whose gray dreadlocks are tangled with gum and wax and perhaps asphalt from the street—he clearly has been sleeping in his frayed and filthy clothes—suddenly becomes agitated. "Donde esta la reina!" he cries. "Donde esta la reina!" Sheba looks balefully at him, and he abruptly subsides. Elsewhere in a dark corner of the courtyard a man who looks vaguely familiar has taken out his penis. A golden stream flows onto a potted plant. He shakes his organ—drops fly about—and looks, perhaps guiltily, over his shoulder. No one notices him except a dog, a bitch with swinging teats. She pauses in her rounds to sniff at his urine. Overhead hangs a media luna. It is very pale in a sky not yet dark.

5.

Outside the air is gray and heavy. In the plaza the leaves of the zapote trees have an aspect of lifelessness. There is dust on the flowers which have opened during the night. Boys toot experimentally at their brass instruments. Meanwhile on the screen the woman lifts herself to one knee. She looks towards the camera. "Is this it? Is this what you want?" *Clang*! A tremor passes through her body. She rises to one knee, then to her feet. She takes a moment to tug at the tops of her stockings. As she does this she points the toes of her black patent shoes. They are triangular, like the heads of vipers. "Is this it? Is this what you want?" Throats clear. In the aisle a legless beggar touches the satin hem of a dress. His knuckle grazes the nyloned surface of a leg. The woman pales. She shuts her eyes. Her companion idly toys with the scarlet nails of her fingers.

The woman Dominique turns to the director seated next to her. Light momentarily reflecting back from the screen makes her visible to us. Have we admired before her profile? She crosses one leg over the other. Even in this crowded auditorium we can hear her stockings hiss as they pass one over the other. It may be she understands perfectly her role in this film. She has read at least the biography the director gave her. "I'm a prostitute? A drug addict? You dont believe in casting against type, do you?" According to her biography she is born in Orange County, California, where there are no oranges, only suburbs. She lives on Foulmouth Street. Her mother groans in the house. She is a fat woman with an underslung jaw. Her face is hairy, mottled. She imbibes in a constant stream cough syrups, thick and sweet, Valiums, Libriums, anti-histimines, Maalox, Phillips Milk of Magnesia—so much richer than her own milk— and pills of every color and several sizes. She is a perfect American consumer, her life controlled by the miracles of modern chemistry. Meanwhile the child Dominique crawls and hides and defecates and pees alone in the backyard until the father comes home and unlocks the back door. He stands looking at her, rocking a bit on his heels, his lips moving soundlessly. Occasionally he clears his throat. Nothing emerges, however, no orotund phrases, no intelligible consonants. One day boiling water is spilled onto the child's face. Details are given, which we have no need to repeat. Dominique reads with her eyebrows arching. "All this?" she says. "And a life in Vegas as a prostitute?" "It is a case," the director says, "of art imitating life." She smiles thinly. She puts her coffee cup on the pile of paper. Its rim is red. *Clang!* A light streaks across the room. After a moment it softens. It clings, like molasses, to the woman who leans now into her mirror. In her mirror she examines her small, pointed breasts. Each arm is bruised. There are track marks, dark subdural bleedings, at each wrist. A scar—the edges are ragged, puckered—has formed itself below her ribs. Each leg is placed correctly before her, exposing to our eyes the marks on her ankles. Is there blood seeping from these wounds? In any case her skin is white, barely tinged by the interior flow of her vital fluids. On her head hair has been scattered like chaff. As she and her director continue their discussion she runs at first fingers and then a brush through this hair which settles finally into its appropriate place. She leans more deeply into her mirror as she guides tubes of waxy colors along the contours of her lips. Eyelashes lengthen and darken. A milky orb moves within its socket. Powder softens a cheek. In the mirror the man gestures with open hands. The discussion has clearly gone into areas in which the woman has little interest. She smiles distantly as she adjusts the garter belt strapped around her waist. Her legs are already sheathed. Her attention concentrates on her image. Even the man falls silent. Finally a twilight dress settles onto her shoulders, and a manto sagrado. They descend together the staircase. They stroll through the casino, where applause scatters right and left. They pass banks of slot machines—the rows are slightly askew—each manned by a small Indian in jacket and polished shoes. A few burly men speak. Indian women squatting on the floor mutter and hiss before stacks of fruit painted in muted shades of reds and yellows and greens. In the courtyard a woman sings. She stands by a fountain, in front of tarnished mariachis. Her flesh is tawny. As she sings she lifts with one jeweled hand the hem of her dress. A silken thigh flashes. Nearby a man in dreadlocks suddenly lifts his head. "Donde esta la reina!" he cries. "Donde esta la reina!" Sheba glowers at him.

"Youre late," she says as the director approaches.

"Are we?"

"You know I hate these occasions."

"Then why do you come?"

"Someone must explain this nonsense you created."

"And you, Garred? Have you found your place in this film?"

"All films are meaningless to me."

"Yes, of course. And I know Osgood's reaction—"

"Really, John. I had hoped this time—"

"Let me have a cigarette," says Dominique. She takes one from Garred. "Isnt this my cue? Havent I something to do now? Arent these people waiting on me? John—take my arm, wont you?"

Crowds follow them. Dominique walks with her usual grace, the grace of a young hoofed animal. She signs programs which are thrust at her. "I've been a fan of yours forever," a young girl says. They stroll down passageways. In the murky light, paintings are barely visible on the walls—the lucent Christ bleeding on his cross, odalisques pearlaceous on their couches, mysterious women dripping as they arise from a black sea. Muted noises come from the catacombs beneath, where, it is rumored, lions pace. Soon the workshops—large adobe rooms with exposed beams—are reached. Here sit the old men bearing chisels and hammers. Here lie the Virgins de la Salud that have been seen in our film, some reclining, some seated, others with arms lifted. Young Indian women drift in the shadows exclaiming over hanging rows of dresses and blouses and skirts and garter belts and flimsy brassieres and panties so fine, so gossamer, they hardly seem to exist. The light in these workrooms has a peculiar glow. There is a thickness to the air. Everything luminesces, especially the mouths and eyes of the women. They try on shoes. They giggle as they teeter about. A group of young men—their eyes are like polished copper—crowd at a doorway, pushing each other, craning necks as they watch. There are no sounds except the ambient voices of the actors and the continued hiss, the reptilian hiss, of the cameras emerging from each crevice, from each darkened corner.

6.

The air seems heavy and gray. Even the flowers appear lifeless. A man in white spats holding a bandleader's baton shuffles in the dust. Finally the doors to the opera house open. A line of campesinos waiting outside in straw hats and straw shoes lift their heads. The band strikes up an unrecognizable tune. Children puff out their cheeks blowing into their instruments. Others bang on drums older than they are. Spilling from the opera house comes a crowd of people—men in Stetsons, women in satin-blinking their eyes as a light, as thick and slow as molasses, flows across the plaza.

The bandleader shouts commands. In ragged rows the boys march tooting and drumming past the abasto municipal and over the bridge which spans the blood-filled river. From above—from the vantage, say, of a soaring bird, wings spread delicately to take advantage of each swirl, each eddy of air—the movement of people is itself riverine. Thus rivulets of people, streamlets of people, emerge from the portales and the warrens of the mercado, joining the main concourse in the plaza beneath the zapote trees across from the opera house from which there continues to exit men, women, children with hands thrust into pockets, municipal dignitaries, etc. These latter proclaim their significance by their stuffed shirts and the coteries of toadies which surround them. The slate sky drops even lower, like a curtain falling on our scene. To the west the sun begins to sink into the miasma rising from the dark water of the lake. As the sun sinks it becomes swollen. The colors become lurid. Later this will be described more exactly. The threat of rain seems now more imminent. Drops coalesce out of the thickening air. These drops disturb the coatings of dust on the open mouths of flowers. Tourists brush at their arms and look at each other with uncertain smiles on their faces. All continue, however, to the ancient hacienda, now a movie set, at the shore of the lake. Bougainvillea and jasmine climb the thick walls. The band forms itself into two segments, creating a passage rather like an aisle.

People pour between them. The casino fills. The party has begun, as promised. Indians in their best clothes pull at the arms of slot machines. *Clang*! A man and a woman are illuminated. She wears a manto sagrado which trails behind as she descends stairs which curve to her left, our right. The heels of her shoes are tall, thin, dangerous. Applause scatters. In the courtyard a madman with gray dreadlocks—they are tangled with gum, wax, perhaps asphalt from the streets on which he sleeps—suddenly shouts: "Donde esta la reina! Donde esta la reina!" La reina appears. She takes a cigarette from Garred. Its white shaft is stained suddenly with red.

"Isnt this my cue?" she says. "John—wont you take my arm?"

He takes it. Sheba growls:

"Do you insist on this?"

"Youve read the script. Osgood? Garred? Youre coming?"

A girl thrusts her program into Dominique's hand.

"I've been a fan of yours forever," she says.

"How nice of you to say so."

A long passageway is dimly lit. Barely visible are the paintings in their gilt frames. A Christ bleeds. Odalisques recline deeply in their own shadows. A black lake—it is visible intermittently as our group passes open windows—ruffles its surface. Oily wavelets spread outward to the shore. Elsewhere, at the mercado, nearly deserted at this hour, tarpaulins heave and swell in the wind like breathing animals. A woman throws back her head. A cry is audible. A bus groans bearing its load up a hill. Rain spatters suddenly against the zapote trees. Within the hacienda, now our movie set, the rain can be heard briefly drumming against the tin roofs of the workrooms. It is here that the young Indian women shift from shadow to shadow in their high heeled shoes, showing off their silken ankles to the coppery-eyed men crowded at doorways. Craftsmen with gnarled hands glance up at the tall tourists whose wallets bulge with credit cards and bills of strange colors and denominations—10,000, 20,000, 50,000 peso notes, all rather pretty in muted shades of yellow, red, green. "Do they bargain?" a lavender-haired woman asks. "Can we haggle?" A man touches a brush to the lips of a pasta de cana figure. Another figure, quite nude, leans against a wall. Black blood has crusted on one thigh. In the amber light which moves in varying intensities through the room these figures seem scarcely less alive than the men bent over them or the woman, the blonde woman with her ruined face, who drifts from one figure to the next, trailing her ornate robe. We admire the way her movements seem to linger long after they have been completed. Her flanks as she walks disturb the surface of her twilight colored dress. When she speaks—commenting, no doubt, on the fineness of the work displayed before her—the sounds seem to phosphoresce in her mouth. Her eyes glow. All this and more is caught by the cameras which descend from the ceilings, which rise slowly from each corner, which emerge, uncoiling, hissing, from each aperture, from each crevice in the ancient walls.

7.

It is sunset. Blackish colors flow on the horizon. A media luna dangles in the sky. Zapote leaves droop. The air is heavy. In the mercado tarpaulins heave and swell like breathing animals. Men, women, children stream into the plaza. They parade past the opera house. At the abasto municipal men in gumboots and rubber aprons smoke cigarettes and watch. Cattle moan within.

A man with gray dreadlocks suddenly lifts his head. "Donde esta la reina! Donde esta la reina!" He subsides as Dominique strolls past on the arm of her director. They are followed by Sheba, Garred Haus, and Osgood Fetters. They continue down passageways. Some of these passageways have lintels so low the people are required to stoop. Sirenos stir in the breeze created by the passing people. Through each window is visible the sunset, now so lurid one might imagine it painted. Blackish colors flow like blood. The sun appears swollen. It is many times its normal size. Because our film is black and white we must imagine the purples, the reds, the yellows which swirl there in the rising miasma of the lake. These colors invest the rooms with a thick, almost tangible density. It is in these rooms that we see the various Virgins de la Salud that we have used in our film. Gnarled men perform last minute alterations on one pair of lips, on the wound on one thorax, on the corona surmounting one head. Elsewhere—the director swings wide a door—Carmalitas Descalzas, or shoeless Carmalite nuns, or at least women playing the parts of shoeless Carmalite nuns, pause in their embroidery to open the mantos sagrados and vestidos sagrados on which they have been working. Gold thread curls into ornate patterns. Many meters of cloth, perhaps kilometers of cloth, all woven to our requirements, have been used. The nuns, or the barefoot women playing nuns, twitter and hum and click in their own language while tourists—their pockets are even now being picked by boys with clever, silent fingers—snap pictures with automatic cameras. "Can we haggle? Do they bargain?" A large tourist—he is so benign he scarcely seems to exist—smiles gently at everyone. We ignore him.

"I have always been fond," Dominique says, "of pale flesh marked with blood."

"I can understand your fascination."

"Do you see that swelling—rather gray, oily—"

"Below her ribs?"

"Exactly."

"A wound, perhaps. A knife—a spear—"

"She looks like a victim—or a sacrifice."

"I can smell death."

"Yes, of course. But you always smell death, it is your nature. I smell semen—but then I always smell semen, don't I? Semen and blood. Don't scowl, Sheba, we depend on you. Tear open your bodice, Sheba. Let us see your wrinkled yellow tits—"

A woman howls in the mercado. Buses labor with increasing slowness up the cobbled streets. The air is now so heavy that the limbs of the zapote trees are forced to the ground. Flowers bend over backwards, like women with their throats exposed. All of this is visible to us. We count each offense. Each crime is one beat of the executioner's drum. There are measured steps being taken. We watch the blood from the slaughter-house mix with the black sewage and the muñecas with rubbery limbs and the half submerged plastic diapers and sanitary pads and the floating empty boxes of texturized soya protein, the occasional corpse of a dog, a swollen rat, all of it flowing into the lake, where it hisses and steams. The Indian women wrapped in their rebozos—some are on their knees, others on their haunches—spread at this shore their offerings, which may no longer be sufficient. All this occurs while the white pasta de cana figures, manipulated perhaps by wires invisible in the dim light, uncoil from the deeper shadows of the workshops. Cameras immediately begin to hiss. They rise like disturbed bees—like the black honey-seeking mucencabs of the forest—from every corner, from every crevice, hover-ing so low that some of the taller tourists inadvertently duck their heads. The hissing sound becomes so loud, so insistent, that we shut the door and withdraw.

290

8.

It is sunset. Because our film is black and white colors are not visible. Yet clearly this sunset is lurid. The inky hues wash back and forth at the horizon, as black as blood. The sun is swollen many times its normal size. It seems to immerse itself into the lake. The black waters steam. Oily waves lap at the shore where old Indian women have bared their breasts. It may be this is some pagan ceremony which has survived into our Christian era. Perhaps it is a ceremony of expiation. If so it is not clear that such expiation is sufficient any longer to ward off whatever evil, whatever catastrophe, the women are attempting to avert. Their exposed breasts, veined and wrinkled sacks, flail right and left, they swell and heave, as the women perform their gyrations. The waves however continue to press at the shore.

In the workshops a man with gnarled fingers puts down his brush. Dominique—swinging her face to a mirror—touches her lips.

"Do you like this color?"

"It looks like blood."

"Blood is sacred to the Indians, isnt it?"

"Blood is a sacred fluid to many people."

"Do you suppose they drink it?"

"I doubt it."

"No, I mean in some secret ritual—like the blood of Christ. I can imagine it—cant you?—perhaps in a symbolic form—"

"Indian women, you mean, gathered in some sacred grove—"

"Yes—or on the shore of a sacred lake—"

"Drinking the bloody juice of the zarzamora—"

"Their breasts stained with it—"

"Why not?"

In the further reaches of the room Indian girls show off their silken ankles. It is a scene we have witnessed before. The girls—some are scarcely pubescent—are swarthy and lithe. They exclaim over the high heeled shoes. They try on one pair, then another. The women lean on each other, at times giggling, then quietly serene, even sombre. The boys and young men crowded at the doorway are more agitated. They crane their necks and jostle for a better look. In the amber light, a light nearly the same color as their bodies, the women seem to glow. Their eyes and lips especially luminesce. This is visible to us and, certainly, to everyone in the room. The tourists, however, are bent over the benches on which they lay out their credit cards and their red and yellow and green peso notes—20,000, 50,000, even 100,000 pesos—as they barter for incised stones, lacquered trays, beaten copper, and the masks carved from the copalillo tree. Dignitaries, for instance the municipal president and his cronies, manage to look important as they strut right, march left. A few policemen drowse in their stiff brown uniforms. Extras whom we recognize from the film are placed strategically. They nod in acknowledgment to each other, the way veterans do. Occasionally they glance at the cameras, as though calculating the best angle at which to present their chiseled jaws or their contoured cheeks or, in the case of the madman in his gray dreadlocks, the angle at which his lunar orbs will best reflect the light entering through the windows to his right, our left. It is at this moment—"La reina, la reina," the dreadlocked man whispers—that the pasta de cana figures begin to stir. Each rises, uncoils, swells. It may be they are attached to invisible wires manipulated by complex mechanisms, or perhaps they are living starlets, carefully imported for the occasion, selected for the pallor of their skin, their long flanks, their pointed breasts. Each has blood seeping from her wounds. The blood has a clarity that is rather like the amber-colored sap that leaks from the trees in the forests. The blood flows from wrists, from ankles, from the crook of each arm, occasionally from a thorax where, revealed coiling from the wound, we see something rather like a snake but which is probably meant to be grayish intestines. Some of these women mount the horned moons, the media lunas which serve as pedestals. They point the black patent toes of their shoes. One of them tugs at her stocking tops. Another strokes with her jeweled hand her hooded clitoris. These gestures, although provocative, are delivered with exquisite grace. Each limb is balanced against another, each movement, that is, counterpointed, so that the pasta de cana figures are never in danger of toppling but remain poised in their very high, very narrow heeled shoes even as the cameras rise swirling around them, emerging from each crevice, from hidden alcoves, from the shadows that have gathered in every corner, hissing with such insistence, such compulsion, that we turn away. Immediately rain begins to fall with such a thunderous drumming that all other sounds are obliterated, even the cries that shake, momentarily, the heavy planks of the wooden door which we have closed behind us.

9.

It is sunset, yes, it is sunset, there is no mistaking that lurid spectacle to the west. We witness the slow immersion into the lake of the sun which swells to many times its normal size. The water bubbles and froths. It is as dark as blood. On the shore Indian women with bared breasts wail. Their offerings, which are perhaps no longer sufficient, are spread before them. We recognize fruit—mangos, zapotes, ciruellos, painted in muted shades of red, yellow, green—and carved faces overrun with lizards. Two-headed catfish gasp on the black sand. A sireno, so waterlogged it barely floats, washes to shore, where it rocks back and forth with each wave. Its wooden mouth is open, its eyes agape. Yet all this time inky colors flow ceaselessly at the horizon.

The casino meanwhile is nearly deserted. A skinny old man in huaraches pushes his broom across the floor. A bartender polishes a last few glasses and puts them into their proper places. A burly man snores in the poker pit, his hairy belly exposed. A couple of technicians pack into black boxes the tools of their trade. In the courtyard children sit cross-legged. A tawny woman sings to them. When she lifts with one jeweled hand the hem of her dress—a silken thigh flashes—the little girls, who are watching with avid eyes, go Aaah, aaah. A bitch we have noted before pants near a wall, her swollen teats laid out in rows, unused. Glowing through the clouds is a media luna. It hangs in the sky like an omen. Slowly, as night falls, it brightens. All this time, meanwhile, the director and his star saunter through the corridors which extend, seemingly endlessly, in each cardinal direction. The lighting here possesses a thick glossiness, an amber hue, that is particularly attractive. The woman Dominique wears her twilight-colored dress—several have been made for her for use in this film—and the manto sagrado, whose long train sweeps behind. Her feet are shod in the black patent shoes we have previously described. Their heels tap sharply on the terracotta floor. Her movements, which are slow, studied, seem to linger long after they are completed. There is a nimbus of light around her, perhaps from the jewelry she wears, the sapphire rings, the carved jasper, the chalcedony and emerald, the sardonyx and sardus. Pearls are around her neck. Rubies are glued to the long green fingernails which curve and taper some distance beyond her fingertips. Many of these jewels are coarsely faceted. Her hair, surmounted by gold resplendor and corona, is particularly elegant tonight. We acknowledge with a nod the horrible beauty of her face. If she is aware of our presence she gives no sign. The director wears his usual khaki shirt. He seems both tired and relaxed, perhaps from the long exertions of bringing his film to its conclusion. Occasionally the two of them stop to admire a painting or a particularly grotesque mask. Once she lifts her head. She says:

"Did you hear that?"

"No."

"I thought I heard cries—or screams—"

"I heard nothing."

"They seemed so real."

"In a place like this anything can seem real."

"It's raining, isnt it? Perhaps I heard the thunder—or the wind."

"The monsoon has arrived."

"At last. That dryness—the dust—"

"How nice to feel moisture in the air again."

They stroll past a hanging sireno which seems to follow them with its protruding eyes. Something drips—perhaps rainwater, perhaps blood—as they pass paintings of sacrificial figures, of lucent flesh torn with wounds, of faces exalted by suffering. At last they come to stairs. In the flashes of lightning, followed by the muted roars of thunder, it is possible to glimpse the heights to which the stairs rise. Elsewhere we see rows of figures slightly askew. Their shadows are abruptly thrown right, thrown left, by the lightning. The flashes are too brief, however, and too startling, for us to distinguish more than muted colors, perhaps reds and yellows and greens, and walls that may or may not be mirrored, and a few shapes which one might imagine, at least, to be living. In any case the man and woman hesitate only a moment. The woman takes the man's arm. "Shall we?" she says. A wind gusts suddenly through an open window, bearing with it the awful odors of the black lake. It brings no sounds, however, no cries, no moans, nothing but the occasional flurries of rain. The audience, if there is one, is silent.

IO.

An amber light moves through the room. It clings to everything it touches. After a moment we hear the click of heels. A woman approaches. She walks like a young hoofed animal. She pauses to pull at the tops of her stockings, pointing, as she does so, the toes of her shoes, which are triangular like the heads of vipers. Her body is bisected. The black garter belt looks like a spider wrapped around her waist. We have noted before her small, pointed breasts, which tremble slightly as she resumes her walk. The manto sagrado trails behind her, loosely attached at her shoulders. Rain drums in a sudden gust against a window. There are masks on the walls and sirenos hanging in corners. The room is ten meters by twenty. A man is visible slightly out of focus in the background buttoning his shirt. If we were in the room doubtless we would smell blood and semen—her blood, his semen. Somewhere behind us a machine chatters, perhaps a projector. The woman, meanwhile, sits on her throne. It is shaped like a lizard. Its eyes are exophthalmic. When the woman crosses her sheathed legs—how her legs luminesce in this light!—we hear their nylon surfaces slide one over the other. She leans towards her mirror, and towards us. The camera, that is—and thus ourselves as viewers—is behind the mirror. We look through the mirror into her face as she paints her eyes and her lips. Powders are applied. Because the film is black and white we must guess at the colors, at a red so dark it becomes black, at the lunar shadowing of each eye socket, at the green which glosses on her fingernails. Her expression as she performs these tasks is indecipherable. We shall have to imagine its significance, just as we imagine the colors which create the mask of her face. In any case we may never understand her. She is la reina de las vegas, the queen of the fertile wastelands. There is no beauty more terrible than hers.

At last she puts down her tubes and brushes. She raises her head. Her left eye looks directly into ours.

"Is this it? Is this what you want?"

"Yes," we say. "Yes, this is it, exactly."

The screen goes blank. Our film is over. After a moment even the hissing stops. There is nothing left to say.